Elaine Bedell was a BAFTA award-winning TV producer before becoming Controller of Entertainment at the BBC a Director of Entertainment & Comedy at ITV. She has nmissioned and produced some of the UK's most popular rtainment shows, including *The X Factor, Strictly Come ng, Take Me Out, Britain's Got Talent, The One Show, Gear* and *Saturday Night Takeaway*. She lives in Hackney d has two children. She is currently Chief Executive of the uthbank Centre. *About That Night* is her first novel.

About That Night

Elaine Bedell

ONE PLACE. MANY STORIES

HQ
An imprint of HarperCollins*Publishers* Ltd
1 London Bridge Street
London SE1 9GF

This edition 2019

1

First published in Great Britain by
HQ, an imprint of HarperCollins*Publishers* Ltd 2019

"YOU'RE MY WORLD"
Words and Music by Gino Paoli, Carl Sigman and Umberto Bindi
© 1964 EDITIONS MUSICALI M. E. C. (NS)
All rights on behalf of EDITIONS MUSICALI M. E. C.
administered by Chappell & Co. Inc

ISBN: 978-0-00-829768-8

MIX
Paper from
responsible sources
FSC www.fsc.org **FSC™ C007454**

This book is produced from independently certified FSC™ paper
to ensure responsible forest management.

For more information visit: www.harpercollins.co.uk/green

This book is set in 11.5/16 pt. Bembo

Printed and bound in Great Britain by
CPI Group (UK) Ltd, Croydon, CR0 4YY

In memory of my dear dad Bert who
should have lived to see it all.

Prologue

Elizabeth Place is packing up her life. The protesting screech of duct tape and the thwack and swoosh of folding cardboard corners have been the soundtrack to her day. She's surrounded by sealed brown boxes. Two muscular men arrived first thing in a white van with its big red boast *'We'll Make the Earth Move For You'* and stomped up the stairs to her first-floor flat, *Where do you want us, love?* Between them they carried a sofa, four chairs, a chest of drawers and her double mattress – *up a bit, right a bit, upsy-daisy, there she goes, easy does it* – while drinking twelve cups of tea with twenty-four spoonfuls of sugar.

Now only the boxes to go.

She sits and surveys her empty flat. She's very tired and a little bit queasy if she's honest (although she has an unfortunate inclination not to be honest, especially with herself). Her entire life has been swaddled, stacked and squashed into eleven cartons: thirty-five years of life, love and loss. Elizabeth isn't much good at maths, but she knows that thirty-five doesn't go into eleven without some leftover bits. What's happened to the rest of her life? Those bits and pieces that might have caused her to tick another ten boxes?

She's thirty-five and single. It wasn't meant to be like this.

She reaches for the last empty box into which she'll carefully stow the few remaining, very personal items. The things she's left until last. Her National Television Award, still on the mantelpiece, sparkling bronze: *Elizabeth Place, Producer: Best Entertainment Programme, Saturday Bonkers;* a framed photo of her dear dad waving proudly at her down the years from the deck of a boat that isn't his; the engraved card from *'Matthew, Controller, All Channels'* which read *'Only you could have got us through that show. Well done! X'*; a black and white postcard of Paris, on which Hutch had written out an extract from Shelley's 'Love's Philosophy' along with the words *Dear Miss Clumsy, I really miss you bumping into things;* Elizabeth and Jamie, framed on their graduation day, carelessly waving their mortar boards in the air. And standing on its spine, propping up the rest, a valuable first edition of Yeats, given to her by Ricky one morning after a terrible night before.

Elizabeth tucks all these mementoes carefully away in the last box and closes the flaps quickly, like a ventriloquist silencing his troublesome puppets. All apart from the Yeats, which she clutches to her chest. She stands for a moment gazing at the empty spaces, thinking of the life she's leaving behind. A life she has loved. A seductive life: of glamour, of glory, of giddiness. An addictive, adrenaline-fuelled roller coaster of a life, with all its exhilarating highs and exhausting lows. A dangerous life.

She's independent, she's strong, she says to herself. She's

really good at her job. She'll do what her bible says and *lean in* (she hasn't worked out exactly what this means, but she imagines it's a bit like the plank, you just have to practice). She's done with being caught in tangled webs of secrecy and lies. She'll heed the warning signs, next time.

Won't she?

Elizabeth wanders back into the bedroom, avoiding the bathroom. She'll deal in a minute with the message in there that might change her life, that's waiting for her in the cabinet, away from the prying eyes of the heavy lifters.

Elizabeth shivers slightly and sinking to the bedroom floor opens up the Yeats, carefully turning the precious pages. And there it is, on the title page, in Ricky's big black sloping writing: *'Dearest Elizabeth, I have spread my dreams under your feet'*. Crazy, comic, complicated Ricky. His story wasn't meant to end the way it did, one innocently blossoming day in May.

A Mayday.

Chapter One

Two months earlier

The audience are settling into their seats. They've been queueing outside the studio in the May drizzle for an hour and a half, an exercise in patience which might have been more bearable had anyone remotely famous walked by. An Ant. Or a Dec. They weren't fussy. But one of the regulars, who'd been to recordings of the show at least twice before and had therefore brought a flask of hot chocolate, said that the stars use a secret tunnel entrance at the back of the studio building. Television stars, she explained patiently, don't use main entrances. 'Not even the Loose Women?' asks a girl, shivering in bare legs and high heels. 'No one,' says the lady with the flask.

They've been herded like soaking sheep into the pens of the audience seating. Their mobile phones have been confiscated and will be returned to them at the end of the show. The lady with the hot chocolate, knowing the form, hangs back a little, watching as they fill the back seats first. She manages to get a seat in the third row from the front and surreptitiously opens up a packet of sandwiches. 'The warm-up won't be on for at least another half an hour,' she whispers to the woman next to her. 'Cheese and pickle?'

The set is much smaller in reality than it looks on the television. It consists of a shiny steel desk, surrounded by bookshelves laden with leather tomes, and a bright canary yellow velvet sofa. Five wide steps run up to the back of the set which serve as the entrance for the guests of the show. Wrapped around the set are a series of huge screens which display drone-captured scenes of planet earth at night, vast cities pin-pricked with glittering street lights, moonlit oceans and mountain ranges crested by stars.

'Or tuna and cucumber?'

The audience is mainly female and they've come dressed for the occasion, eyeliner and foundation thickly applied, in case, just in case, there's a fleeting shot of them clapping on camera. They're hardened, battle-worn fans of the star of the show, the primetime entertainment king, Ricky Clough. They've been with him since he was a youthful breakfast DJ, have seen him through his career highs and lows. They've grown up through the years of his primetime, live, television show, *Saturday Bonkers*, watching it faithfully before going out to hit the weekend bars and clubs. But in recent months, Ricky's audiences have been thinning, along with his hair, and a transplant on both counts has been necessary: he's now been given his own chat show, *The Ricky Clough Show*, but not live, not on Saturday nights, and in the graveyard slot of 22.40.

The warm-up guy bounds on to the set, dressed in a tartan suit. He's carrying a stick mic. 'Right, ladies – and you few brave gents – are we ready to get this party going?' he says.

'ARE WE READY?' The studio lights blaze on his entrance; for a brief moment he's king of the court. He parades up and down the set, relishing the spotlight. The sound guys turn up the volume to DJ Fresh and the audience begin to shift in their seats, itching to get up and dance.

'Okay. Five minutes till we start recording the show! Put your make-up on, ladies! Oh? You already have? Sorry, love. Now then. Take a good look at the person next to you. Is anyone here with someone they shouldn't be? Because you're about to be on telly – a television studio's no place for people having affairs!'

Elizabeth Place, Ricky Clough's producer, allows herself a small smile at this. She's watching the warm-up from the comforting shadows of the black drapes that surround the studio. The entire audience is up on its feet, dancing along to 'Ain't No Stoppin' Us Now'. Middle-aged women have shed their coats and their inhibitions and are dancing like teenagers. Elizabeth likes to watch them; she loves to hear the pre-show excitement build to a crescendo of hysteria. She thinks they might be in for a good night: Ricky was in a better mood than usual when she checked on him in his dressing room earlier. A bottle of white wine was open, but still full, and he didn't drink at all while she went through his script with him. (Nonetheless, she had taken the precaution of hiding another unopened bottle under the sofa when he wasn't looking.)

She turns to the black-shirted cameraman nearest her, Phil, leaning against his pedestal camera with his arms folded, his back turned firmly away from the disco-dancing divas. 'How is he this evening?' he asks her drily with a raised eyebrow.

'Very lively,' says Elizabeth with a smile.

'Think we're in for a good show?' Phil asks.

'Actually, yes.'

She skips up the spiral staircase that leads to the studio gallery, a rectangular box of a room with a long desk facing a bank of television screens, each offering different angles on the studio below. The director, Robin, is sitting in the middle of the desk, with the vision mixer beside him. He's wearing a silk cravat and a velvet blazer. Elizabeth kisses him lightly on the cheek then takes her seat at the far end, next to the gallery assistant, Lola, who prints all the scripts, does all the timings and entertains the camera crew with stories of her recent breast enlargement procedure. She has platinum blonde hair piled impressively into a beehive on her head and is perfectly made up: heavy kohl eyeliner, white powder, bright red lips (Lola is in a perpetual state of mourning for the 1940s). She's wearing a tight pencil skirt and a cropped knit sweater which shows off to full advantage her perky new breasts. She has an array of dangerously sharpened pencils in front of her, as well as two stopwatches.

Elizabeth never feels more alive than when she's in the gallery, producing a show, sitting side by side with Lola. They've worked closely together for seven years, sharing every beat of every nail-biting show. Shoulder to shoulder they've somehow kept the show on the road, through all the ups and the downs, and have become firm friends. Elizabeth loves her job and she loves these moments just before a show most of all. She loves the precision of the preparation and the execution, the fact that everyone must move in synchronicity. She loves all the little meaningful rituals and habits which bind them all intimately together, like a professional family. She loves the thrill, the adrenaline, the buzz. She loves the way her heart beats painfully in her chest during a show and the fact that her brain never feels clearer.

Lola squeezes her hand as she sits and whispers, 'I saw him in his dressing room. He seems on really good form. I don't think he's been drinking or anything.' Lola's eyes are shining, she's happy. Elizabeth smiles and nods. As far as she knows, she's the only person on the production team who has any clue as to the true nature of Lola's relationship with Ricky.

'Stand by studio floor, coming to you in two minutes.'

Elizabeth puts on her headphones and presses the button of the small console in front of her, saying softly into the small microphone, 'Hello, Ricky. This is me. Just testing talkback. Can you hear me okay?'

'Loud and clear, Mrs T,' comes back the familiar voice of the star of the show in her ear. She can't see him yet, but can hear from his breathing that he's walking quickly down the corridor from his dressing room. She knows that his wardrobe assistant will be running along beside him carrying his jacket, which he never puts on until the very last second.

'They're a rowdy bunch tonight, can you hear?'

Elizabeth glances anxiously at the television screens that show her wide shots of the studio audience, up on their feet and dancing to 'The Macarena'. They're very pumped. She decides to ignore, as she always does, his reference to Mrs Thatcher. 'See you on the other side, Ricky.' She puts a smile into her voice.

'See you on the other side,' he replies, as he always does. And then, as he reaches the back of the set, before he leaps into the heat and glare of the spotlight, he addresses all the crew. His voice is deep and close into his microphone. 'Elizabeth? Guys? Let's make this a show to remember, eh? Let's rock and roll!'

'Fifty seconds!' Lola announces loudly in the gallery.

'Are the food props all standing by?' Elizabeth asks and the clipped vowels of her young Etonian researcher, Zander, return in her ear. 'Yes, ma'am, they're under his desk.'

Elizabeth gathers the pages of her yellow script together and tidies them into a compact tome, her very own *War and Peace*. She glances at her mobile phone. There's a thumbs-up emoji from Hutch and a picture of a double bed with a question mark. A shiver of pleasure and anticipation prickles all the way down her spine, but she puts her phone away. She finds her foot is tapping incessantly underneath the desk.

'Twenty seconds,' says Lola, placing her hand reassuringly on Elizabeth's arm, but never taking her eyes from her stopwatch.

'Have a good show, everyone!' Elizabeth says, smiling down the desk at Robin. She gives him a mock military salute, which he solemnly returns. Everyone in the gallery is on the edge of their seats.

'Ten seconds,' says Lola, with a new warning note of urgency.

'9, 8, 7, 6, 5, 4, 3...'

'Roll titles!' shouts Robin. The central screen, in front of the gallery desk, bursts into life with a cacophony of bright graphics, lurid yellow and blue shapes, which gradually form themselves into a giant head, the silhouette of a man in profile, with longish curly hair and an aquiline nose. The head dissolves into jigsaw pieces which re-assemble themselves into letters and finally words: The Ricky Clough Show.

In the studio, Ricky bounds down the stairs and runs to the front of the audience, as they whoop and cheer in concert with the warm-up who is conducting them from the sidelines. As he draws his hand across his throat they stop immediately as if they've been switched off and they sit back down, a bit disappointed and suspicious that the party might already be over.

'Hello! Good evening and thank you for that warm hand on my entrance. Welcome to my show! Wanna know who's on my sofa tonight?' Ricky Clough is wearing his trademark purple suit, Doc Martens and a peacock blue custom-made shirt. His hair has been neatly combed to cover the seam of his transplant, but the curls reach down to his collar. He's tall and his expanding girth is held in check by a clever combination of belts and expensive tailoring. His face is a light entertainment shade of polished conker. He has that unusual combination of camp and lascivious heterosexuality shared by so many successful performers. He paces restlessly around the set. His fizzing energy is almost electric. He's an Icarus, Elizabeth thinks, you will burn if you get too close. It's impossible not to look at him. He smiles brilliantly, revealing startlingly white teeth, as he ad-libs to the audience and cracks a joke at each of his guests' expense, so that even Elizabeth – who's seen it all before and knows his every facial tic – feels lost in wonder at his magnetic pull.

She presses the talkback button and says very quietly, 'Ricky,

Paolo's ready – let's bring him on to the sofa now.' Paolo Culone, a young celebrity chef, is to be the first guest.

Ricky can hear Elizabeth's instructions through an earpiece invisible to the audience and he responds smoothly by turning to the autocue camera that discreetly displays his script. He begins to read the words of his introduction. But as he moves towards his desk, he catches his foot on the step and stumbles, his arms momentarily flailing. The audience titter.

'Whoa, babe, steady,' Lola mutters under her breath.

Puzzled, Elizabeth kicks back her chair and goes to stand behind Robin, resting her hands on his shoulder, and they both lean forward, staring intently at their star's face on the close-up cameras. His eyes are glittering in the studio lights and a sheen of sweat is already moistening his forehead. Nothing unusual in that, they're used to seeing him in states of overexcitement, pumped by adrenaline, or wine – or worse. But as he arranges his cue cards on top of the desk, Elizabeth notices that his hands are shaking. His mouth is still moving but he's stopped looking at the nearest camera. Instead, he's looking down and his voice has dropped to a mumble. Elizabeth finds her heart beating faster. She doesn't understand this unusual lack of grip from Ricky. Even when very inebriated, he can always keep the show going.

Robin jumps up crying, 'Camera 5, pull wide! No close-ups. Stay wide!'

Elizabeth walks quickly back to her seat and Lola turns, her face full of panic. Elizabeth leans over the talkback microphone, presses down the button and reads from her script carefully and slowly, 'Okay, Ricky, say after me... Now, most of us when we fancy a snack, think about a toastie, a steak bake or maybe some fish fingers…' She turns her eyes to the bank of television screens and watches as Ricky slowly lifts his head and fixes his eyes, now glassy and unfocused, on camera 5. Out of his mouth, mechanically, come the words she recites in his ear…

'But not my next guest, the man who invented the fish eyeball brioche! Ladies and gentlemen, Paolo Culone!'

'Cue Paolo!' cries Robin and the young whizz-kid of nouvelle cuisine comes running down the stairs and on to the set to wild applause, generated furiously by the floor manager. Only the lady with the flask and those sitting in the very front rows have noticed Ricky shaking and fumbling for his words and they are now sitting up very straight, alert to the exciting possibility of being witness to a proper show-business meltdown. Ricky doesn't move from his desk chair as Paolo bounds on, but with a sort of superhuman effort, shifts in his seat so that he can greet the chef from a sitting position.

'Ricky,' Elizabeth continues, low and encouragingly in his ear, 'the food props that you asked for are under your desk. You remember, we're going to see if he recognises his own dishes by their smell. It's a great idea – it was your idea, Ricky! Let's do it now. They're under your desk.'

Paolo sits down but is clearly uncomfortable with the surprising lack of a welcoming handshake. Nothing that the researcher backstage told him would happen appears to be taking place and so to fill the empty air-time, he begins to jabber nervously about meeting an *X Factor* finalist backstage. As he speaks, Ricky slides down in his chair and with a trembling hand, produces one of the dishes hidden underneath and places it shakily on top of the desk.

'Mate, have some water,' Paolo suddenly says, reaching for a glass decanter of clear liquid on a low side table. He pours a glass and hands it to him. Elizabeth puts her head in her hands and Lola cries, 'No! Not the gin!'

But Ricky ignores the offered glass and instead eats with his fingers from the dish and licks them ostentatiously. He says, suddenly loud and clear, 'Mmm, what do you call this dish again?'

'Well,' Paolo sits forward on the sofa excitedly, 'that's cockle ketchup and…' but he stops mid-sentence, his mouth dropping open.

Ricky's trembling hand, holding the dish, has suddenly dropped to his side and the plate falls to the studio floor with a clatter. His cheeks are bulging, as if with extreme exertion, his face is contorted and turning a dark purple. His shoulders suddenly seem to give way and his whole body sinks, as if loosed from its moorings. Up in the gallery, Elizabeth flies out of her chair as Lola cries, 'Oh God! What's the matter with him?'

The back rows of the studio audience are struggling to get into their coats and scarves because Elizabeth, taking no chances, has turned the air-conditioning glacially high in order to keep them awake. But an amused muttering begins to build amongst them – they're clearly enjoying the extravagantly comic turn. The front rows on the other hand are half out of their seats, craning their necks to get a better look at the now slumped star of the show. The lady with the flask is foremost amongst them, the considerable weight of her experience sitting bored and cold in television studios telling her that none of this seems planned.

Under the heat of the studio lights, Ricky is momentarily motionless and a shimmering sliver of spit glistens its way down his chin. With enormous effort, it seems, he lifts his head and his bloodshot eyes search out his close-up camera. He holds its unforgiving gaze for an instant. But then his body twists and writhes, caught in the pitiless rhythm of its own maniacal dance, until one jerking spasm throws up his head and Elizabeth cries out in horror at his distorted face, his mouth gaping and gasping for air. Paolo leaps from the sofa with a scream, but still some people in the back rows are shrieking with laughter.

Elizabeth turns on her heel to run down the spiral staircase that will take her back to the studio floor. 'Stop recording!' she cries over her shoulder to the gallery. 'And for God's sake, get the warm-up back on.'

By the time she's groped her way around the heavy black drapes that enclose the set and the audience, the warm-up is on the studio floor and calmly announcing that the show has been suspended. People are reluctantly gathering their things. On set, Ricky has slithered to the floor beside the desk. The floor manager is trying ineffectually to shield him with her own body from the openly gaping stares of the front rows. Paolo Culone is being ushered politely off the set by Zander, the researcher, whose face creases with alarm as he passes Elizabeth running in.

'Ricky?' Elizabeth bends low over her presenter's head and

gently touches his shoulder. 'Ricky – can you hear me?' Her touch seems to topple him, he rolls on to his back and she can't help herself, she shrinks back in horror. The whites of his eyes have yellowed and a sudden spasm forces his head back, but his hand seems to find her wrist and his grip is like a vice.

'Phone 999. Where's the St John Ambulance attendant?' Elizabeth shouts. She tries to find Ricky's pulse. The flesh around his wristwatch is pudgy and his shirtsleeve is stuck to his skin with sweat. She sees Lola running into the studio and tries to restrain her but Lola sinks to her knees beside Ricky. She bends low to stroke his soaking forehead and whispers in his ear, 'It's okay, babe. Someone's coming. Hold on. It's going to be alright. It's going to be okay.'

Elizabeth straightens up and says, 'Get the audience out the back way. Now! Quickly! Keep the scene dock clear for the ambulance.'

She notices the cameramen are still standing by their cameras, watching curiously. They've seen people die in television studios before – they worked on *Celebrity Wrestling* – but this is definitely more sensational. Phil on camera 5, when he catches her eye, holds out his hands, palms upwards, as if to say, *Who'd have thought…?* She turns back in despair to Ricky and sees that Lola is kneeling and rocking beside him, almost in prayer. He is lying on his back, his arms and legs splayed, as if completely spent.

Then there are uniforms, men in hi-vis jackets saying, 'Clear a space please, coming through', and a stretcher. Ricky is laid out flat on the floor, behind the desk hidden from view, but he's stiff and unresponsive, an oxygen mask over his nose and mouth. A machine is placed on his chest.

Elizabeth steps aside and takes a deep breath. She wants to be calm and capable, but she can barely think straight and her heart is pounding. She steels herself and pulls out her mobile to phone her boss: the Controller, All Channels.

'Elizabeth? Um. Hi. Everything okay?' Matthew sounds sleepy, slurred, like he's just surfacing.

'Ricky's collapsed in the studio. The ambulance is here. They're working on him now.' Her voice is unnaturally high, but steady.

'Jesus Christ! Working on him? What, like resuscitation?' Matthew is suddenly alert. He hasn't got where he's got to without recognising a crisis when he's just been told that there is one.

'Yes. He just keeled over at the desk.'

'Was he drunk?'

'No. Well. Definitely no more than usual.' The paramedics are standing up. Ricky is lying inert on the floor. She whispers into the phone, 'Um, I think he's – dead.'

'Dead? Oh God! Poor Ricky. The poor old bugger. You know, I feared it might come to this... Christ – what did the audience see? We need to manage this. Call the press office. I'll be with you in half an hour.'

'Um, we should ring Lorna. His wife? Do you want to ring her...?' There's no response on the end of the phone. 'Or shall I?'

Matthew hesitates. 'Can you do it, Elizabeth? As you were there, you know. In case she wants any details. You've worked with Ricky for so long, she knows you two were close. And you were there, at the house the other week, at Ricky's party. I think it might be better coming from – you know – a woman.' He pauses and Elizabeth can't help thinking that Matthew was at that party too – he was the one who gave Ricky his big break in the first place – he's known them for years. But she says nothing and so Matthew adds with some relief, 'Right, I'm leaving now. Elizabeth?'

'Yes?'

'You okay?'

Elizabeth presses her cheek against her phone. 'Yes,' she says finally, 'I'm alright.'

The ambulance crew lifts the body on to the stretcher. 'We'll take him to St Thomas's, love,' one of them says to Elizabeth. 'It's Ricky Clough, right?'

'Yes. Thank you. Does someone need to travel with him?'

'No, not necessary.' The ambulance man looks at Elizabeth carefully to see if she has understood and she nods. 'I'll phone his wife and tell her that's where he is.'

Once the ambulance has gone, the cameramen pack up their equipment in respectful silence. The last few members of the audience are filing out of the side doors, whispering in hushed voices. They're unsure what they've just witnessed, but it was definitely more eventful than the last Ricky Clough show they saw. Lola is sitting in the front row, crying into some paper napkins from the canteen. The rest of the crew have also gathered on the studio floor and are standing about looking stunned. The researcher, Zander, tells Elizabeth that Paolo Culone is now in the Green Room, happily drunk on the show's warm white wine and has the *X Factor* finalist sitting on his lap.

'He thinks it's all a planned joke.' Zander's solemn grey eyes turn towards her, searching for guidance. He's in his late twenties, tall and very lean, with broad bony shoulders; good-looking in that well-bred way with soft curly hair – neatly and expensively cut – and a warm, charming smile. His impeccable Etonian manners make him an excellent booker of celebrity guests: he's unfailingly polite but incredibly thick-skinned, and simply never takes no for an answer, without ever seeming to offend.

'Tell them all to go home,' Elizabeth instructs him. 'And tell them Ricky's gone to hospital. Don't tell them anything else.'

She moves to a dark quiet space at the back of the set and spools through her contacts to find Ricky's home number. She peers round the drapes that separate her from the set and sees that Lola is still sitting in the audience, her head in her hands, her shoulders shaking. Elizabeth has met Ricky's wife Lorna a number of times over the last six years, although she no longer comes to any of his shows. Elizabeth presumes Ricky put an end to her visits once he grew close to Lola. She was a former dancer and they met on the set of a music show, back in the days when he was the UK's most popular breakfast DJ. They've been married for eighteen years and Elizabeth reckons Ricky managed to stay faithful for at least four of them. Lorna Clough picks up immediately and Elizabeth gives her the news slowly and carefully: Ricky collapsed, he seemed to have trouble breathing, there was nothing anyone could do… Her voice cracks and breaks in the end. Lorna, however, is composed. She takes a short, sharp intake of breath, but then says quietly that she will go straight to the hospital. Once Elizabeth has established Lorna can get a friend to drive her there, she tells her that someone from the television network will meet her when she arrives.

Elizabeth takes a moment to compose herself before hurrying to find her team in the Green Room – a saloon furnished with plump sofas and a bar that groans with wine bottles and buckets of beer. The Green Room is a sort of celebrity farmyard pen, there to hold the guests before a show and keep them well watered. She joins the rest of her production team, most of whom are red-eyed and speechless, and she hugs each of them in turn. She spots two of Ricky's old schoolfriends in the corner, including his sometime manager and mentor, Deniz Pegasus. Deniz left school in East Ham and became a brickie during the day and a roadie for his DJ mate Ricky in the evenings, but he soon found a gap in the building market by supplying low-cost 'affordable' housing estates for council tenants. It proved to be more than very affordable for him, and he quickly made a fortune from careless councillors whose political ambitions he fed and watered in various clubs around town and who afterwards couldn't be bothered to check his books. Recently, Deniz has started coming to all of Ricky's shows and afterwards offering Elizabeth his opinion, which she finds annoying.

Deniz is holding two Pomeranians in his meaty arms, staring at her. She beckons to Zander. 'What are we going to do about Hiss and Boo?'

Zander turns and looks puzzled at the two leather-jacketed men.

'Ricky's dogs,' Elizabeth says patiently. 'The ones with the four legs.'

'Oh!' Zander says in relief. 'Shall I ask them if they can take the dogs home with them?'

Elizabeth nods. Deniz Pegasus steps forward as if to speak to her, but she firmly turns her back on him to face the network's Head of Press, Kevin, who is talking into his mobile with his hand over his mouth. He tells her the police have arrived and want to talk to her. They've been put in Ricky's dressing room. Elizabeth wonders whether Kevin has been brazen enough to do a quick clean-up before the police went in – she wouldn't put it past their wily head of press. Then Matthew, the Controller, bursts into the Green Room, ready to do some controlling. Elizabeth, truly glad to see him, moves quickly towards him and is pleased to see his arms opening to receive her. He hugs her and for a brief moment, Elizabeth longs to rest her head on his chest and weep but instead, she straightens and stiffens.

'Elizabeth! The police are here! They want to see the most senior person here. That's obviously me. But I think you should come too, you know, to fill in some of the detail.'

'Yes, Kevin just told me, I was about to go and see them.' She's aware that she's sounding overbrisk, even though she's on the verge of shaking uncontrollably.

'Okay. Let's go.' Matthew's voice is now also curt in response to hers and he turns away.

'Do you think you should maybe say something to the team? They're all quite upset.' Elizabeth gestures to the researchers, who are now mostly sitting silently on the floor, staring at them. Robin is posing palely against the wall, an embroidered handkerchief in his hand. Lola is curled up on the sofa, clutching a glass. Matthew immediately squares his shoulders and begins:

'People, listen up! I realise tonight has been traumatic for everyone involved in the show. Ricky was a great guy. I've known him for years.' He pauses for effect, which fortunately gives him just enough time to remember that this speech isn't really about him. 'Many of you will know how much Ricky cared about the show and how hard he worked.' A few of the researchers shuffle their feet and Matthew decides to err on the side of honesty. 'And of course, he had his demons – but we loved him for it, right?' A few miserable heads nod. 'Needless to say, we have to keep this absolutely confidential at the moment while Kev sorts it.' Elizabeth looks across at Kevin, Head of Press, who is feverishly texting, and wonders if sorting it means that he can somehow miraculously bring Ricky Clough back to life. 'So please stay off Twitter for now, nothing on Facebook, don't talk to ANYONE about this yet. Okay?' Matthew looks to Elizabeth for approval and she raises an eyebrow questioningly. 'Oh,' continues the boss graciously, 'and don't worry about coming in tomorrow. Take the day off.'

'We always have the day off after recording the show,' says one fearless researcher.

'Yes, exactly,' says Matthew. Elizabeth adds gently, 'I'll call you all in the morning, when we know more.' She hugs Robin, blows a kiss to the rest of the team, her eyes full of tears, and then follows her boss out of the room.

Chapter Two

The police officers, a man and a woman, are sitting uneasily on the leopard-print cushions in Ricky Clough's dressing room. His day clothes, a crumpled sports shirt and some jeans, are hanging on a hook and the desk is piled high with weekly magazines, scripts, his laptop, as well as empty bottles of white wine. Two scented candles still burn by the mirror and the air in the small room is thick with the smell of hairspray, aftershave (Colonia, Acqua di Parma) and something else, something sticky and fetid. If Kevin managed a clean-up sweep, Elizabeth thinks grimly, it was fleeting.

As they walk in, Matthew immediately holds out his hand to the policeman, who is looking hot and bulky in a padded vinyl bomber jacket, but he simply looks anxiously across at his female colleague. Matthew continues to address the policeman. 'Hello. I'm Matthew Grayling, Controller, All Channels, here at the network. Sorry about this, we can go upstairs to my office, if you'd prefer?'

'No, this is fine.' The policewoman speaks. She stands up. She is really quite tall. 'I'm Detective Inspector Watson and this is Detective Sergeant Rafik.' She turns her back on the Controller and instead looks directly at Elizabeth. 'And you're Elizabeth Place? The producer of the show?'

'Yes.'

'Right. We're going to need to talk to you again tomorrow morning when we have the results from the hospital. But if you wouldn't mind just answering a few questions now?' DI Watson has an estuary accent, the missing t's giving her voice an abrasiveness which Elizabeth suspects works rather well in her line of work. Although she's technically asking a question, Elizabeth understands there's only one possible answer.

'Of course not.'

She sinks on to a velvet stool and remembers that she'd hidden one of the still-full wine bottles under the couch. She can't help glancing down and sees that it's still there, unopened. DI Watson's eyes follow Elizabeth's.

'So I'm afraid that the emergency services were unable to save Richard Clough when he collapsed on the floor of studio 4 at 20.15 this evening. I believe you're aware of this?'

'Yes,' Elizabeth says faintly.

'And how had Mr Clough appeared to you earlier this evening?'

'Well, I'd say, better than normal. Ready to have a good show.'

'And what was normal, for Mr Clough?' The DI glances at the empty wine bottles.

'Yes, erm, well, on studio days, he liked a drink, you know. Or two. Um. Well, on other days, as well, if I'm honest.'

'And so he'd been drinking this evening?'

'Well actually, I'm not sure how much he had... Until he started shaking and slurring his words, I thought he was sober. But then he just keeled over.'

'And other than wine, did you notice Mr Clough take anything else this evening?'

Elizabeth looks across at Matthew, who is staring back at her with an unreadable expression. She chooses her words carefully. 'Well, um, he never eats before the show. He likes to go out for dinner afterwards. I mean, he's got quite an – appetite. So he picks at stuff before the show – Percy Pigs mainly, Yellow Bellies, Smarties...'

Elizabeth glances around the room. She can't see any of the usual sweet-shop detritus, just one bowl of fruit slowly mouldering under its cellophane wrapping. 'We did have some food props on the show. We were going to do a tasting because we had the celebrity chef, Paolo Culone, on the show.'

'Never heard of him,' DI Watson says flatly.

Elizabeth looks at her helplessly. 'I'm not sure if Ricky actually ate any of it. I mean, he made out like he did, for the show, but...' DI Watson looks at her sceptically.

The Controller has had enough of not being included. He adopts a pose and an expression Elizabeth knows only too well and speaks as if addressing a small child instead of a senior officer of the law. 'Detective Inspector – Watson, is it? As I'm sure you know, Ricky Clough was a man in his late forties, erm, early fifties, who was quite a bit overweight and drank too much for his own good. I've known him for years. He was also under a lot of stress, you know, ratings and so on. I think you'll find that's a classic coronary case, right there.'

Elizabeth understands that Matthew wants nothing more than for the network to escape any further interrogation. He doesn't want Ricky's appetite for the high life exposed and examined. He wants the police off the premises and the network's reputation unsullied.

The policewoman looks at him without saying anything. The silence hangs heavily in the room and Elizabeth begins to feel hot and itchy. The sergeant is looking miserably at his boots. 'You may be jumping to conclusions, sir.' The detective inspector is icily sarcastic. 'It would be foolish for us to do so. And as yet...' she nods briefly at her colleague, who struggles thankfully to his feet. 'And as yet, the cause of death is not established.' She looks stern as she turns at the door. 'So we'll see you both tomorrow morning. We'll come to your offices first thing.'

Elizabeth glances anxiously at her boss. Matthew clearly doesn't like the idea of the police arriving in full view of everyone at the TV studios. He says very hastily, 'We'll come to the police station.'

DI Watson looks at him as if considering this, but then shrugs. 'Alright, if you prefer. Paddington Green, 10 a.m. Don't expect any tea. It goes without saying that this is an ongoing investigation so please say nothing in the meantime. Our press people are liaising with yours. This room is now being sealed for evidence. Goodnight.' And with that, DI Watson strides out of the room, ushering Elizabeth and the Controller ahead of her, and slams the door behind her with an almighty bang.

Back in the Green Room, most of the production team have left for a spontaneous wake at the King's Head, except for Lola, who's being comforted on the sofa by Robin. His eyes are also red-rimmed but, as Elizabeth comes in, glitteringly alert to the prospect of further drama. Kevin, the Head of Press, is still in the corner, talking into his mobile. Matthew moves to the drinks table, now laden with empty wine bottles, and shakes a few to see what dregs are left. 'Christ, is there no whisky here?'

'It's a banned substance.' Elizabeth reddens at the sudden realisation that the principal reason it's banned is now lying in a hospital morgue.

'Banned? Who banned it?' He turns on her accusingly.

'You did.'

Various measures, not many of them successful, have been taken to curb Ricky's excesses. A complete ban on alcohol was deemed unworkable – providing it for the guests before the show produced the sort of loose-tongued talk that gives a chat show its headlines – so they'd tried instead to empty Ricky's dressing room of all bottles, but he'd simply taken to stealing them from the Green Room. In the end Matthew decided a firm line needed to be drawn – and he had drawn it at Scotch.

Elizabeth realises that their intern, Sam, is sitting miserably on the sofa by herself. She's always the last to leave because although she isn't awarded a London Living Wage, she is awarded the responsibility of locking up the Green Room at the end of the night.

'Sam,' Elizabeth says pleadingly and the intern jumps up,

grateful that someone has finally spoken to her. 'Please could you find some whisky... somehow... somewhere?' Sam nods quickly and runs out of the room. Elizabeth puts her arm around Lola while Matthew sits on the edge of a chair, uncertain how to interject himself into the emotionally charged scene. He hasn't got where he's got to without previously keeping all his presenters alive and kicking.

Lola begins to sob on Elizabeth's shoulder. 'I mean, Ricky seemed so fine this afternoon! Like really normal, you know? He's not been drinking or you know, doing – anything else.' Her mascara begins to run in deep black rivulets down her cheeks. Elizabeth has never seen her friend so unkempt. She's always impressed that Lola can turn up for any crisis with her face done, her hair plaited or piled, and in clothes so tight and heels so high that Elizabeth is surprised she can move or breathe. Elizabeth, in contrast, keeps her hair cut short so that she can simply dry it by running her fingers through it each morning and wears a combination of short skirts and pumps that allow for running, since she always seems to be going at twice the speed of everyone else. ('We should put a battery pack on you,' Hutch once said as she came hurtling down the street, bumping into passers-by and tripping into his arms. 'I could plug into you and charge my mobile phone at the same time.')

'Ricky was really together and just – well, you know – not that tipsy, really.' Lola gulps.

Elizabeth nods. The dress run had gone well in that Ricky hadn't had a tantrum. He'd managed to keep the camera crew on side with a couple of well-aimed quips against his guests, especially the celebrity chef Paolo Culone, whose very fashionable and pretentious Soho restaurant had just opened. It was Ricky who'd come up with the idea of bringing some of Paolo's food on to the show for a tasting and, he promised, a pasting. 'Piquant cockle ketchup?' he'd sneered in the rehearsal. 'Little nuggets of calf's tail? Blimey! Who wants to eat this stuff? What's wrong with a tidy pie from Greggs?' And the crew had laughed and egged him on, surprised at the host's new-found enthusiasm for his show. Many of them had been at the receiving end of Ricky Clough's bad humour over the last few weeks, when he'd found everything wrong and everyone else to blame. This was a welcome change.

Matthew begins to pace around the Green Room. He's small and completely bald but muscular and full of a kind of attractive adrenaline. Two weeks ago he was the victim of a mugging and has since developed a slight limp. He's in his mid-fifties and every morning a personal trainer comes to his Hampstead Heath mansion with a gym bag full of rubber resistance bands. As a result, Matthew has gained some nicely bulging triceps, a flat(ish) stomach and, Lola claims, a new-found interest in S&M (she'd heard it from his secretary, who found a bag of sex toys stashed in the secret, locked, bottom drawer of his desk – a drawer to which she'd taken the precaution of cutting a duplicate key). Matthew hasn't got where he's got to without flexing a few muscles and he likes people to notice them.

'Christ, we'll have to put out a repeat this week instead of the show,' he says despairingly, but then his eyes brighten. 'Maybe a compilation? The Best of Ricky Clough? Only the early shows, obviously. Kev – would we have enough time to publicise it? Get everyone to watch it while they're still upset? We could be in for bumper ratings!' The two men huddle together around Kev's vibrating mobile.

'Lola, what time did Ricky actually arrive at the studio this afternoon?' Elizabeth tries to think back over the day's routine. She'd been in the production office till the early afternoon, trying to sort out next week's show. She'd only joined for the dress run when Ricky was ready to rehearse his monologue at the top of the show.

Lola looks at her miserably. 'I didn't like to call him.' She looks defensive. 'You know, it's not MY job to chivvy up the presenter...' Her eyes well up again and Elizabeth strokes her back.

'Of course it's not. It's just that you do it so well. Normally.'

'But he was only an hour late. And you know, sometimes it's been worse than that. And he was in such a good mood when he arrived.'

It's true that Ricky had seemed much more his old self and Elizabeth had been hopeful the show might improve. It was very unlike the last couple of weeks, when he'd been bored and bullying. She'd had to have words with him after she found a camera assistant in tears. Yesterday, he'd missed the production meeting because he'd failed to return from lunch. Elizabeth was getting fed up with it and had begun to think about leaving the show and leaving Ricky Clough.

As if reading her thoughts, Lola turns to Elizabeth, her face streaky with grief. 'I thought he was getting better. You know...'

'Yes, I did too.' Elizabeth pauses, but the whisky has done its job. 'Lola, hon, when did you last…um…you know, with Ricky?'

Lola screws her soaking napkins into a tight ball. 'Not in the last few weeks. He hasn't wanted to. He didn't seem to want company – or at least, not my company. To be honest, I'd wondered if there was someone else.'

'Oh, Lola. You didn't tell me! So no more late-night visits after the show?'

'Not for a few weeks, no.' Lola looks up, sharply. 'You won't tell Matthew, will you?'

'If you haven't seen Ricky – I mean, alone – for a while, then I don't see how it could be relevant,' she says slowly, glancing over at her boss. 'But Lola, I'm not sure it's as secret as you think it is…'

'Has anyone from the team said anything to you?'

Elizabeth considers this for a moment. When she'd first gone to discuss her presenter's bad behaviour on the show with Matthew, he'd asked if Ricky had 'inappropriately' propositioned anyone on the team. Elizabeth had said, truthfully, that no one had complained and Matthew seemed very relieved. But she's wondered a lot since about that word 'inappropriate'. Was it inappropriate that Lola should phone Ricky late at night, when she 'unexpectedly' found herself close to his Kensington house? Or inappropriate that she should accept his offer of a nightcap – and then a bacon butty? Or inappropriate that she should then go back for more at Ricky's urging? Inappropriate maybe, but definitely consensual. Over the years, Ricky had entertained a number of dalliances – Lola was merely the latest.

They'd all lived with it, condoned it, covered for him, even. And Lola is her best friend. No, Elizabeth isn't about to tell tales about this affair.

'No, no one from the team.' (Elizabeth decides that Matthew doesn't really qualify for this distinction.) 'Why don't you go home, Lo? Nothing's going to happen here. Let's speak in the morning. I've got to see the police again at 10. I'll call you after that.'

'Promise?'

'Of course.' Elizabeth hugs her. 'By the way, hon – do you know who Ricky had lunch with yesterday, when he missed our planning meeting?'

Lola bends down to pick up her vintage peep-toes, which she'd dramatically discarded in the heat of the crisis. 'Oh yes. Didn't you know? He had lunch with the boss.'

Elizabeth turns to her in surprise. 'With Matthew?'

Lola nods.

'Oh.' She glances over at the whispering two men in the corner of the room. 'Funny. Matthew didn't mention it.'

Lola looks at Elizabeth ironically and she smiles ruefully back at her. 'Yeah, you're right, hon. Of course, knowledge is power.' She kisses Lola on the cheek.

'Will you be okay yourself? I mean, going home to an empty flat?' Lola looks at Elizabeth meaningfully.

Elizabeth feels her sides constrict and her heart sink as she thinks of the deathly silence waiting for her: the unlit rooms, the unoccupied double bed. 'I'll be fine,' she says, turning away.

'Well, if you're sure. Speak tomorrow. Call me.' Lola squeezes her hand and leaves.

Elizabeth makes a half-hearted attempt to stash the empty bottles into an already overflowing recycling bin. She realises her silk shirt is clammy and clinging uncomfortably to her flesh. There are some unidentifiable stains on the front of it. She leans against the sofa and runs the shaking fingers of one hand through her fringe – her forehead is damp and strands of dark hair fall wetly on to her cheeks. The waistband of her skirt suddenly feels tight and restrictive; she feels she might have trouble breathing. She catches Matthew looking across at her, his face creased with concern. Kevin leaves the room with a brief nod in her direction.

Matthew puts down his whisky glass and moves towards her. 'How you doing, kiddo?'

Elizabeth is thirty-five but it's somehow become accepted between them that he will occasionally confuse her, his most senior female producer, with his teenage daughter Millie. It's a subtle but useful reference to the power play between them and Elizabeth is perfectly aware why he does it. And equally, she knows that occasionally she finds it comforting to treat Matthew like a dad. For too many long years now, she hasn't had a dad – and the older she gets, the more she realises what a void this is in her life. She's genuinely fond of her boss; she indulges all his foibles (as you would a dad) and allows him to tell his celebrity anecdotes uninterrupted, even though she's heard them a hundred times before. It's a purely professional partnership but it works well and she's grown to feel genuinely fond of him, especially given his recent trauma. But she's no longer sure she needs Matthew – or any boss, in fact. She's begun to harbour dreams of setting up a production company of her own. It's high time, she thinks, to call the shots herself.

'Is someone going to the hospital to meet Lorna?'

'Yes, Kev's organising it. She'll need help with the press — word is creeping out.'

'I hear you had lunch with Ricky yesterday.' She speaks more sharply than intended.

Matthew raises his eyebrows. 'Is that a question?'

'Yes, I think it is. Especially as he missed our programme planning meeting because of it.'

'Did he?' Her boss moves to open the door in an elaborate display of chivalry and gestures for her to lead the way out. 'Well, yes, I had lunch with Ricky. At The Ivy actually. I suspect there may be paparazzi shots, which are bound to get used once the papers hear about this. Kevin's checking it out now.' Matthew seems quite pleased at the prospect of some intrusive evidence of his celebrity lunch.

Elizabeth hesitates at the open door. 'Will you be telling the police?'

'Well, yes. If it comes up.' Matthew pauses. 'Actually, as lunches with Ricky Clough go, this wasn't so bad. He seemed, well, reconciled to the inevitable.'

'The inevitable? Did you tell him we're making a new show without him?' Elizabeth stops in surprise.

'Yes, I did. Although actually I think he knew anyway. He just wanted confirmation. But yes, Ricky took it remarkably well. He asked if the new show was with Hutch, and I said it was. He had quite a few very nasty things to say about Hutch and what he thought were his fatal flaws. Nothing I wasn't

33

expecting.' Matthew gestures that they should continue walking and Elizabeth, whose face is aflame at the mention of Hutch's name, avoids looking at him as he continues. 'But you know, Ricky seemed more relaxed about his future than I've seen him for a while. There was none of that recent aggression. He had a few ideas for new shows himself – they were all terrible, of course – but I got the impression his heart wasn't in it. I think maybe he was beginning to think about other things he wanted to do in life.'

Elizabeth doubts this. She can't imagine Ricky enjoying a life out of the spotlight. And she isn't entirely sure they can judge him, notorious as he was for his volatile mood swings, by just one day's good behaviour. But of course it's irrelevant now. Pointless. Poor Ricky. She suddenly finds her eyes welling. 'Well... That's a real shame, given...' A tear creeps out of the corner of her eye and she rubs it away, fiercely.

Matthew grabs her hand. 'I know, I know. It's terrible, Elizabeth. I'm going to miss him too. He was brilliant in his heyday. Unbeatable. But he was living on the edge – you know he was. His appetites were too large. He was caning it, night after night. He's not a child, he knew what he was doing. It's not your fault. It's not our fault.'

'But he *was* a child in so many ways... We indulged him just like we would a child! And it feels like my fault. I was supposed to be in charge this evening. Why didn't I spot it? Why didn't I see that he was so ill?' A shuddering sob escapes.

'Elizabeth, listen. In this business, we're all control freaks. But there are some things we simply can't control. No producer – not even one as good as you – can stop nature taking its course.' He smiles at her. She knows that she will tuck away his rare compliment for a future rainy, otherwise unrewarding day, but for now she gratefully accepts the neatly pressed hanky he hands her.

'Have you got a car to take you home?' he asks, still smiling.

'Take mine. I might walk for a bit.'

'Are you sure?'

The Controller is very sure. Elizabeth's phone call had pulled him away from a meeting in a discreet hotel room where the irresistibly long-legged hostess of his lunchtime consumer show is waiting to consume him. She's blonde and favours the sort of wrap dresses that show just about enough of a luscious cleavage (although some viewers have written in to complain that her breasts are putting them off their sandwiches). He figures that he'll get more comfort there than he will from going home to Hampstead and his wife, the history don, who despairs of absolutely everything to do with his job – other than its considerable income.

Tears are now falling freely down Elizabeth's cheeks and she allows herself to be ushered into Matthew's Mercedes with its deep leather seats and the heady smell of aftershave. Winston, Matthew's driver, tilts his mirror to look at her in the back seat and then silently hands her a box of tissues. As the car pulls away from the kerb, she sees Deniz Pegasus, Ricky's friend and manager, lurking in the shadows of the building. He steps out and moves towards the car but without saying anything, Winston gently presses down on the accelerator and they glide smoothly past him. Elizabeth turns and looks out of the back window to see Deniz standing in the street, his legs apart, his arms outstretched, watching her go. 'Thank you,' she says to Winston. He nods at her in the rear-view mirror. She pulls the hood of her parka low down over her face, sinks back into the seat and Winston turns up some soft jazz. The car slides like a snake, stealthy and smooth, through the London night.

Chapter Three

Elizabeth woke alone in her flat the following morning, having had no more than a couple of hours' sleep and feeling parched and nauseous. The day was already bright and spring-like. The cherry blossom in the street was showering dusty blooms, leaving a pale pink underlay on the pavement. She reached for her mobile to check her messages. The blank screen was a stark reminder of how changed things already were and brought with it a fresh wave of grief. She couldn't remember the last time she'd woken to a morning with no texts. Especially none from Ricky. He'd spend his nights sending her random ideas for the shows, feverish thoughts – and the occasional ridiculous demand. There had been middle-of-the-night phone calls as well, always in theory about some urgent piece of show business, but quite often giving way to monotone, paranoid monologues, where he lectured her on the failings of her production team.

There was no text from Hutch, either. Over the last few months, he'd sometimes send her funny, sexy, late-night messages – usually comments on the poems she was making him read ('I've got that old letch John Donne in bed with me tonight. Unruly son. *He'll do/ But he's not you.'*) Elizabeth didn't always respond to these suggestive texts; she was uncomfortably aware that they were sometimes sent when he was hiding in the bathroom or lurking in the shadows of his back garden. But there was nothing today. It was possible that he still hadn't seen any of the gossip circulating on social media, and she hadn't called or texted to tell him the news last night. She'd felt too drained somehow, too tired, too sick; she hadn't wanted to talk about it. Over the last few weeks – since Ricky's party – she'd felt that in every conversation with Hutch she was dancing on eggshells.

She pulled on a jumper he'd left in her room the night before last, when he'd told her that he loved her and she'd allowed herself to believe the world was still rich with possibilities. She wandered barelegged into the tiny kitchen, opened the fridge door and drank milk straight from the bottle. Then she leaned against the long sash window, gazing down at the street, where a road sweeper was wheeling his barrow of blossoms while jabbering away on his mobile in Polish. The jumper still smelled of Hutch and she hugged it round her, closer. Ricky dead! How was that possible? The man who had seemed so much larger than life!

Elizabeth knew something about loss. She knew that things can be snatched away when you're least expecting it, perhaps when you're still not grown up, not fully the person you're going to be. That you might get a phone call in the wrong place or at the wrong time of day and that moment will not only change your life, it will change your entire view of life. Elizabeth was seventeen when her dad died out of the blue.

She was at school and she had to go and see the headmistress, who sat on the wrong side of the desk and looked very sad. She handed her the phone and Elizabeth could hardly recognise the voice of her mother, cracked and hoarse, the terrible words strangled in her throat. The school organised a taxi to take her home and Elizabeth knew even then, in the back of the cab, that she'd just learned a lesson many people escape ever having to learn: that the world can be very fragile and your grip on it uncertain.

Elizabeth made some tea and forced herself to eat some dry toast. She was always astonished to find her kitchen empty of anything resembling butter or jam. She knew these things had to be purchased with forethought from a supermarket – she just never seemed to have the forethought. Jamie, when he'd lived with her, had been good at keeping up the supplies, religiously filling out the Tesco order online, taking care to seek out all the organic options, replacing Elizabeth's Jammie Dodgers with nourishing seeds and nuts. At times like these, Elizabeth hated living alone. She didn't want to be by herself, this morning of all mornings. She missed the lie-ins, the cuddles, the cups of tea in bed, the cleaning of teeth side by side, spitting in unison into the basin. She missed Jamie.

Jamie! The day that should've been her happiest – her wedding day – was a year ago, almost to the day. Another terrible May day.

★

39

When Elizabeth told her mum the date of her wedding six weeks beforehand, the corners of Maureen's mouth had drooped and she'd murmured, *'Marry in May and rue the day.'* Elizabeth had been furious. But later she had to acknowledge that her mum, through some spooky umbilical instinct, seemed to know something then that Elizabeth barely knew herself.

The whole wedding had been a whirlwind, although she and Jamie had met in their first week at uni and had shared a flat for the last ten years. Elizabeth had assumed they'd just continue to live together and then – quite soon, she hoped – have a baby. Jamie had often described marriage to her as an outmoded, patriarchal, state-imposed institution and as a full-time feminist, Elizabeth felt that she ought not to feel excited about the idea of a day when everyone would treat her like a fairy-tale princess. (Although she and Lola did quite often find themselves poring over wedding dresses in *Hello!*, and she had really quite well-developed ideas about what she would wear, in the very unlikely event that the occasion might arise.)

So the proposal, when it came, caught her completely off balance. She'd been up to her eyes producing the latest series of *Saturday Bonkers* and was out of the door early in the morning and always home late. She and Jamie were hardly ever in the flat at the same time. He'd grown exasperated with her job, her hours, the Ricky Clough antics. He worked for a charity which educated women in Ethiopia about the spread of HIV and he quite often travelled abroad. He'd shown Elizabeth photos of the prostitutes lining the road to Djibouti, a long ribbon of tarmac known as HIV Drive, and she'd often wondered what those women in their brightly coloured kemis and embroidered shawls thought of her blond, earnest boyfriend, in his button-down denim shirt, squatting in the dust talking to them about condoms.

In an attempt to spend more time together, Elizabeth had suggested that they go to her nephew's birthday party and stay the weekend in Manchester with her sister, Vic. Elizabeth adored her two small nephews and Vic in turn was fond of Jamie. Elizabeth had thought a family party might be healing, but in the end she and Jamie argued all the way up the M6 about whether or not they should sell the flat and buy a small house (Elizabeth was keen – she was secretly hoping they might soon have a need for a second bedroom – but Jamie dampened her hopes by arguing it was too acquisitive and bourgeois) and the tiff cast a cloud over the family reunion. Jamie was mostly sullen and distracted from the moment they arrived, and Elizabeth found herself overcompensating by being exceptionally lively and drinking too much. But during the birthday party on Saturday – just as she was acting out an elaborate scene from *Toy Story* with her nephews – Jamie suddenly seized her round the waist and murmured into her hair, 'Hey Lizzie, you're good at this. Let's get married and have one of our own.'

Elizabeth looked up, puzzled by his change of mood, and in her best Buzz Lightyear voice said, 'Excuse me, you are delaying my rendezvous with star command.' But Jamie was looking at her very seriously. It wasn't a joke. Vic paused in her pouring of lemonade and looked over at them anxiously.

'Well?' Jamie said more loudly.

Her nephew, Billy, who was Woody to her Buzz, took

off his sheriff's hat and threw it across the room, frustrated that the game had stopped. He looked up at Elizabeth with a chocolate-smeared mouth, eyes round and impatient. Jamie's face paled. He looked suddenly young, very like the hopeful blue-eyed boy she'd met on a freezing anti-war march in her first term at York, when he'd offered her some soup from his flask and some socialist leaflets from his rucksack.

But *marriage?* Did she want to be married? To wear a ring that signalled *I belong to someone else*? And they'd been so distant with each other recently! She glanced over at her sister, whose mouth formed a small questioning O. Billy tugged at her skirt and she looked down at his sweet face. But oh yes, oh God, she so wanted *that*! She did want one of their own. She took Jamie's hand. The hand she knew so well, every contour and lifeline, almost better than her own. How could she not accept that hand? Things would be better if they were husband and wife. She'd go home more. He'd be more communicative. They'd have a baby. Everything that felt wrong now would feel right once they were married.

'Yes,' she said, smiling at him. 'Yes. Yes. YES.'

★

Elizabeth drained her mug of tea and wandered over to the mirror that hung over the fireplace. Her face was unnaturally pale, the fine dusting of freckles across the bridge of her nose more pronounced than usual, her lips colourless, her short brown hair standing on end where she'd run her fingers through it, again and again. Hollow eyes were framed by dark circles and looked back at her accusingly: *Why didn't you know? You were meant to be in control. Why didn't you spot how ill Ricky was? Was it just like it was with Jamie? You simply didn't notice what was wrong?*

Her phone rang and she hesitated, thinking it would be Hutch. It was her mum. Elizabeth imagined her in her Essex kitchen, pottering about in the inappropriate silk robe Elizabeth had bought her when on a shoot in Rome, more suited to a bordello than a bungalow in Frinton-on-Sea. It sat uneasily on her, as did a number of other things Elizabeth had bought on her travels: the sofa throw that she'd brought back from Colombia, or the Costa Rican mugs, or the Galapagos tortoise paperweight. None of it suited the home of a woman who had spent most of Elizabeth's childhood holidays on the Costa del Sol searching high and low for Branston Pickle and Cheddar cheese. But that's what parenting was like, Elizabeth imagined: you cherished unsuitable gifts just because your children had thought about you for the briefest of moments while shopping in a South American street market.

And you stood by them no matter what they'd done.

Thoughts of home were comforting and Elizabeth wished she was with her mum now, being made cups of strong sweet tea. Tea had got them through so much over the years.

'Hello, dear. How are you? I wasn't sure if you'd be up... Elizabeth, are you still not sleeping properly?'

'Well...' Elizabeth realised her mum wouldn't have seen the news swirling on the internet. She kept the old android phone her daughters had bought her in a knitted sock in her bedroom drawer 'for emergencies'.

'Mum, Ricky Clough's dead! He died last night.'

'Oh no! Elizabeth! Really? How awful! How old was he?'

It was a relief finally to be able to talk about how terrible it had been, without having to put on a show of being capable and in charge. 'Oh, Mum, it was so horrible! And do you know, I'm not sure how old he is… I went to his birthday party a few weeks ago and people said it was his fiftieth but I think he was a bit older.'

'Yes, he looked a lot older.' Maureen had got to the age where the death of friends was most often the reason for a phone call before breakfast, but news of an unnaturally early death was much less run-of-the-mill. 'What did he die of, do they know?'

'We're not sure. Mum, it was during the show! I was there.'

'Oh, Elizabeth! Did you see it happen?'

Elizabeth thought of Ricky's body writhing on the studio floor, his eyes bloodshot and his mouth distorted, his hand gripping her wrist. And then she thought of her mum, running in from the garden on another glorious May morning, dropping to her knees with a small scream and cradling her husband's head as he grasped hopelessly for his last breaths, his heart clenching itself into an unyielding fist. Tears rolled down her cheeks. 'Yes. I've got to go to the police station this morning for an interview.'

'The POLICE? Good heavens! What on earth for? Oh, dear, are you in trouble?'

Elizabeth wiped her eyes with the back of her hand. Was she? 'No, I don't think so, it's just that they don't yet know what he died of… I think they just want to speak to everyone who'd been with him.'

'Well, I imagine it was his heart. I mean, he didn't pay much attention to his health, did he? He was quite heavy. And for a man of his age…' Her mum faltered and Elizabeth thought again of her dad at his office desk, gazing miserably at the Tupperware box of cottage cheese and pineapple chunks her mum had carefully prepared for him, longing for his egg-and-chip lunches of old in the City Road café. Not that it had helped in the end. *Fat lot of good that low-cholesterol diet was*, Maureen had said, sobbing, as they buried him, aged fifty-four.

'I guess it'll be on the BBC News by now.' Elizabeth reached for the remote.

'Oh yes, I'll take a look. But are you okay, in yourself? I mean, I know you'd worked with him for a while but I was never sure if you really – well, you know – liked him? Was he a nice man?'

Elizabeth thought for a moment. 'No, Mum, I don't suppose he was what you'd call a nice man.' Who wants to be *nice*? 'But Ricky was interesting. He could be very good company. In his heyday.' Elizabeth realised how easily she had let Ricky slip into the past tense and tears pricked her eyes again. He was already gone from the present and he would be gone from the future.

'Well, I only really watched his shows because you were working on them, you know.' Elizabeth's mother seemed very happy to dump Ricky now that he was dead. 'He wasn't really my cup of tea. You know, a bit shouty and well, a bit crude sometimes.'

There had been many versions of this conversation before. Elizabeth sighed. 'Yes. He wouldn't have been right for *Countryfile*. Mum, I've got to go – I'll call you later.'

'But listen, your sister's coming down to Frinton tomorrow for the weekend with the boys because Mark's away. Why don't you come too? I don't like to think of you there, alone.'

Elizabeth very much wanted the comfort of home – even her mum's neat seaside bungalow, with its limited provision of alcohol and pervasive smell of potpourri, and she longed to see Vic. Her sister was a successful divorce lawyer and had built a thriving practice in Manchester redistributing the wealth of Premier League footballers. Their chances to get together for boozy confessions had been much curtailed by Vic's move up north. It would be good to see her – she had a lot to tell her.

'I don't know, I'll see what the police say… Maybe I'll come.'

'Yes, do. And darling, can I tell Maggie? And Judy? I mean, it'll be all over the news, won't it?'

Elizabeth could only imagine how distracting this latest piece of information would be to the Zumba class in Frinton-on-Sea. It would surely trump the story of her wedding that wasn't.

She showered and let the hot water run over her face, streaming down her strained neck, and wondered what not to wear for a meeting with the Metropolitan Police. A pile of discarded clothing in the middle of her bedroom floor included PVC trousers, a pinstripe trouser suit from Kate Moss at Topshop that looked nice and boyish but had a wine stain on the jacket, and a summer dress from Zara that in sunlight was entirely see-through and always made her think of that photograph of Lady Di, standing coyly in the sunshine holding the hands of some toddlers. Maybe too demure? She rather suspected that the penetrating gaze of DI Watson would see through it all.

Elizabeth picked up the pinstripe jacket and stared at it. She remembered where the wine stain came from. A few weeks ago Ricky had invited her as his plus one (she was, after all, technically single) to an exhibition in a private gallery of the animal sculptor David Farrer. After swigging Chablis straight from the bottle, Ricky had bought a life-size papier-mâché head of a white cockerel, for which he paid over the odds on the basis that the gallery would let him take it home right there and then. Between them, they'd carried the cock's head – and the wine – home to his house in Kensington, stumbling drunk along the streets with Ricky crying to anyone who would listen, 'I've got an enormous cock!' The next morning she woke as usual to four texts from him, alluding in various ways to his purchase (*'Isn't it awfully good to have a cock?'* and *'I'm going to call him Percy'*), but the final text said that he'd been disturbed at an unearthly hour by some crowing and so he'd got up and thrown the papier-mâché head into his neighbour's skip. The texts had made Elizabeth laugh but in the cold light of day she found herself feeling sick and unhappy about his cavalier waste of fine art and money.

Elizabeth sat very still, clutching the jacket, fighting back tears. She thought her memories might drive her mad. She wished she wasn't alone; she wanted someone to make it go away. She wondered why Hutch still hadn't called and reached for her phone to check. There was a text, but it was from Matthew and it warned her that all news outlets were about to run the story. By the time she'd settled on a subdued navy blue skirt and a crisp white blouse, she was ready for the 8 o'clock headlines:

News just in of the sudden death of television and radio personality Ricky Clough. It's thought that he collapsed last night in the studio where he was recording his chat show, and that paramedics were unable to save him. No details have been released as to the cause of death but it is reported that police were also called to the studio premises. We'll bring you more news on this as it comes in.

Her phone buzzed.

'Elizabeth.' Hutch's voice was early-morning deep and gravelly. 'Really? He died during the show? Well! Not for the first time, eh?'

Elizabeth wondered if this was what she'd been avoiding: Hutch's need to say the unsayable. The very thing that attracted her to him in the first place was now the very last thing she wanted to hear. She also realised it was a time of day they rarely spoke. But nothing was usual, today. 'I'm not up to it, Hutch. Not now. Honestly. It was horrible.'

His voice was softer. 'Yeah, I bet it was. Poor you. Poor Miss Clumsy. Did you have to take charge?'

'Yes. Matthew turned up – after it was all over. I tried to do what I could, but you know, the drill, first aid – those things just go out of your head when it's really happening. He seemed so out of it, almost immediately. I've got to go to the police station this morning. But Hutch, none of us saw it coming! I mean, he didn't seem ill or pissed – not at all! If anything, he was more relaxed. It was just like the old times. We'd got Paolo Culone on – remember, I told you I'd booked him for the show after you and I went to his restaurant? And Ricky was firing on all cylinders, taking him down for his overly poncey food – the stuff he used to do in the past, that everyone loved. It was all going well... until...' Elizabeth's voice wobbled dangerously.

'So it was a heart attack?'

She thought again of Ricky's bloodshot eyes and violently contorting body. Was *that* what had happened to her dear dad? A half moan escaped her. 'I guess it must have been. Oh God, Hutch, I don't even know how old he was! I mean, officially.'

'He was fifty-two.' His voice was flat, certain. He seemed unaware of her distress. 'He's exactly ten years older than me. We're both Aries. And that's where the similarities end.' She could hear him yawning. 'Or should I say, ended.'

'Hutch! Please.' Elizabeth refrained from saying that a cruel wit was at least one other striking similarity between the two of them. She was struck by the fact that he was yawning, stretching, drinking coffee – as if waking up to a normal day. All the ordinary morning things she'd never seen him do. 'Hutch, Ricky knew about the pilot! He knew we were trying out a new show with you. I was so worried about him finding out – but he already knew. So it's even more extraordinary that he should be so fine in the studio yesterday.'

'Really? Who told him?' Hutch's voice had a sudden sharpness, a hack's nose for a source.

'Well, Matthew did actually. The day before, at lunch, apparently.'

'Did he indeed! That's interesting.' There was a pause.

'You didn't call or text last night.' Elizabeth gazed at Hutch's jumper on her bedroom chair.

'Yeah. Sorry. I was at the match and then went out to dinner with Sue.' Her name hung in the air. Like a stale smell.

'Oh.' And behind that 'oh' was an entire avalanche of suppressed emotions: hurt, dismay, jealousy. Resignation.

'Are you around later? Can I buy you lunch? After you've been to the police station?'

Elizabeth paused, but her heart began to beat faster. She desperately wanted some arms around her. She wanted someone to be there for her. But she tried to sound as casual as he did. 'Yes, I think I can do that. Usual place?'

'Yes. Usual place. One o'clock. Oh, and Elizabeth? Don't confess. Even if they waterboard you.'

Elizabeth couldn't help herself, she smiled. He still had the ability to do that, despite everything, to make her laugh.

'Fuck off, Hutch.'

Chapter Four

Elizabeth took the bus to Paddington Green Police Station. She liked the unusual sensation of sitting up top on a bus and watching London crawl beneath her. She had a car, a Volkswagen Beetle Convertible, which she drove furiously and much too fast. (She once drove Hutch down the Embankment and around Parliament Square and afterwards he said he needed a brandy and a lie-down.) But in the trauma of last night she'd left it parked at the production offices, where it was currently acquiring the undesirable accessory of a sticky plastic parking ticket. It was Elizabeth's fourth ticket in six weeks and on each occasion she'd made up her mind that she would renew her acquaintance with Transport for London. Her family had strong links with public transport: one grandad had been a linesman on the railways, the other a bus conductor, all his life on the same route – the 38. As Elizabeth's nan had said rather bitterly after he died, 'Never got promoted. Never got to do the 176 or the 55. Never got to go up Park Lane, or down Piccadilly. Never got to be a driver, neither. Always the same bloody route. Every day of his life.' But her grandad hadn't sought promotion, he'd been perfectly happy with his lot. And

Elizabeth thought there was much to be said for being happy with your lot. You never know when it might all disappear.

As the 73 chugged and chewed its way down Euston Road and through the early morning rush hour, it shaved some overhanging horse chestnut trees, showering the roof with pale white blooms that fluttered down past the window like the ghostly remains of a bridal bouquet. Hutch once took her for the night to one of those five-star hotels that turns your towels into origami animals and scatters petals across the bed (the bed was the size of a small continent) and in the middle of the night, Elizabeth found pale pink petals stuck between her thighs and in her armpits. Later, in the waterfall shower, she found another one between Hutch's buttocks. It was there that Hutch first told her he loved her and promised that he would leave his wife.

And in turn, she had finally told him about Jamie, and about the wedding that wasn't.

*

Her wedding day turned out to be a perfect pink Magnolia May morning, just as she'd imagined it would be. It had been just four weeks since Jamie's surprise proposal. They'd decided there was no point in waiting – after all, they'd waited ten years. Jamie didn't want the full pomp and ceremony of a church wedding and thought it a waste of money, and Elizabeth had convinced herself they were just getting the right piece of paper before having children. So she'd approached the production of her rushed wedding as if it was a last-minute live television programme. She came up with a strictly limited guest list, she wrote out a running order and she had an Excel spreadsheet on which she eked out their wedding budget. Their honeymoon was to be a two-day mini break in a Cotswolds spa hotel. She would be back in the office on Friday. They bought her a wedding ring in Hatton Garden for £35 and every so often she took it out of the little blue velvet box and tried it on her finger. She'd never worn rings and the wedding band felt tight and restrictive. She couldn't stop staring at it.

On the way to the register office, sitting with her mum Maureen and her sister Vic in the back of a London black cab clutching a hand-tied bunch of daffodils and irises (Vic had insisted she take something blue), Elizabeth realised she hadn't heard from Jamie since the previous afternoon. They'd spent the night before their wedding apart and she'd assumed he was just sticking to tradition. In the end, she'd texted him a jokey photo of a bride in an enormous meringue dress with a smiley emoji. But he hadn't replied. They'd gone for more than twenty-four hours without speaking and she couldn't remember a time in the last ten years when they had done that.

She was wearing the vintage lace garter Vic had laughingly given her the night before (something old) and it was chafing the soft skin on her inner thigh. Elizabeth had scratched it irritably several times already and now as she surreptitiously lifted the hem of her dress, she saw that the flesh around the garter was red and angry. Her dress was a vintage 1960s sleeveless shift and was the colour of apricots. She thought it would be a statement dress – look at me, I'm in a fun, flirty, fruity frock – but now she regretted it. The dress was creasing terribly in the traffic jam on the Euston Road. The plastic comb of flowers she'd tried to weave through her hair wouldn't stay in place and was now hanging drunkenly by a thread around her ear. The daffodils started to droop. She noticed her left hand (no engagement ring) was resting on the cab door handle and that she'd clenched it tight, as if about to open the door.

'What are you doing?' her sister asked sharply and Elizabeth's hand dropped, lamely, back to her lap. Vic had got married in a country church wearing a long cream silk dress that melted over her curves like liquid silver. She'd looked stunning. 'Won't be long now.' Her sister had smiled brightly at her, as Elizabeth imagined Vic must smile at her clients before she led them into the dock to be sentenced. Of course they should have known the traffic would be terrible, it was a Wednesday afternoon. A woeful workday Wednesday. Who gets married on a Wednesday? Vic's face softened when she saw Elizabeth's brimming eyes.

'Mum, tell you what. You keep the taxi. We'll walk. I feel a bit sick and could do with some fresh air and it would be good for Elizabeth to get a quick breather.' Vic was all lawyerly efficiency. She was wearing a smart navy blue coat dress. ('It'll always do for court afterwards,' she had told Elizabeth on the phone after she'd bought it. At the time, Elizabeth had felt hurt, as if her wedding wasn't excuse enough for her sister to buy a new shocking pink dress, but now she couldn't help thinking how wise it was.) Vic had inherited their mum's fairer skin and hair – although she'd dyed it so many times during her flirtation with the post-punk revival that Elizabeth could barely remember its original shade – and she had it cut short and pixie-like, a style that served her even better now, when she was almost in her forties and the mother of two small children, than when she'd flirted with The Libertines.

Elizabeth tumbled out of the cab trailing her posy of wilting daffodils as Vic led her firmly to one of the round tables nailed to the pavement outside the Globe pub on the Euston Road. The few hardened drinkers still on their feet turned to stare at them over their pints. Vic put her Hermès bag on the table and Elizabeth noticed a yellow lawyer's pad poking out of the top, as if her sister might find time during her wedding to catch up on a bit of casework.

'What's up?' Vic had said briskly.

'I don't know… It just doesn't feel right…'

'Look, Lizzie, it's just last-minute nerves. It's fine. It's Jamie! You've known him for ever! Being married isn't any different.'

Elizabeth had torn unconsciously at the daffodil petals. She raised her panic-stricken face. 'Vic, I know it's ridiculous, but I feel we've rushed into this wedding. It was so lovely, being with your boys at the birthday party and in that moment, when Jamie proposed, I wanted that life so badly. The life that you have, Vic. A domestic life. Babies. So I organised the wedding really quickly, I thought Jamie was right, we'd waited long enough. But oh God…' Elizabeth looked desperately at her sister. 'I panicked, Vic. I panicked about Forever. About it being Jamie, and no one else, ever again.' She lowered her eyes. 'I met this man at a work party, just a few days after Jamie proposed. And, Vic, he was so unlike anyone else I've ever been with! He was funny, he made me laugh and he was so interested in me and my job – and I don't know, just so different to Jamie!

He made me feel so good about myself. I thought I could have one last fling, I thought it wouldn't matter. But of course it *does* matter – and I've felt so guilty ever since. But Vic, I can't stop thinking about him!'

'Oh, Lizzie! But it's just the once? Just this one time?'

'Yes. You know there's never been anyone else, Vic. I've been longing to find the moment to tell Jamie, but the days seemed to race past and I couldn't find the right moment. And every time we confirmed another detail of this wedding, I didn't see how I *could* tell him! But now it feels like we'll be starting our marriage all wrong.'

'Oh, hon.' Vic hugged her. 'Look, Lizzie, let's try and be practical. There are ten people waiting in that building over there for you to turn up like a blushing bride. And one of them is Jamie. Jamie, the boyfriend you've been with since uni. Jamie, who's trying to save the world and who's good and kind. You do want to marry him, right?' There was a long pause. 'Hello?'

Elizabeth looked at her sister in desperation. 'Yes, I do. But oh, Vic, it feels so final! And I've only had sex with seven people! I keep thinking – is that enough to last me a lifetime?'

'Well, I'm not sure it's all about the maths, Lizzie. But I bet lots of brides go through this. I'm sure it's really usual to panic about committing yourself to one man, for better or worse. Look, I'll do whatever you want, but are you sure now is the time to tell Jamie? You made a mistake and you regret it. Maybe he never needs to know? Or maybe you can tell him, in time. But now? I'm not sure.'

Elizabeth nodded, numbly, and Vic was suddenly businesslike

again. She found herself being propelled along the Euston Road towards Marylebone Town Hall. Large splashes of rain began to stain the apricot dress. Vic ran up the wide stone steps, half dragging Elizabeth behind her. At the town hall doors, she turned suddenly and said, 'Who was it?'

'What?' Elizabeth was almost breathless. She tried to smooth down the damp creases in her dress.

'Who was it? That you slept with?'

Elizabeth bit her lip. 'Harry Hutchinson.'

'Harry…? Wait. You mean Hutch? The guy who does that late night football show?'

'Yes. And Vic, he's married!'

'Oh, Lizzie,' was all that Vic said as she pushed open the doors to the town hall.

★

Elizabeth took two quick brisk turns around the block to pull herself together before walking into Paddington Green Police Station. The only time she'd been in a police station before was when she had to take in proof of her insurance after she'd been caught doing 89 mph down the A12 and sent on a National Speed Awareness Course ('As if you need to be taught about speed, Miss Clumsy,' Hutch had said consolingly, as she threw herself on to his bed, clutching a new copy of *The Highway Code*.) She was greeted by DS Rafik, the young sweating sergeant who'd been in the dressing room the night before. His eyes were like two brightly polished buttons in the fleshy cushion of his face. He walked quickly, despite the extra pounds, and she had to half run to keep up with him, down the bland, windowless corridors, doors all closed, walls devoid of any kind of decoration. She found herself babbling nervously. 'You could do with some pictures. Maybe a cartoon or two. You know, something to help innocent members of the public, like me, who have to come in and give statements feel more at home.'

'I hope your home isn't anything like this.' The sergeant opened the door to an office with two desks crammed together underneath a barred window. An uncovered light bulb was hanging from a ceiling rose. Someone had put a cactus plant on one of the desks, which simply added to the general feeling of dismal discomfort.

'Wow!' said Elizabeth. 'Did you get your inspiration for interior design from Guantánamo Bay?'

A pink flush crept upwards from the folds of the sergeant's neck, but he stopped himself from smiling. He moved a pile of folders from a hard-backed chair, dropping some papers as he did so, and flustered, gestured for Elizabeth to sit on it. He offered her a coffee, pointing apologetically at a kettle on the window sill and a box of Nescafé sachets.

Elizabeth grimaced. 'No chance of a skinny double shot latte, I suppose? Maybe a basket of muffins? Haven't you got a runner?'

He looked at her, bemused. She shrugged off her raincoat. 'I'm sorry. I think I'm making terrible jokes because I'm nervous.'

He nodded, but before he could speak the door opened again and banged into Elizabeth's chair. It was Detective Inspector

Watson. She smelled strongly of apples. Her blonde hair was loosely swept up into a knot and fastened with a surprisingly girly pink scrunchie. She was wearing black trousers and a shirt the colour of cornflowers. Her arms were toned and tanned. She wore no make-up and, fresh-faced, looked younger than she had last night. Elizabeth guessed they must be about the same age.

'Hello, DI Karen Watson. Sorry, not much room.' The detective inspector went to sit at the remaining desk, the one with the cactus. She flipped open a notebook, picked up a pen, inspected it, and then lobbed it across the room, where it tipped neatly into a waiting wastepaper basket. She picked up another pen, inspected it again and wrote something on the open page. Finally, she looked up.

'Good shot,' offered Elizabeth.

'County netball team. Wing attack.' DI Karen Watson leaned forward, resting her elbows on the desk.

'Still plays,' added the sergeant proudly.

'Tuesdays only,' the DI said pointedly.

Elizabeth found herself saying, 'What's wrong with Saturdays? Or Sundays? I've heard weekends are good for sport.'

The DI looked at her sharply. 'Well, you see, the women I play with mostly have husbands, some of them have kids, and so they can't play netball at the weekend. Tuesday is their only opportunity to get out of the house.'

'Gosh,' said Elizabeth, genuinely struck. 'And they spend their only evenings off playing netball? When they could be necking sauvignon blanc in the wine bar? That's dedication.'

'Ah, well you see, most of us don't drink,' the DI said, and the implication was clear.

Elizabeth shifted in her seat. She realised that the volunteering of some personal information by the detective must be a well-rehearsed ploy. She noticed DI Karen Watson's body was taut, wired, finely tuned.

'So, tell me, how long had you been working with Ricky Clough?'

'On and off for seven years.'

'Producing all his shows?'

'Yes, this one and his Saturday night entertainment show…'

Elizabeth looked carefully at the DI to see how much of this television history she knew. Her face, however, was a perfect blank. But to her right, the sergeant said helpfully, '*Saturday Bonkers.*'

DI Watson looked nonplussed.

'Yes,' said Elizabeth. '*Saturday Bonkers.* Which was, well, a bonkers show! Partly a variety show but with other anarchic stuff going on in the studio, games and live OBs – um, outside broadcasts. And Ricky is – was – very good in it. You know, he's probably best known for *Shower*? The secret camera pranks on celebrities. And the song and dance finales every week with Ricky and guest stars. We had the Shadow Home Secretary on once, that caused quite a storm… Anyway, it's been running for years and last year it won Best Entertainment Show at the National TV Awards.' Elizabeth looked at the policewoman, hopeful of a congratulatory nod, but DI Watson remained expressionless.

'But, well, we've had some difficulties over the last few

months. The show's not been doing so well and Ricky was reluctant to try out new ideas. He couldn't believe it was losing its audience, he blamed the viewers, not the programme. He'd become quite difficult – a bit, well, bonkers himself.' Elizabeth smiled half-heartedly, but the DI's face was serious.

'Bonkers? How?'

'Well, you know, he could be very unpredictable.' Elizabeth twisted in her chair. How could she begin to describe, in this soulless office, to this ramrod straight policewoman, the sort of daily mayhem that had for the last few years passed for her professional working life? 'Um, well, let's see. He'd bring live animals into the office – I seem to remember there was a serious incident with some rats. And he'd wear clown's trousers to production meetings and then let them drop. He liked holding meetings in his underpants. There was an occasion when he went to a meeting with the network's chief, carrying a water rifle… He quite regularly used a water pistol during script meetings. And there were the late-night phone calls…'

The DI frowned and Elizabeth rushed on. 'But you know, people loved working with him. It was exciting. He had a loyal team. I liked working with him. That's why I agreed to produce this new chat show with him as well. I mean, you had to dismiss half his ideas, but at least he had some. And he could be very generous – he used to take the entire team out for lunch and pick up the bill. And he was very entertaining when he was on form… It was exhilarating to try and harness that sort of creative energy.'

'Tell me about the recent difficulties.'

'Well, I'd had to have words with him about his behaviour with the team.'

DI Watson nodded and Elizabeth got the feeling that despite the professionally blank expression, she knew more than she was letting on. 'Yes, tell me about that. His bad behaviour.'

'Oh, you know, he'd get stressed and angry and take it out on the researchers. He reduced a couple of them to tears. Nothing was good enough. He'd find fault with the guest bookings, the scripts, the props. In a way, it came from the right place – his ambition for the show – but it got to the stage where he was never going to be satisfied unless we booked Barack Obama and preferably got him to sing a duet on the show. He'd lost perspective somehow. He couldn't understand why he was having to work with reality show contestants instead of the leader of the free world.'

'Did he reduce *you* to tears?' The DI looked at the pad on her desk and Elizabeth realised she'd made quite a few jottings.

'Not in his presence,' Elizabeth said truthfully. 'But I must admit, I've had quite a few nights where I've been awake at 3 a.m., eating Marks & Spencer custard.' She looked at the policewoman's lean, netball-toned figure and doubted that Karen Watson had any nights when she succumbed to a tub of crème anglaise. But the detective looked up and half a smile played across her lips. Her eyes were lively and bright.

'And who's your boss?'

'Matthew Grayling, the Controller. The man you met last night.'

The DI's smile vanished. 'Ah yes, the man with the limp.

So he runs the whole network? He's in charge of all the programmes?'

'Yes. He's been there fifteen years. He knows Ricky of old. He got him to do *Saturday Bonkers* in the first place. He recently gave him the chat show to try and ease him into a new slot – you know, it's not on Saturday nights, it's not live, so we can always go into the edit and cut out the worst bits.'

'And was Matthew in the studio all evening?'

'No, I rang him, once Ricky... once he'd collapsed.' Elizabeth felt suddenly tearful. She bent her head and DI Watson sat silently for a moment before saying more gently, 'And now you've had time to think about that night, time to think over everything that happened, you can't think of anything that was unusual? Nothing about Ricky Clough that struck you as strange or different? He didn't seem ill?'

'No.' Elizabeth reached for a tissue from the box on DI Watson's desk. 'If anything, the thing that was unusual was that he was actually in a good mood. He seemed upbeat. I thought we were in for a good show. He didn't seem in any discomfort, wasn't complaining.'

'And you'd actually started recording the show, I think, when he fell ill?'

'Yes, that's right. We'd done the introduction and we were about to do Paolo Culone.'

The DI look across at the sergeant. 'We're seeing all the guests from the show later, is that right?' Ali Rafik nodded and listed the names of a few minor celebrities. Elizabeth winced at the poor quality of the bookings, but the DI appeared to register nothing. Eventually, she said, 'I don't watch much television. There never seems to be anything on that I want to watch.' Elizabeth nodded. It was true. There was a criminal lack of coverage of women's netball in primetime.

'So tell me about the chef – Paolo Culone?'

'Well, he's young, very brash. He's just opened his third London restaurant and it's all about smell. He puts a different scent around the restaurant entrance because he says it influences your mood and he wants his guests to be happy when they come in. So the week it opened, he made sure it smelled like an old-fashioned sweet shop – sugary and lemony – so that people coming in would feel nostalgic for their childhoods.' Elizabeth took a deep breath. She'd been to Culone's new restaurant a few weeks back. She'd gone there with Hutch and it had smelled of Curly Wurlys. Later that night in bed, Hutch had said she smelled deliciously of caramel and he'd licked her agonisingly slowly, all over.

The sergeant made a sound that was half cough, half giggle. Elizabeth recovered herself and nodded at him. 'Ricky thought it was all bollocks, too. He wanted to take the piss out of Paolo. We were going to bring on some of his restaurant dishes hidden in boxes and get Culone to guess what they were by their smell.'

The DI wrinkled her nose and frowned, as if trying to understand how such an idea might constitute primetime entertainment. 'And so it's likely Ricky Clough might have eaten something before or during the show?'

'Yes. We had some of Culone's food in the Green Room, where we entertain guests before the show. Ricky went in to say hello. I think he was trying to put Paolo at ease. To praise his food and sort of lull him into a false sense of comfort.' Elizabeth shrugged apologetically as if to distance herself from the sheer cynicism of the move, although it had actually been her idea.

'And so others might've eaten the food, in the Green Room?'

'I'm not sure. I wouldn't be surprised if some of the team had some. We don't pay our junior researchers much. They mostly live off scraps.' Elizabeth pulled a face at Sergeant Rafik and was delighted to see him try to hide a smile. DI Watson's expression was stony.

'We're running tests on all the food that's been left over. We'll have to interview everyone on your team as well.'

'Really?' Elizabeth sat up straight. 'Is that honestly necessary?'

The DI put down her pen. 'Yes, it is. But they don't need to come in here. We'll come to your offices this afternoon and talk to them individually.'

'Well, I guess you'll have to talk to Matthew about that...' Elizabeth realised her boss's attempts to keep the network out of this were hopelessly optimistic. 'I guess he may want someone from Legal there.' She looked at the DI anxiously. 'Can I ask, do you know the results of Ricky's hospital tests?'

The sergeant cleared his throat. The DI looked down at her pad, as if considering something, and then looked up at Elizabeth. 'Not all of the results, no. But we've got reasonable cause for concern at this stage.'

Elizabeth felt sick. The colour drained from her face. 'Concern about what?'

'It would seem from all the tests so far that Ricky Clough

did not die of natural causes. In fact, it appears that his seizure was the result of a highly toxic substance in his bloodstream.'

Elizabeth gripped the arms of her chair, her knuckles whitening.

DI Watson leaned back in her chair. 'I'm afraid, Elizabeth, we have very good reason to believe that Ricky Clough was poisoned.'

Chapter Five

When Elizabeth staggered out of the police station an hour later, the smoky purple sky was threatening rain. DI Watson had let her go after some very detailed questioning about the studio schedule and routine. She'd asked Elizabeth to produce an exhaustive list of all the people present, from the camera crews, the sound guys, the lighting team, to all the production staff – anyone who might have had direct access to Ricky Clough. Elizabeth supplied it all, her mind whirring with obscene possibilities: could it have been the cameraman who'd been shouted at by Ricky once too often? Was it the make-up girl who used to service Ricky on her knees in his dressing room? Was it a prank gone wrong from the sound guys, who every week had to clear the wax out of his earpiece? Who on earth would do such a thing, to Ricky Clough, the king of entertainment?

She walked slowly towards Café Cecile, her usual meeting place for lunch with Hutch. They'd been seeing each other for nine months now, but still in secrecy. Hutch was beginning to get increasing recognition on the street; his football show was becoming very popular. He was now getting invited to every celebrity party, gallery opening and first night. He was witty, he was tall, he wore mostly black, he suited a baseball cap, he stayed late and drank a lot – he'd won his place on the A-list. He also went to most of these events alone, which made him popular with every hostess, because although it was well-known that he was married – to a sports PR girl he'd met when he still lived in Manchester – her own work commitments seemed to entail her spending most weekdays up north.

Elizabeth was wearying of the subterfuge. She'd initially gone along with the secrecy, had even found it exciting: slipping into his flat through the car park's side door, leaving restaurants minutes apart, walking in opposite directions. Only her sister Vic knew about the affair – she hadn't even told Lola. She'd been swept up in the giddiness of being adored – it had been a great solace after the break-up with Jamie. Hutch seemed fascinated by her, it was very gratifying: she felt clever and self-confident in his company. He was interested in her job, asked lots of questions, watched all her shows, minutely observing. He'd told her from the beginning that his marriage was over, they were living separate lives – he was simply waiting for the right moment. But here they were, nine months later, apparently still waiting for his right moment, and in the last few weeks Elizabeth had begun to believe that his right moment might never come. She was fed up with hiding in the shadows. She wanted a relationship that could be public, open, lasting. She wanted to be loved, enough.

That was what Jamie had said inside Marylebone Town Hall a year ago: *I don't love you, enough.*

★

He had been waiting for her as she came through the town
hall doors, standing alone and apart, unfamiliar in his grey
suit, his shaggy blond hair newly washed and combed. He
looked very pale and grave. Elizabeth held out her arms to
show off her ridiculous apricot dress and did an apologetic
mock pirouette. But Jamie didn't smile. Instead, he grabbed
her hand and pulled her with him out of the nearest door and
into a municipal corridor. Portraits of former councillors, all
of them men, gazed sternly down at them with their heavy
chains of office.

'Jamie… I… I'm sorry.' Elizabeth's heart was pounding
against her ribs.

Jamie looked at her, surprised. 'You're sorry? What…? Oh,
for being late? It doesn't matter.' He now looked at his feet and
she noticed he had new shiny shoes. 'Elizabeth, I…'

She suddenly felt she couldn't breathe. She leaned against
the wall. He must know! Perhaps dishonesty was like a scent;
it lingered around your ears, on your neck, so that when he
kissed her, he could smell her treachery? Surely, now, she had
to say something? What if Vic was wrong? Perhaps it would
be better to confess.

'Elizabeth, I'm so sorry.' His voice was quiet, almost a
whisper. Unconsciously, she leaned in to hear him. 'I don't
think I can do this. I don't think we should do this.' His breath
came in gasps. 'I don't want to marry you. I'm so, so, sorry.
I… I don't think I love you. Enough.'

Elizabeth reeled back as if struck and her knees buckled; she slid slowly down the wall to the floor, still clutching the stems of her disintegrating bouquet. Enough? What did 'enough' mean? Jamie knelt beside her.

'Lizzie, listen to me. I know you hate me right now. But I think, once you've had time, you'll realise I'm right... We're just doing this because the alternative seems so scary. But it's not the right thing to do, Lizzie. We don't love each other enough, we've just got used to each other. And that's not the same thing.'

Elizabeth's head sank to her knees. Suddenly, she felt very tired. She realised she hadn't eaten anything. She wanted to curl up in a ball on the municipal floor and make everything disappear. But Jamie was still talking, low and urgently, in her ear. She couldn't make it stop; this torrent of words from him, they kept on coming.

'I know this is all my fault. I know I suggested we got married. I thought we needed to change something and that marrying would do it. But I've been very unhappy for a long time, Lizzie. You've been too busy to notice it. We've stopped talking. But I've been feeling very lonely and confused. And stupidly, I thought we'd sort things out by getting married and having kids. But as the days went by, I realised it was just a sticking plaster. And that isn't right – that's not what marriage should be. I kept thinking I'd say something these last few weeks, but I wasn't brave enough, I suppose. But I can't do it. I can't go through with it. I'm still unhappy. I'm sorry. I'm very sorry.'

Elizabeth struggled to get to her feet and Jamie tried to help her, but she pushed him away angrily. Vic came running, with her husband Mark close behind her, and as they got to her, Elizabeth was feverishly shredding the flowers, a carnage of dismembered blue and yellow petals scattered around her like confetti. Vic lifted her by the arms and it was as if she was drunk, she couldn't stand. Her mother appeared, crying, arms outstretched as if to catch her. Then Vic and her mum were steering her back down the town hall steps, her feet tripping crazily against each other. Mark was yelling for a taxi, and Elizabeth looked around, bewildered, for Jamie. But he was nowhere to be seen.

*

Elizabeth pulled her coat around her, feeling shivery. She had dawdled too long – she was late for Hutch. Café Cecile, at the wrong end of Ladbroke Grove, was a faded patisserie which served tired croque monsieur and stale pastries. Madame Cecile herself had also seen better days and she was more often than not to be found sitting on the back step of the kitchen, puffing on a cigarette and rubbing her swollen ankles. But she stocked a reasonable cache of very drinkable wine and being still mostly French, she allowed Hutch to smoke the odd Gauloise inside, at the table nearest the back door. But the main attraction of Café Cecile was that no one Elizabeth and Hutch knew would ever dream of going there. In the early, heady, getting-to-know-you days, she took to wearing a French beret and once presented Hutch with a copy of James Fenton's 'In Paris with You':

Do you mind if we do not go to the Louvre,
If we say sod off to sodding Notre Dame,
If we skip the Champs Elysées,
And remain here in this sleazy
Old hotel room,
Doing this and that
To what and whom,
Learning who you are,
Learning what I am.

Their relationship had blossomed, along with Elizabeth's astonishment that Hutch knew not a single poem, not even a limerick, resulting in her consequent determination to introduce him to the Romantics. And so his poetic education had progressed in tune with their affair, so that in time he became used to having not only Elizabeth in his bed, but also Keats, Byron and the Liverpudlians. Hutch liked her reading aloud to him and she liked to show off, and so they'd idle away hours over the poetry, the wine, and each other. It was almost as good as a dirty weekend in a backstreet hotel in Le Marais, a weekend they often talked dreamily about, but which had so far failed to materialise. Café Cecile would have to do.

By the time she arrived, Hutch was sitting at their usual table, an empty glass of red wine beside a plate of crumbs and a half-drunk bottle. She looked at him through the glass and the raindrops that separated them. His blue eyes were narrowed against the light, but they didn't move from her face. His face seemed fuller; Elizabeth noticed his neck was creasing into the collar of his shirt. He'd had a haircut – it was clipped close to his head, like an army buzz cut. It seemed to make his features, his nose, his chin, more obvious. His forehead was furrowed, his dark, almost black, eyebrows raised in that familiar ironic expression, his mouth suggestively half open, those full lips inviting. She stood still, hands thrust deep into her pockets, her hair clinging limply to her face. He was wearing the pink checked shirt she'd once bought him and she wondered if he'd chosen it deliberately or if it was an accident of fate. Or maybe Sue had chosen it for him? Elizabeth imagined rows of freshly laundered shirts on padded silk coat hangers, his wife running her hands over them, lifting one down, laying it carefully on the bed for him. She clenched her fists in her pockets. There was still something unreachable about Hutch, some bit of him she couldn't penetrate. She hesitated. She could run away, right now. But then Hutch half stood up, still not taking his eyes off her, and his arm was stretched out, his hand open like a supplicant, and she felt the familiar enticing pull. She shrugged as if to say, here I am, the old fool, back again. She opened the door and stepped inside.

Hutch had sat back down and she had to bend to kiss him. He was unshaven and her lips brushed the rough surface of his cheeks, the familiar hard corner of his mouth. His shirt was open at the neck, revealing dark curling hairs. She often found looking at him unbearably tense: he would hold her gaze for seconds too long and she would feel her insides dissolving into liquid anticipation. She would feel that she couldn't breathe. He poured her a glass of wine and she took off her raincoat. He looked at her navy skirt and white blouse, now clinging damply to her skin, nodded slightly and said, 'School uniform?'

Elizabeth took a long swig of wine. 'Well, it turns out I don't actually have a wardrobe for all occasions. I'm missing the "What to Wear for a Police Interrogation".'

'So you thought carefully and came up with an outfit more suited to a twelve-year-old on her way to choir practice?'

'Well, if I look virginal and innocent, that was half the point.'

'Virginal? In that bra?' Hutch looked at her long and hard, and in the end Elizabeth looked away first and self-consciously crossed her bare legs.

'So how was it?'

Elizabeth looked over to the café counter, where Madame Cecile was slamming down a cup of coffee, clearly irate that someone had dared to come into the café expecting a hot drink. She lowered her voice. 'It's bad. They think it's suspicious. It's become a criminal investigation.'

He looked at her quickly, glass paused halfway to his lips. 'What d'you mean? They don't know what caused the heart attack?'

'They're not even sure it was a heart attack.'

He was staring at her very intently. 'Go on.'

'Well, it seems he had something in his bloodstream that wasn't – natural.' Hutch put down his glass and let out a short, mirthless laugh. She went on quickly, 'Or at least, something he wasn't used to.'

'You mean someone gave him some bad stuff? Well!' He leaned back in his chair and his shirt stretched against his chest, gaping slightly over his belly so that she caught a glimpse of the line of strong, dark hair. 'Tell the police to call me. I could give you the names of quite a few people who'd like to have Ricky Clough bumped off.'

'Come on, Hutch! Sure, he had enemies. I know he's been badly behaved these last few years.' He raised his eyebrows. 'Okay, really badly behaved. But it's a big stretch to say he had enemies who wanted him dead! Or even the sort of enemies who could pull that off – actually killing him.'

'I've wanted to kill him,' Hutch said flatly. 'And so have you, Elizabeth. The truth is, he'd become a jerk and a boor. He wasn't even funny any more. He was just rude. It was good of you to go and produce this new chat show with him, but he'd lost it. You know it.'

Elizabeth gazed out of the window. Poor Ricky. How had it come to this?

Hutch reached for his glass and deliberately brushed her fingers with his. His touch reverberated through her like a bolt of lightning. He smiled at her, his eyes half closed and softening. 'What d'you think will happen? To our show?' He leaned on the word 'our'.

She knew this was coming. But still, she wasn't ready for it and she felt the tastelessness of the question burn in her throat, in her gut. 'Hutch, I have no idea.'

'Well, the network's going to be needing a new show, now more than ever!'

She looked at him, horrified, and he laughed out loud and sank back in his chair. 'C'mon, Elizabeth. I'm teasing you. I don't want to step into a dead man's shoes. Anyway, there'll be an outpouring of sympathy for the old git – you watch. Everyone will forget his ratings were shit. There'll be a big nostalgia wave for *Bonkers* – they'll all talk about how they used to watch it while getting ready to go out on a Saturday night. "Oh, it was part of my growing up," tabloid hacks will write. He'll get the best reviews he's ever had.' Hutch's tone was surprisingly bitter and she found herself defensive in response.

'Well, he deserves some good reviews. Most of his career, he was funny and original.'

'Yeah, we all admired him. Until we knew what an arse he was. Come on, Elizabeth, don't lose sight of the truth just because he's died unexpectedly. He had it coming.'

'You know, you're not the first person to have said that to me in the last twenty-four hours.'

'Well, there you go.' He glanced around the café, then held her hand, lacing her fingers between his. 'Mind you, you have to pity Lorna in all of this. Poor love! She didn't get much out of that marriage.'

Hutch and his wife Sue knew Ricky and Lorna Clough. They mixed in the same celebrity circles and occasionally attended the same parties. The two wives had another connection: Lorna Clough had employed Sue Hutchinson to do the PR for the horse shows she held at their home in Surrey. Hutch and his wife had been at Ricky's birthday party a few weeks ago and had sat on one of the top tables. Couples. Elizabeth had once been part of a pair. She'd been a significant other. But now she was a secret other. She felt something hard and painful in her throat. Abruptly, she pulled her hand away from his, and in doing so knocked over her wine glass so that it spewed across the table and dripped into his lap. She reached to grab a napkin to dab at the wet patch and then realised that it would look entirely inappropriate. She dropped the napkin and sent a knife flying to the floor with a clatter. Hutch caught her wrist and held it firm.

'Whoa, Miss Clumsy! You are in a state. Is it me – do I turn you to jelly? Or are you like this with all the boys?' He winked at her and she stuck out her tongue at him.

'I don't know what you mean. I'm completely in control of all my limbs.'

'Well, later, I intend to get you undressed and count your grazes. I'm keeping a record. Last time, I seem to think there were four unexplained bruises. Either you're still bumping into furniture, or you're having an affair with a sadist.' He smiled at her. She loved that smile. He took her hand again. 'I'm sorry I wasn't there for you last night. I wish I could have been. I just couldn't get out of that dinner with Sue, you know how it is. But I'd much rather have been there for you.'

Here it was. The old familiar swing of the pendulum, back and forth: just as she was melting, he mentioned his wife. And actually, she didn't know any longer how it was. Being with Hutch felt a bit like groping your way forward through a maze. Every so often, she thought she'd found a way out into the open, confident that she was on the right path. And then she'd meet an unexpected dead end. And just as her despair reached crisis point, another secret track would open up and she would be on the move again, groping her way blindly back into the light, into his arms. It was so often like this, the weight of what they were doing and what she felt but hardly ever said, threatening all the time they were together to burst their delicate bubble, splinter their fragile peace.

She dropped his hand, pushed her chair back. 'I've got to go. The team's being interviewed back at the office. I need to be there.'

He didn't like his hand being dropped. 'But I moved things around for you. I've got to file a piece but I got them to extend the deadline. For you, Elizabeth.'

She burned with embarrassment at his petulance, but he looked back at her without any trace of self-consciousness. She snatched up her coat, struggling to get one arm in a sleeve. 'Maybe I shouldn't have come. I'm all over the place. But I think with good reason.'

He stood up and opened his arms. 'Of course, with good reason. Come here. Stop fiddling with your coat. Stop babbling. It's me, it's okay.' Gently, he disentangled her from her sleeve. She let herself be pulled into his chest. It was of course what she wanted, why she'd come. He smelled good, of Sancerre and sugar and smoke.

'Can't we go to the flat?' Hutch said against her hair. His hand slipped under the waistband of her skirt and his fingers crept down to stroke the base of her spine. She felt the familiar ache. Her breasts hardened against his chest. He was breathing more heavily and she felt him press against her legs. She pulled back and glanced around the café. Madame Cecile was slapping a wet cloth backwards and forwards along the counter. There was only one other customer, an old man who was reading the *Metro* with an eyeglass.

'Hutch, we can't have sex. It would be so wrong. Ricky's just died!'

'I think that's exactly why we should have sex. To celebrate being alive. And anyway, sex and death – they go together well. One climax, or another. Ricky would approve, you know he would.'

He pulled a twenty out of his pocket and waved it at Madame Cecile, who gave him a knowing nod as he tucked it under the empty wine bottle. He nudged Elizabeth gently towards the door and she felt an exquisite sensation as she skipped beside him, his hand reaching for hers, their heads bent against the rain, hurrying towards his Paddington bolthole, the place he'd owned when he was single that still had his bachelor Habitat leather sofa, his bachelor futon, his bachelor black sheets. The flat that gave nothing away about the fact he was a married man with a wife called Sue.

Indoors, dripping on to the polished pine floor, he kissed her all over, sweetly, slowly, sensitively, as if she might break. Every bit of her body responded by aching for him. He slipped down her zip, never taking his eyes off her, and carefully undid the buttons on her shirt. She reached for his neck and pulled his face to hers, their tongues searching out the further corners, the loose, wet insides. Hutch lifted her on to the breakfast bar and stood in front of her, spreading her knees apart as she unzipped his flies. He smiled a lovely, lopsided, knowing smile. He pushed her undone skirt up over her hips and stood staring at her pale naked thighs, the dark mass of curling hair. His mouth found her breasts and tugged on the nipples until she shivered and rocked beneath him, sliding further and deeper into him on the tiled counter so that he had to clutch her buttocks with his hands to hold her steady, as she wrapped her ankles around his hips. Then he lifted her down and spun her round so that she was facing away from him. She stretched out her arms across the counter and lifted her pelvis so that he came into her from behind. He was mouthing filthy words into her ear, his fingers in her mouth, using them to slide between her legs and stroke her.

Of all sexual positions, Elizabeth's favourite was on top: she liked Hutch pinned and helpless beneath her. It was, she felt, the most properly feminist position to take. But he was never more excited than when he took her from behind and was always very grateful afterwards, as if she'd bestowed on him some kind of honour. And she couldn't help herself, she liked how surrendered it made her feel, spread-eagled face down on the breakfast bar. Now, he slowed his rhythm to coincide with hers, reaching down to stroke her until she groaned and cried his name out loud.

Afterwards, Elizabeth got dressed while he watched her, leaning against the counter, smoking. She loved this quality of stillness he had, the way his eyes never left her, as if he were transfixed by her. As he stood there, naked, watching, she was aware that her own movements were theatrical. She was performing for him, slowly buttoning here, lazily zipping there, swaying with an exaggerated deliberateness. She smoothed down her hair, smiled self-consciously and leaned in to kiss his chest, his unshaven cheeks. This was what they were good at; here was where they were at their best. Away from the world, hiding from reality. He ran his hands up her thighs and under her skirt. He was physically unlike any other man she'd been with. Jamie had skinny hips, narrow shoulders and a long, lean back of pale creamy skin with a smattering of freckles across his shoulder blades. Hutch was much broader and more solid. Jamie had always been restless, his knee bobbing up and down when sitting on the edge of his chair, his eyes darting, as if at any moment a global catastrophe might cause him to bolt. Hutch's movements were slow and measured. He was comfortable in his own skin, confident in his rootedness.

'Let me make you something to eat – you can't deal with the police on an empty stomach.'

Hutch, still naked, gently pushed her away and opened his fridge, which was wonderfully full. He wrote occasional restaurant reviews and their relationship had involved a lot of eating. In the first few months, giddy with love and lust, her stomach full of butterflies, Elizabeth had lost weight. But Hutch had gradually encouraged her to embrace gluttony and she reckoned she was now half a stone heavier than she was a year ago. He'd learned to love food from his Jewish mama in Manchester – he'd grown up in a home where latkes would be frying in the pan when he got in from school, the table laden with cholla, pickled herring, matzo balls, chopped liver. For Elizabeth, he'd cooked creamy scrambled eggs and grilled pink juicy rib-eye; he'd made salads with mango, and ice cream with loganberries. He'd taught her where to find the best matured Cheddar, which he'd melted on top of some sweet-tasting Italian tomatoes and sourdough bread. He'd taken her to Culone's, where they'd eaten pork cheek and pampas petals, with yacon root and small black things floating in a white sauce. ('Gosh, these peppercorns are crunchy!' Elizabeth had said, bravely. 'They're ants,' Hutch had said.) He'd made her try tocosh – fermented Andean potato, which she assured him she'd never touch again, and percebes (Iberian gooseneck barnacles), which she'd loved. He once made her eat a dish called Spiders on a Rock: 'limpet, crab, sea snail, served with sarcasm'.

'Sarcasm?'

'Sargassum. Seaweed. Although your version's better.'

Now, he pulled out some eggs, smoked salmon and a bag of bagels. She took one bagel, and a strand of smoked salmon, which she held above her head and dangled slowly into her mouth. 'I'll have this on the run. I can't stay and eat, much as I'd like to.'

He leaned over to lick the salt from her mouth. 'By the way, I've got a new poem for you.' He looked at her slyly.

She shook herself free and clapped her hands, delighted. 'Go on then!' she said. Hutch made as if to recall the words, then slowly recited, his eyes never leaving hers:

As the trees reach for the sun above
So my arms reach out to you for love
With your hand resting in mine
I feel a power so divine
You're my world, you are my night and day
You're my world, you're every prayer I pray
If our love ceases to be
Then it's the end of the world for me.

She frowned, trying to place it. He winked at her and turned back to the eggs, which he expertly cracked with one hand into a Perspex bowl.

'Wait, I know I know it!' she said, frustrated. He shrugged, whisked, and began humming to himself. Elizabeth searched the compendium of collected works she had studiously stored in her head but she just couldn't locate the wretched poem. She was sure it was twentieth century – she knew Hutch favoured Modern – and she'd schooled him from Auden to Wilde. She felt she knew it so well – she could almost come up with another verse. But it had gone.

He turned away, amused at her frustration. She reached for her coat and then paused. The crushing weight of anticlimax was already clouding their encounter. She went where she'd promised herself she wouldn't. 'So how was dinner with Sue?'

A flicker of something close to irritation washed over his face. He reached for his jeans and in a few quick, rough movements, pulled them on.

'It was boring. Okay? We talked about the Aga, which isn't working, and that seems to be my fault. You know, it was all just domestic stuff. I kept thinking how different the conversation would have been if you'd been there with me instead. We'd have talked about poetry and sex and I'd have tested you on the defensive back three for Man City and run my hands up and down your naked legs under the table.'

'You've got an Aga?'

When Elizabeth thought about the Soho loft that she and Hutch would eventually occupy, with its Crittall windows and crowded bookshelves, she imagined that centre stage would be an Aga, perhaps in a tasteful shade of duck egg blue. The sort of clever, permanently warm appliance that could miraculously produce both hot scones and lamb stew, so that you might casually refer both to your *simmering* oven and your *baking* oven, while barely mentioning your four hotplates. The sort of appliance around which friends would sit cosily and laugh and gossip and drink wine. You might sit beside it and nurse your baby, like a Madonna. Perhaps with a curly-haired toddler at your feet. Yes, *all that domestic stuff.* The Aga was another small piece in the broken jigsaw of Hutch's marriage that she would think about over and over, once she was alone. They still had an Aga. They were still together.

'Have you spoken to Matthew about the plans for our show?' Hutch's tone was equally sharp in response.

'No. Obviously, I'll see him now when I get back to the office.'

'But he still wants it, yes? He's still keen on the pilot?'

'Yes. He thinks you're great. The next big thing,' Elizabeth said drily.

'Good. I've had some more ideas about items for the show. You know, we're really on to something. It's a different kind of talent show, I know, but I think I'll be a very good judge. I think we could make the opening much bigger. And I know this sounds strange, but maybe introduce some music numbers – perhaps in the finale?'

Elizabeth looked at him quickly. 'You mean, like Ricky did on *Bonkers*?'

'Well, not quite. I'll do it better.' He kissed her lightly on the cheek.

As soon as she left his flat and irritated by his small poetic victory, she texted him this:

When I am sad and weary
When I think all hope has gone
When I walk along High Holborn
I think of you with nothing on.

(Adrian Mitchell, in case you're wondering.)

She was aware that once again she'd sent a jokey text, as if nothing important needed to be said. She'd gone wanting some comfort, but she didn't feel comforted. She worried that the more she got to know Hutch, the more she wondered whether they were really a match. She was embarrassed by his lack of subtlety, by his obvious self-interest – qualities she'd previously excused as being part and parcel of his seductive and abundant self-confidence. But she couldn't really blame him for trying to steal some of the ideas that had made Ricky's show so popular. She knew it was her fault. It was she who'd suggested Hutch appear on *Bonkers*, on Ricky Clough's show, in the first place.

And that was really when it all began to go wrong.

Chapter Six

Six weeks earlier

'Hello, everybody! I said, Halloooeee, everybody?! It's Saturdaaaaay! Are we ready to do something really Bonkers? Ready to do something Bonkers with Ricky Clough? Of course we are!' The warm-up guy was wearing an electric blue suit that sparkled under the heat of the television lights. 'Now then, anybody single tonight?'

A laughing blonde two rows back from the front put up her hand, goaded by her mates. 'Hello, darling.' The electric blue suit was all insinuation. 'Where are you from?'

'Watford,' the girl shouted back and the warm-up guy turned his back. 'Forget it, love. I don't go north of Finchley. Not for you, anyway.' The girl and her mates are left to scream with mock hurt and offence.

In the shadows of the studio floor, Elizabeth pulled a face at the warm-up guy and drew a finger across her throat. She wanted him to back off the blondes – this was, after all, a family show. She ran up the spiral staircase to the gallery above the studio floor, where Robin, the director, resplendent in his cravat and a lucky silk waistcoat, a cloud of Paco Rabanne settling around him like a shroud, was giving notes to the cameramen, who were listening on talkback. Lola, with lucky yellow bows in her beehive, was bent over her script, rubbing out her previous notes and carefully making new ones with a sharp pencil. Matthew, the Controller, was also in attendance, in a dark recess at the back of the gallery, lounging on the sofa wearing a suit and demolishing a bowl of Haribo.

Ricky strode into the gallery. His eyes were thick with eyeliner. He shook Matthew's hand and then called out to the rest of the gallery, 'Aye aye, watch out – the Suits are in!'

'Have you met all the guests?' Elizabeth asked Ricky. She made sure he spoke to each of the show's guests in the Green Room before the show.

'I saw Beverly in her dressing room.' He winked at two young researchers who, basking in the glow of his direct appeal, winked back. Beverly Hunter was the Puerto Rican member of an *X Factor* girl band (they came fourth) who had latterly made a name for herself on the West End stage.

Elizabeth frowned. 'And have you seen Hutch yet?'

Ricky looked at her quickly, but she steeled herself to return his stare. No one, she was fairly sure, knew about her secret relationship with Hutch. Certainly not Ricky, nor her boss, Matthew. And not Lola, the hardest person of all not to bring into her confidence. But on so many levels, Elizabeth was nervous about the show tonight. Ricky had resisted booking Hutch as a co-host on *Bonkers* until a few days before, when even he'd had to accept that David Beckham wasn't going to turn up. But he'd said warningly to Elizabeth, 'It won't work. Hutch is too clever-clever for our show. He's all about irony.

He can't do proper entertainment. He gurns at the camera like a weathergirl.' And she'd had a moment's panic that he was right. But Hutch, when she'd coached him in bed later that day, proved to be eager to please, up for anything, keen to appeal to the large mainstream *Saturday Bonkers* audience.

'Have you seen Hutch?' she repeated in the gallery.

Ricky looked at her cynically, his fists tightening around his rolled script. 'Sure, I've seen him. All eager like Tigger, he is. Bushy-tailed. Very keen to please the producer is what I hear...' He looked accusingly at Elizabeth, who ignored the dig, although she felt Lola turning to look at her and she could sense that Matthew had paused in his hoovering up of the Haribo.

'No tricks, please, Ricky,' Elizabeth said firmly. 'Nothing unrehearsed, okay?' She didn't get the reassuring nod she was looking for. Instead, he moved towards the staircase that led down to the studio. They could hear the warm-up shout, 'Okay, ladies and gents! Are you ready to greet the star of the show?'

Ricky blew out his cheeks and loosened up his shoulder blades, as if on the starting blocks for a 100-metre sprint. Elizabeth moved closer to him and gave him a hug. 'Enjoy!' she said, at the same time covertly checking his pupils for dilation. He kissed her on the cheek, as he always did and said, as he always did, 'See you on the other side!' And then he waved to the rest of the gallery, 'Let's have a good one!' He opened the door that led down to the studio floor and they could hear the audience roar in anticipation.

She took her seat at the gallery desk. Lola handed her a mint, announcing to the crew on talkback, 'One minute till we're live on air. One minute.'

Elizabeth had been to see Hutch alone in his dressing room half an hour earlier to take him carefully and one more time through her plans for the show. He was amused at her anxiety, kept trying to kiss her when she was at her most serious, slid his hands underneath her top when she stood beside him pointing out his cues in the script.

'Elizabeth, I love it when you're this strict.' He breathed into her ear. 'And when you're dressed to kick ass. Tell me, have you split any seams yet? Got any coffee stains? A new bruise? Be careful, you're live tonight, and liquids can play havoc with that vision-mixing desk.'

She smiled to herself in the gallery and surreptitiously moved her glass of water out of harm's way. She was excited to show Hutch off, to prove to everyone how good he really was. She picked up her cans and pressed the switch on the talkback console in front of her. 'Hi, Ricky, this is Elizabeth. Let's have a great show. Just checking the level's okay?'

His voice came back in her ear. 'Hearing you fine, Lizzie. Lola? Speak to me.'

'Hello, Ricky. Thirty seconds till we go on air. Thirty seconds.' Lola held one stopwatch and had another simultaneously counting down on the desk in front of her.

Elizabeth felt the familiar shiver down her spine and her heart began thumping in time to the loudly ticking watch. She desperately wanted this show to go well. She was sure Hutch could pull it off, but she also knew that Ricky was increasingly unpredictable. She arranged her script and notes on the desk and said loudly in the gallery so that all the crew could hear her on open talkback: 'Have a good show, everyone.'

'Good luck, gallery!' Matthew added from the dark recess. It made Elizabeth more than usually jittery to have her boss sitting behind her, watching and listening.

'10, 9, 8, 7…' Lola's voice was clear and firm.

'Roll titles! Coming to camera 4. Stand by,' Robin called. 'And – cue Ricky!'

The host of the show came galloping down the stairs to an ovation from the audience. The crane cameras swept back and forth over the audience, an effect that made the excitement seem even greater and the audience twice the size. He moved quickly to his solo spot, marked on the studio floor with a piece of barely visible black tape. Here, he could be shown to best effect by some strategically placed uplighters, which shone directly under his chin, lightening the bags and the shadows, suffusing his whole face with an attractive glow.

Elizabeth said quietly in his ear, 'Okay, Ricky, they're a great audience. No need to ramp it up. Take it nice and slow.' He went smoothly on, not missing a beat, so that she was worried for a moment that her talkback wasn't working, then she felt him slow down and she had to admire his skill in simultaneously listening and speaking. But just as she felt him respond to her invisible reins, Ricky unexpectedly hesitated, his head reared up, his eyes sweeping the front rows. He spun on his heel and went off script. 'Phew! What an opening, Madam!' He moved with a wink towards a very large lady in the second row. Elizabeth felt herself growing hot and she sensed Lola freeze beside her. Was that an intentional innuendo?

Robin cried, 'Okay, we're off script, folks. Go with him. Camera 3 quick, give me a close-up of the fatty.'

Ricky sat on the lap of the girl next to the large lady. 'And what's your name?'

The floor manager ran to him with a stick mic and Ricky pointed it at the large lady, who was laughing and wiping her eyes. 'M… m… Moira.'

'Are you nervous, my love? Don't be nervous. What have you got in there?' Ricky pointed to her lap, where she was clutching her handbag. Moira twisted the bag in her hands. 'In here?' she asked.

He smiled at her. 'Yes, in there.' But he seemed to point to her belly and the audience laughed, although Moira's smile was fading. She hesitated.

'Got a bun in there, have you?' Ricky looked round at the audience, who roared, but Moira decided to trust that he meant her handbag and so opened it with trembling fingers.

'Do NOT get a close-up of that bag!' Elizabeth said loudly in the gallery.

Robin followed with, 'Cameras, stay wide, please.'

On talkback Elizabeth said urgently in Ricky's ear, 'Right, let's get back to the script. We're going to item one. Item one. The lad whose grandpa died this week on the very day he got a place at the Arsenal Academy.' She spelled it out for Ricky in an effort to distract him. 'He's in row four, wearing an Arsenal shirt.'

'Moving on to item one,' called Lola optimistically, throwing a page of unread script on the floor.

But Ricky was still poking about in Moira's handbag and had pulled out a long satiny make-up bag. Moira's hand flew to her mouth and her eyes widened in terror. 'Shall we have a look in here?' Ricky asked the audience. They roared their approval. He unzipped the bag and peeked in. 'Moira!' he admonished in mock horror. 'Moira! You naughty lady!' He held the bag high, pinched between his finger and thumb. 'I think I might have to confiscate this – perhaps we can use it later in the show, eh, Moira?'

Moira shook her head, her face crimson. Ricky tucked the bag under his arm and then said, 'Right! Let's meet my sidekick this week, my wingman – please welcome Harry Hutch Hutchinson!'

'Shit. We're going to Hutch early!' Elizabeth cried in the gallery. 'Is he standing by?'

The dislocated panting voice of her researcher came back on the talkback. 'Running into studio with him now, boss... Shall we send him on? He's confused.'

'Yes, send him on.' Elizabeth said, and then muttered to Lola, 'We're all fucking confused.' She turned around. Matthew was now out of his seat and standing, watching the screens intently.

Lola scrabbled around in her script. 'Item three, everyone. Item three. The chat with Hutch. Cameras 5 and 6.'

The audience were clapping for several minutes too long before Hutch finally walked on, his hand aloft, waving sheepishly. He strode towards Ricky, his arm outstretched, but the host caught him unawares with a bear hug. Elizabeth caught his lips moving as he said something in Hutch's ear. Hutch shrugged, but then turned again to smile at the audience. They cheered and she had a moment's satisfaction that they seemed pleased to see him. Hutch was wearing a smart dark suit jacket over a pale blue shirt and some black jeans. He looked relaxed, cool, sexy. Ricky, prancing around him in his purple mohair suit, looked like a colourful clown.

'Hutch, my man! Welcome to the show!' Ricky was restless; he made no attempt to sit down so Hutch also stood beside him, uncertainly. He was supposed to have come on through the back of the audience and was meant to pick out a predetermined audience member to play a large-scale game of table football they'd built especially for the show.

'Okay, let's keep it light, Ricky. Table football standing by… If you could just move camera right with Hutch, we can clear the shots so that the crew can get it on.' Elizabeth tried to keep her voice level.

Ricky put his arm around Hutch's shoulders again. 'Now, mate, there's a kid in our audience who wants to meet you. You support Arsenal, don't you?' This was a well-aimed insult – the one thing most people knew about Hutch was that he was a lifelong Manchester City fan.

'Well, I would if they played better football.' The audience laughed.

Ricky, his arm still draped around a visibly uncomfortable Hutch, led him to row four and the kid in the Arsenal shirt. Lola turned, her face creased with concentration and alarm. 'Back to item one?' she said. But Elizabeth had no idea where Ricky was heading. He had shrugged off the reins, the halter and the saddle. She had been completely thrown, and she felt sick.

'We'll have to go with it, for now,' she said. Lola quickly picked up the sheets of script she'd previously thrown on the floor.

'Okay, Ricky, the lad's called Kieron.' Elizabeth struggled to keep her voice low, despite the combination of fury and panic that was pulsating through her body. 'He was brought up by a single mum and his grandad. It's a sugar item, remember.'

Sugar items were the beating heart of the *Bonkers* show. These were the key moments where they sentimentally patronised paragons of the community: carers, fundraisers, dead grandparents. Elizabeth found too much of this sort of thing made her queasy but Ricky had a large appetite for sticky things and was always trying to put more saccharine into the show than she could stomach. But he usually handled them with warmth and charm. They were his items, he excelled at them.

'Kieron, mate, meet Harry Hutch Hutchinson!' Kieron was sitting at the end of the row, next to his mum. Without prompting, Hutch immediately sat down on the step beside him so that he was level with Kieron's eyes. He held up his hand for a high five and Kieron returned it with a crooked grin, revealing a row of braces.

'Who's your favourite player, mate?'

'Ozil,' said the boy.

'Yeah, he's good at passing the ball but he's got to work harder in defence,' Hutch said comfortably as if it was just the two of them chatting at a bus stop. 'What would you do about the back four? They didn't hold up last week against Chelsea.'

Kieron turned in his seat to fully face him, his eyes excited. 'I'd take Mustafi off, get Mertesacker back on.'

Hutch nodded thoughtfully. 'Good idea, mate. They could do with you on the bench.' The audience laughed.

Ricky tried to wrestle back the steering wheel. 'Well,

Hutch, this lad might be meeting them all sooner than you think. For this little star has just won a place at the Arsenal Academy. Isn't that right, Kieron?'

Kieron nodded shyly. Hutch smiled at him. 'Is that your mum next to you?' The boy nodded. 'And are you the proudest mum in the world this week?'

Kieron's mum was very thin and pinched. But her face lit up as she gazed at her son. 'Yes, I am. Kieron's been such a good boy.' The researchers had rehearsed this several times with her and it came out in a rush, as if learned off by heart. 'It's always been just the two of us, you see – plus Kieron's grandad, who always took him to football. Never missed a match or a practice. And then,' her face creased with genuine grief, 'Grandad fell ill two weeks ago and couldn't make Kieron's final trial. And he died the day we found out Kieron had got his place. He never knew...' She dribbled to a halt and the audience as one all sighed, 'Aaah.'

Hutch looked at Kieron feelingly. 'Tough, right?'

Kieron nodded numbly, his head down. Hutch shifted his sitting position so that he was cosily close to Kieron's seat. He bent his head towards him – he knew the microphones would pick up his quieter tone. The audience was silent.

'You know, Kieron, I was brought up by just my mum.' Kieron looked at him intently, mouth slightly open. 'And my grandad was big in my life, too. He took me to Maine Road when I was four years old – we went every Saturday. Just me and him. He used to let me have a bag of chips on the way home.' Kieron nodded more vigorously. 'Well, he died just before I wrote my first football column for the *Evening News*.

I didn't make the Man City trial – I wasn't as good as you, mate – but I know a bit how that feels. And I think of him all the time. Especially at football. And you know – the first time you walk on that pitch at the Emirates, your grandad will be right there with you.'

The gallery was hushed and Elizabeth heard Matthew say quietly, 'Good man.'

The audience was still and solemn. She watched Ricky carefully on his close-up. He was professional enough to know he had to let this moment rest, but she knew his facial tics too well and she could see an irritable crease at the corner of his mouth and an impatient twitch to his eyes.

The stage crew had managed to get the table football on to the set while the cameras were focusing on Kieron, so Elizabeth said briskly on talkback: 'Ricky, let's play the game now. As rehearsed. It's ready to go.'

Ricky stood up and spread his arms wide. 'Ladies and gents, shall we get Kieron and my man Hutch here to have bit of a kick-about? In honour of their dear dead grandads?' The audience cheered, oblivious to his sarcasm. Up in the gallery, Elizabeth banged her balled-up fist on the desk. Kieron was not the pre-determined audience member who was meant to play the game. Ricky was abandoning the minutely rehearsed segments of the show and creating something of his own, on the hoof. She had never felt so helpless in a live studio before. But Ricky was now ushering the boy, his mum, and Hutch back down the stairs and on to the set.

The props team had made a giant-sized table football, with mini-me figures of current Premier League footballers, who each stood about three feet high. They were attached to giant levers, which the players could operate by running up and down the length of the pitch. When a goal was scored, a bucket of gunge suspended from the ceiling was poised to tip over the losing player. It was pre-agreed that Hutch would be the loser in the first instance, so he was aiming not to score a goal until his opponent had. Ricky would be referee and chief clown.

He put Kieron's mum on the sofa and handed her Moira's make-up bag. 'Here, love, play with that. It'll cheer you up no end.' The audience tittered but her face was creased in puzzlement. Kieron looked anxiously over at his mum, rigid with fear that she might be about to embarrass him on primetime television. Hutch, noting it, moved to interpose his body between Kieron and the sofa. 'Okay, Ricky, come on, we're ready to play.' Hutch shot him a warning glance.

But Ricky smiled saucily. He turned to Kieron's nonplussed mum. 'Love, remind me, what are those animals called with bushy tails that love carrots?'

'Bunnies?'

Those in the audience who understood, mainly female, guffawed. Ricky winked at them. Up in the gallery, Elizabeth groaned and Matthew whispered in her ear, 'Is that what I think it is?' but she pretended to search through her script for the game cues. Ricky suddenly leapt into action and took up his referee whistle. 'Okay. Let's plaaaay!'

The game got under way and Kieron and Hutch began running up and down, chasing the bouncing ball and swivelling their cumbersome levers as best they could. The audience were yelling and cat-calling, unaware of the highly charged atmosphere on set. Kieron scored a goal, to a huge cheer from the audience and the first bucket of gunge fell, as planned, on Hutch's head. It was a gooey green sludge – the sort of liquid mess that the finest craftsmen working in television spend hours trying to concoct – and good sport that he was, Hutch let it slowly trickle down from his head to his shoulders.

'Ricky's asked for another bucket of gunge,' the floor manager said on talkback. 'Shall we let him have it?'

'No!' Elizabeth and Robin cried simultaneously. But they watched their screens helplessly as Ricky went running over to the floor manager and snatched the bucket from him. The audience could see what the host of the show was up to, dancing about like a hot-roofed cat with his extra bucket, and were egging him on. In the end, Hutch seemed to resign himself to the inevitable and scored a goal. The guys on the lighting rig had replaced the first bucket and Kieron cowered in anticipation. But the second bucket had only confetti in it and Kieron stood amazed as tiny bits of glittering silver paper softly crowned his head like an angel. Hutch barely had time to turn before Ricky swung his bucket and the green goo slapped him smack in the eyes, into his open mouth and then splashed messily down his T-shirt, pooling at his feet.

'Ladies and gents!' Ricky cried. 'Let's hear it for our two good sports – Kieron and Harry Hutchinson!' The audience roared and clapped.

Hutch stood, soaked and sticky. He looked ridiculous. Elizabeth could hardly bear to look at him, dripping green slime and wrath. The audience were laughing at him. He wiped some of the goo from his mouth but resisted Ricky's efforts to shuffle them off the set. He turned instead to Kieron, at the same time holding up his hand commandingly for silence from the audience.

'Mate, fair play,' said Hutch to Kieron. 'Tell me, have you ever seen Barcelona play? The best team in the world, in my view?' Kieron shook his head. 'Well, I've got tickets next week – Barca v Real Madrid. Ever been to Spain?'

Kieron shook his head, his eyes bright and excited.

'Well, I'd like you – and your mum – to come with me, as my guests. Let's have a night of footie in Barcelona, the city where it's still a religion.'

Kieron looked happily over to his mother, who was standing open-mouthed, still confused by the object she'd seen in the bag. The offer of a genuinely free gift was so far out of her compass that she looked suspicious and a little bit sullen, as if she was about to be the victim of another joke she might not understand.

'Wow!' breathed Lola in the gallery.

Matthew had ceased pacing behind them and slapped his rolled-up script triumphantly against his thigh. Elizabeth could see Ricky biting his lip. But then, quick as a flash, he cried, 'And all of us here at *Bonkers* will throw in a night in a five-star hotel and a slap-up meal. For you and your lovely mum!' He managed to ignore Hutch and now put his arm round both Kieron and his mum, so that Hutch was left outside the heart-warming circle, an isolated, dripping, green gnome.

Once Ricky had despatched his victims, the second half of the show passed without incident and Elizabeth had to acknowledge her presenter was on ebullient form. His childish manic energy had become an entertainer's exuberance. He displayed all the relentless optimism of the successful game show host: the promise that life might actually have some prizes in store. This was the chief quality that endeared him to millions. It was almost as if his goading of Hutch had released some sort of pressure valve.

Then came the popular finale – a version of 'Singin' in the Rain' sung by an eighties pop star and accompanied by two former boy bands yoked together – a retro combo that Elizabeth hoped looked intentionally ironic, rather than what it was: a failed attempt to book Michael Bublé. Ricky and Hutch had rehearsed a quite complicated dance routine with buckets of water and umbrellas. They were to be joined on stage by long-legged lover Beverly, wearing a white raincoat and thigh-length silver boots, whose taxing role it was to twirl around the lamp post.

Hutch had worked hard at not looking like a fool – he'd even taken some secret extra lessons with the choreographer. Elizabeth had allowed herself to believe (with a secret thrilling sense of pride) that it was because he wanted to impress her, show her that he could be just like Ricky. He came on, as cued, in a yellow plastic mac and hat. But as he and Ricky joined together to dance their steps in unison, Ricky suddenly flicked open his umbrella so that it fanned across Hutch's face and completely masked him. They danced the steps for another few beats, Hutch's legs only visible beneath the open umbrella. The audience hooted with laughter. Ricky closed his umbrella again as they both turned on their heels to move upstage with their backs to the audience. As Hutch stepped ahead of him,

Ricky leaned forwards and jabbed the point of his umbrella hard into his arse so that Hutch stumbled with the force of it. On talkback Elizabeth heard several of the crew say as one: 'Ouch!' The audience cheered.

Hutch and Ricky had now turned at the top of the set to dance back down towards the audience and Elizabeth could see on the close-up camera that Hutch's face was grim with fury and pain. Robin cried, 'Cameras, stay wide, nothing on Hutch.' Beverly danced towards them at the front of the stage and Ricky turned to her, once more suddenly opening up his umbrella in Hutch's face so that he had no choice but to rear backwards, losing his footing on the wet, sticky floor and falling heavily on to his back, his yellow wellington boots waving pathetically in the air.

Elizabeth cried *No!* out loud. Robin was also out of his chair and shouting at the cameras. Matthew called out, 'Is he hurt? How badly is he hurt?' Hutch lay for a dangerously long moment on the floor, while Ricky and Beverly danced smoothly on, bringing the finale to its conclusion. The audience were on their feet, positive this was all part and parcel of the entertainment. Ricky took the applause, then reached over to offer Hutch a hand, but he preferred to stagger to his feet unaided. He stood, tottering and dazed, as the audience gave them an ovation, Ricky bowing elaborately: 'Ladies and gents! Let's hear it for our good sport, Harry Hutchinson! Hutch, mate! Thanks a billion.' He smiled at his damaged guest and then, as the clapping subsided, asked, 'Is your wife here tonight?'

Up in the gallery, Elizabeth's heart stopped. Hutch also

sensed danger; he looked warningly at Ricky. 'Um. No. No, she's not.'

'Ah. Just as well, mate, not sure she'd forgive me! Busy is she? Out somewhere else? With someone else?' He winked at the audience and they laughed along with him. He was the ringmaster. 'Fair enough, mate. Not sure she'll want you home tonight looking like that, eh? Okay, folks! That's all we've got time for! Thanks to Bev, to Kieron, his lovely mum and of course, Mischievous Moira! And of course to Harry Hutchinson, who I don't suppose will ever come again! See you all next week, same time, same place!'

In the gallery, Robin screeched, 'Roll the credits!' and Lola began her countdown to 'Okay, guys, we're off air. We're OFF AIR!' Elizabeth sank back in her chair and the entire gallery let out a collective sigh of relief. Lola dropped her head into her hands and Elizabeth reached over to rub her tense, strained neck. 'Well done for keeping us on time, Lo. You did brilliantly. Honestly. It's a miracle we didn't fall off air.'

Lola lifted her head and blew out her cheeks. 'Lizzie, what's *wrong* with him? Why does he do it?'

'Because he thinks he's untouchable.'

Matthew came over and put his hands on each of their shoulders. 'Christ! That was tight. Well done, both of you. Elizabeth, a moment, please?' She got up from her chair, knowing what was coming, and nervously followed him out.

'I take it that was a vibrator, live, on my primetime family show?' His voice was quiet but venomous. An angry pulse was beating under one eye.

'No one saw it,' she said quickly. 'I checked all the cameras

– there were no close-ups. Otherwise I'd have got him to apologise. But there was no point; hardly anyone understood what he was talking about.'

'Okay, but this is serious, Elizabeth. He's way out of order. You did brilliantly to keep up with him, but we have to put an end to it. Hutch has been a class act. But Ricky is way out of line. Now is not the time, but I want you both in my office on Monday at 9 a.m.'

Elizabeth nodded miserably. Matthew hesitated, but then reached over and kissed her on the cheek. 'Look, Elizabeth, there's no one else I would've trusted to get us through that. Only you could've done it. I'm not blaming you. You made the right calls.'

Elizabeth pulled herself together and then ran down to the studio floor, tearing a seam in her skirt. Ricky was standing, accepting the congratulations of the departing audience, to all intents and purposes the king of entertainment at the centre of his court. Normally, she would run to hug him, but this evening she ignored him and searched instead for Hutch. The floor manager said that he'd refused all medical checks and had limped off to his dressing room.

He was standing naked, a towel wrapped round his waist. His hair was wet and plastered to his head. She couldn't help noticing that there were still flecks of green goo stuck to the dark hairs on his chest and his forearms. He was unsmiling. Elizabeth moved towards him to give him a hug but he side-stepped it.

'Hutch, you did brilliantly.' She was aware she was gushing. 'That Barcelona offer was so sweet. So well judged. It was so clever of you to come up with it on the spot, like that.'

He looked at her coldly. His eyes were very blue and steely. She pressed on brightly. 'You can really think on your feet. You're wasted on Channel 4! Honestly. And the finale! You handled it so brilliantly. Like a real pro. Um. You're not hurt, are you?' She could only begin to imagine how bruised his ego was.

'Elizabeth.' His voice was icy. 'None of that was as we rehearsed. What the fuck? What was Ricky playing at?'

Trying to upset you, humiliate you, expose you, Elizabeth thought. But she said lightly, 'Well, you know, Ricky loves live telly – he likes to switch things up a bit. He doesn't like the show to be too slick, too obviously rehearsed.' Hutch's eyes narrowed and he shook his head. 'I did say it can be a roller coaster sometimes,' she finished, weakly.

'You did NOT prepare me for that.' He pulled a black T-shirt from a hanger and slipped it on. Elizabeth noticed a ripple of muscle and a tautness across his chest. She sat down.

'I'm sorry. Truly. He went off script in a way that was – unacceptable.' She smiled up at him but he'd turned his back and was rummaging through his things. 'But when you watch it back, I think you'll be pleasantly surprised. You came out of it really well – you behaved like it was all perfectly planned. The finale was…' she hesitated, trying to find the right words to describe his very public humiliation. 'Well, it looked like well-rehearsed slapstick.'

'I will not be watching it back.' He still had his back to her and Elizabeth heard the venom in his voice. She could also see a purple bruise beginning to take shape at the bottom of his spine, below his T-shirt, on the smooth upward curve of his buttocks.

'And what was all that crap about my wife? For God's sake, she's friends with his wife! We were out together just last week! How dare he make such insinuations? What does he know, Elizabeth? Does he know about us? Have you been careless?' He turned on her accusingly and she recoiled from his fury.

'No! Of course not. He doesn't know anything, I'm sure of it.' She found in trying to placate him, she was treating him like a child. A bit like she treated Ricky. 'I am sorry. I realise I talked you into this. I think he's just jealous. He knows how good you are, and he wanted to show you up, but he ended up showing you off. He's probably furious.'

Hutch looked at her quickly. She thought she detected the faintest twinkle in his eyes although his mouth was still unforgiving. She moved towards him and slowly reached for the towel around his waist. There was a knock at the door and almost immediately it opened. Elizabeth just had time to inch away, as Hutch quickly repositioned his towel. It was Matthew, who had come to do some Controlling.

'Fabulous show, mate.' He strode across the dressing room, not acknowledging Elizabeth, and grasped Hutch's hand, who had to juggle his towel with the other. 'You were a star. You kept Ricky Clough on his toes, I'll say! Brilliant stuff. Listen, Hutch, who's your agent? Let's get talking about a show of your own, yes? Elizabeth here can produce it. She's great. I've got this idea. Let's meet for dinner and talk about it.'

Matthew hadn't got to where he was without knowing the value of a cosy sole meunière at The Ivy. Elizabeth, meanwhile, was hovering uncertainly behind the sofa, trying to compose herself. She wondered whether she was expected to speak up, perhaps to agree that she was, indeed, great.

Hutch was all smiles and modesty. 'Matthew, that's very kind. I don't know if I can do anything more on television than talk about football, but we can certainly chat.' He didn't look at Elizabeth and she felt cross that he hadn't included her. Wouldn't he like to reiterate that she was great?

Matthew slapped Hutch quite hard on his back. 'That's my idea, mate! Sport meets entertainment – let's combine the two and do, what do they call it? One of those Tough Mudder shows. You'll be head judge. It'll be brilliant. And it'll work really well on Saturday nights.'

Elizabeth felt the familiar rush of excitement at the talk of a new show. Immediately, her brain began racing through the possibilities for something brand new, an unconventional show. Hutch was cut from very different cloth: he was casual about the way he looked, he was caustic and outspoken. He wasn't Ricky. But she could see that he could be a star if only someone knew how to produce him, knew how to smooth out the rough edges, the gurning at camera. Yes, a new show with Hutch could be transformational – it could make her the most successful producer of the moment. She opened her mouth to express her opinion, but Matthew was on a roll.

'You see, mate, you can do mainstream. And you're northern, aren't you? Manchester, isn't it? That's great. You'll really appeal to our northern heartland. Isn't that right, Elizabeth?'

Hutch did have a soft Mancunian accent that served to make him sound classless. Elizabeth, who was very much from the South, felt there was nothing that she could trust herself to say. But Matthew was now busy exchanging diary dinner dates with Hutch – it seemed that there was no room at The Ivy for Elizabeth. It wasn't until Matthew had left the room that she got a chance to speak. 'Make a pilot show together?' she spluttered. 'You and me? How on earth are we going to pull that off?'

'Well.' Hutch pulled her towards him. His earlier fury had entirely dissolved in the face of Matthew's flattery. 'No one knows about us, you just said. Matthew clearly doesn't. And we're a great team. We've proved it in bed, and now we can prove it in the office. You're going to get the best out of me – because apparently, you're a great producer – and now you're going to get to know what it's like to have a real presenter to deal with.'

Elizabeth couldn't help herself; she laughed and rested her head on his chest. She felt his heart beating beneath her lips. 'Okay, but you do realise now that you're going to have to do everything I tell you? I'm going to be your master and you're going to be my puppet.'

'Mistress,' Hutch corrected her. 'You're my mistress.' She looked up to chide him and he stopped her with a kiss.

'You know, you've never told me that stuff about your grandad before… You don't often talk about your childhood. Was he like a dad to you?'

Hutch shrugged. 'Well, no one's really like your dad, except your dad… You know what that's like. You and I have that in common, at least. It's why we're soul mates.' He smiled at her. 'I told you, my dad died when I was ten. It was tough, but Mum was amazing. The family all clubbed together. Football saved me, though. No one could tease me about being a mummy's boy if I could out-run them on the pitch.'

'But what about your grandad?'

Hutch paused. 'Okay… That… I maybe embellished a bit on the show.'

'Embellished?' Elizabeth took a step back and looked at him sharply.

'Well, I had a grandad. Obviously. I had two. But they were both dead by the time I was six.'

Elizabeth stared at him, realisation slowly dawning.

'Are you disappointed that I made it up, or that you didn't know I made it up?' Hutch looked at her through narrow eyes, his mouth curled into a crooked smile.

'And you accuse me of cynicism! Harry Hutchinson, you are learning fast.' She bit her lip. 'What did Ricky say to you when you first walked on the show?'

'Ah, you noticed that, did you? Wait. Did the cameras catch it?'

'No, not really. Not long enough for lip readers. Why? What did he say?'

'He said something about Marcus McManus. He's a striker for Manchester City.'

'What?' Elizabeth didn't think Ricky knew anything about football.

'I'm not sure. Something like, "This is for Marcus McManus." I put it down to his version of bullying – you know, locker-room banter. Everyone knows I support Man City – and McManus is a bit of a lightning rod, on and off the field. He's the bad boy of football.'

'How well do you know him?'

'I've been going to Man City all my life. My job means I know a lot of footballers. But I try not to socialise with them. Their idea of a good time – threesomes in some dismal motel – isn't really mine. Unless, Elizabeth, you fancy a threesome?'

He opened his arms. His towel fell to the floor. Elizabeth couldn't help it, she laughed out loud. 'You're so hammy,' she said, moving back into the circle of his arms.

'And you're so yummy,' Hutch murmured into her hair, his fingers finding the torn seam of her skirt.

Later, much later than she intended, Elizabeth marched down the corridor to Ricky's dressing room. Half her production team were inside enjoying the show hospitality, together with two old schoolfriends of Ricky's, including the low-cost building merchant, Deniz Pegasus. Ricky had at least four bottles open and several more were waiting in a bucket of ice. He was liberally pouring wine into paper cups. Ricky was still in his show clothes but had removed his trousers and was parading about in a pair of canary yellow Y-fronts. He and Deniz were also smoking large Cuban cigars, in open defiance of the smoking regulations (expediently, Ricky had taken out the battery in the smoke alarm overhead). His two dogs were curled up asleep on Union Jack cushions under the table. Scented candles were burning under the make-up mirror. Ricky was standing on a coffee table, the tail of his shirt didn't quite cover his crotch, and Elizabeth was forced to notice from the prominent bulge that there was probably a sock in his pants. He offered her a cup of wine. She shook her head. 'Oh, come on, Elizabeth. Don't be a party pooper.

Let your hair down, the show's over. I got us off air on time. We had a bit of fun. The audience fucking LOVED it! Let's raise a glass.'

Elizabeth took the cup and raised it in the direction of her team. 'Thank you, everybody, as ever, for your hard work keeping this show on the straight and narrow.' She looked pointedly at Ricky and downed her wine. 'Has anyone spoken to Kieron's mum?'

'Sorted!' said Ricky smugly.

'What do you mean?' Elizabeth said sharply.

'I've sorted Kieron and his mum. By the way, darling, her name's Tracey. They're on their way to The Dorchester for the night. In a suite.'

'But Ricky, we don't have the budget for that!'

'It's paid for.'

'What do you mean, it's paid for?'

'It's on my account. It's my treat. Look, Elizabeth, maybe I went too far with the mum. I see that. I don't want her to feel bad. And the kid's great. So I thought I'd make a gesture. They don't need to know it's me that's paying – they'll just think well of the show.'

'And, Ricardo, may I say, it was bloody great telly,' added Deniz Pegasus who, rather horribly, then winked at Elizabeth.

Elizabeth shot him a sarcastic smile. 'It was totally inappropriate telly, that's what it was.' She turned to the door. 'I'm still worried that once the mum – um, Tracey – realises in the cold light of day that what you were doing was teasing her with a vibrator, we may get a formal complaint, although a night in The Dorchester will probably help. However, you and I need to have a chat.' Her disapproving glance took in the empty glasses, 'I can see that now is not the moment. But talk we must.'

'Fire away, Mrs T. I don't mind these guys hearing what you've got to say and Deniz is all over my business these days. He's looking out for me.'

'No, Ricky,' Elizabeth said firmly, determined that for once he would not have an audience for this showdown, nor would it be conducted when he was in his pants. She was also irritated by his reference to Mrs Thatcher, as he knew she would be (but he was, she realised, very short of any other female authoritarian role models). 'We'll do it later. The Boss wants to see us in his office on Monday morning at 9.'

'Oh, don't worry about Matthew,' Ricky said airily. 'I'll sort him out.'

'I doubt that.'

'How's the Hutch? Still cocky? Or is that bushy tail a little bit droopy now? A bit bruised?' The men all laughed uproariously. Elizabeth stalked out and made as if to slam the door, but Ricky caught it and followed her into the corridor. He shut the door behind him and stood there, unconcerned, in his stuffed canary pants.

'Look, Ricky, I get that you never wanted Hutch on this show and then you decided to try and humiliate him. To prove me wrong, I guess. But you can't just score personal points on a live show! It's not fair on the team, the crew – or on me. And anyway,' she couldn't resist saying, 'it didn't really work, did it? You thought Hutch would be all at sea – you thought he'd be too clever, too self-conscious... But he handled it well, he thought on his feet – he came up trumps! And as for that stuff about his wife! Ricky, that was really rude. What on earth were you thinking?'

'Yeah, well, he's a hypocrite. The worst kind. Working-class Man City, ooh, me grandad bought me a bag of chips, blah blah. You know what? Everyone knew the Hutchinsons in Manchester. Big in the clothes trade. He grew up in a bloody huge house – there was plenty of money there, believe you me. And let me tell you, I've seen both of them – him and his lady wife – out with other people where they shouldn't be. Lorna's invited them to our party – but I've warned her, they're not what they seem. I just fired a warning shot over his bows, that's all. He'll get it. He'll know.'

Elizabeth swallowed hard. She tried to keep her gaze level. What did he mean? Who had he seen out with Hutch? 'Look, let's have a coffee before we see Matthew on Monday and get our story straight.'

Ricky nodded. 'Although I'll say then what I always say to him – that you're a great producer, Elizabeth, and I know I drive you mad, but I love working with you.'

'Is that an apology?'

Ricky laughed. 'Yes, Headmistress, it is. See you Monday.'

Chapter Seven

Ricky had died too late on Wednesday night for the morning papers, but as Elizabeth hurried back to the office after leaving Hutch's flat, she saw that he was on the front page of Thursday's *Evening Standard*: 'RICKY CLOUGH DEAD AT 50'. She picked up a copy and stood in the drizzle, gazing at his photo on the front page. He was wearing a purple trilby and a candy striped jacket and was winking at the camera. The article said police were investigating his 'unexplained' death and then went on to recount his career highs and lows. Hutch was right: mostly, the article contained phrases like 'the king of entertainment' and 'epoch-making television' with only a glancing mention of his declining audiences. There were just a few subtle references to the 'party-loving guy' and 'generous host'.

As she searched desperately for a black cab, her phone rang. She hesitated for a few seconds and then answered it.

'Hello? Elizabeth? Hi. It's Lorna Clough.' Her voice was hesitant, soft. Possibly a little defensive.

'Lorna, oh God, how are you bearing up? And the boys?' Elizabeth felt bad. She should have called Lorna this morning.

She regretted leaving the press team to meet Lorna at the hospital last night – she and Matthew ought to have gone.

'The boys are up in their room playing music. They're going through Ricky's old record collection. You know, he has so many old vinyls...' she faltered and then cleared her throat. 'Elizabeth, I spoke to the police...'

'Yes, I have too.'

'Oh, okay. Right.' She pressed on more confidently. 'Elizabeth, I'd really like to talk to you... about... about it all. I want to try and make some sense of it... You know, I didn't speak to him at all yesterday. But I'd like to get some idea of – well, how he was, in himself?'

Elizabeth could hear rustling, it sounded as if Lorna was crumpling up some paper in her hands, and then her breathing came too quick and fast.

'Lorna?'

'Yes. Sorry. It's um... Look, would you mind coming down to the house? I can't leave the boys. And the tabloids are outside. The kids have spotted some of them in the bushes. Waiting for the first photo of us, I guess. But I'm not ready, I can't face them...'

'Of course I'll come to you,' said Elizabeth hastily. 'How about this evening? I can easily jump in the car.'

'That would be great.' Lorna sounded relieved. 'You know the house, of course. See you later then, thanks.'

There were still no taxis. Elizabeth began to run, her coat flailing behind her, regretting that she didn't have her car. Her phone buzzed again. This time it was Kevin from the press office. Elizabeth couldn't tell whether Kev knew about her and

Hutch. He made it his business to know pretty much everything else. A few weeks after the wedding that wasn't, she had kissed him drunkenly during the carnage that was an end-of-series party. Kevin had responded by holding her strongly and she had understood that sex with him would be confident, slow and studied. But she'd pulled back, laughing and embarrassed, and he had turned away and said softly, 'Any time, Elizabeth. Any time.' Ever since then, she felt he was watching her back, that she could go to him if she needed to at any time.

'Where are you?'

'I'm running to the office now. I can't find a cab. I've been at the police station.'

'Yes? Earlier, you mean?' Slight pause. 'Don't talk to anyone.'

'I'm not going to. So, you know what they now think about Ricky?'

'A contact of mine from the Met told me early this morning.'

Elizabeth stopped by a park to catch her breath and watched some skateboarding kids freewheeling into the wind and the drizzle. 'What do you think, Kev? Do you think Ricky was – *poisoned*?'

'No, I don't,' Kevin said flatly. He was a man used to dealing with daily exaggeration – he spoke to the tabloids every day – but this was a step too far even for him. 'I expect the poor bugger had taken more than he should have – or some new version of what he usually takes – and it backfired on him. You know what he put away, Elizabeth. God knows, it could easily have been some bad shit.'

The kids were skidding, laughing, going back for more.

'I just can't believe someone – someone we might know

– would really have it in for him. I mean, have it in for him that badly.'

Elizabeth had a sudden memory of a red-faced female researcher rushing out of Ricky's dressing room two weeks ago, just as she was walking in. 'Are you okay?' Elizabeth had called as she went flying past. The researcher looked back with wide eyes and a half-laughing face and as she ran, made a gesture with her hands as if she was shaking a bottle. 'He's WANKING? Really?' She'd marched into the dressing room without knocking as Ricky was leaning back on his leopard-skin cushions, his shirt lazily undone, zipping his flies. His obsession with exhibitionist flashing, Elizabeth thought, had become offensive and wearying in equal measure. He'd tried to persuade his production team over the years that a bit of disruptive, socially deviant behaviour was entirely conducive to the creative enterprise. And sure enough, they'd all found ways of dealing with it – mostly by laughing at him behind his back. But now she was icily business-like. 'Put it away, Ricky, no one wants to see it – and don't get it out when there are female researchers around. It's pervy.'

'Clothes are the last barrier. We should all get naked. We'd all have better ideas without them. And it makes meetings more exciting.'

'No, Ricky. It makes meetings extremely uncomfortable. Your penis is of no interest to anyone working on this show. Keep it to yourself.'

'Well, granny pants, I *was* actually keeping it to myself – it's not my fault if she didn't knock. And also,' Ricky had winked at her, 'it's not strictly true that my penis is of no interest to anyone on the team.'

Elizabeth took a quick breath, her heart beating fast, remembering Lola bent over Ricky's prostrate body, whispering in his ear.

'Ricky knew some pretty weird people.' Kevin was resolutely unemotional. 'I mean, dealers and shit. Could be he owed someone and they just wanted to teach him a lesson by dealing him some rogue stuff.'

'Wow, that's quite a theory!' Elizabeth said doubtfully, although it was true that there had been a sizeable contingent of shifty-looking men in cheap suits and shades at Ricky's party. He liked to collect people. 'I can't see DI Watson falling for any crackpot theories. And she's not a fan. She doesn't watch telly. Well, maybe the Olympics. But she clearly thinks we're all mostly drunks and tossers.'

Kevin let out a cheerless laugh. 'Well, she ain't wrong. You alright though? No one calling you?'

'No one's called me. But I'll let you know if they do. Thank you, Kev.'

There was a slight pause. 'Okay. Well, don't be too long.'

The network's production offices were located in an old banana warehouse with a cobbled courtyard in north Kensington. It was all carefully exposed pipework and industrial ducting. Today, the atmosphere inside was subdued. The team were at their desks, bent over the internet and barely talking. Lola was in the kitchen, sorting out a tray of teas. Elizabeth ran to hug her. She looked terrible: she didn't seem to have fully removed the traces of make-up from the day before, her face looked grey and streaky and her hair was tumbling out of its nest. Elizabeth felt again the injustice she was doing to Lola, not telling her what was going on with Hutch. Perhaps she would tell her, perhaps she'd suggest they go out for a drink, like they used to.

'The police are already here. They're in the scriptwriters' meeting room. I thought that was best.' She sniffed and Elizabeth winced at the unspoken criticism of her late arrival. She tried to imagine the coolly observant Essex girl, DI Watson, sitting on the cartoony plastic yellow chairs around the writers' glass table, with Hedda the Shredder in one corner, ready to devour rejected scripts. She thought of her staring at the basketball net, the large poster of The Young Ones and the writers' graffiti accumulated over the years: *I don't know what the question is, but sex is the answer* and *I said, just blow the bloody doors off!* and in one corner, in red crayon: *Ricky is a Cunt*. She had to congratulate Lola for choosing the place most likely to offer the police an insight as to how they spent the majority of their working days.

'Good girl. How is everyone?' Elizabeth glanced around the office.

'We're being called in one by one. HR have done the list. I'm next in line.' Lola slopped boiling water into a series of mugs which said *Have a drink with Ricky Clough*.

Elizabeth picked one up and wrapped her hands round it. 'Ricky is a mug,' she said ruefully. 'I guess it's one kind of immortality.'

Lola smiled thinly, but it was a smile at least.

'Is the boss here?'

'Yes, he's been pacing about, trying to pat people on the back.' Lola slammed the fridge door. 'He doesn't know what to say. He never knows what to say. He's too bloody public school and uptight to talk about feelings. Remember last week when we went to see him at home after his mugging? He was so embarrassed, kept turning his head away so we wouldn't see that bloody great shiner. Couldn't talk about it! I don't know how blokes like him cope with being so repressed.'

After the mugging, Elizabeth and Lola had been told by Matthew's wife that he didn't want any visitors for the two days he was in hospital. So they'd gone round to his house the moment he was back home and despite his wife's admonitions, took a crate of Frog's Leap and the board game Twister – jokes they thought he'd enjoy. But when Elizabeth saw him struggle to get to his feet and limp painfully across the room to greet them, she realised it had been a joke too far. It was true that he hadn't wanted to talk much (not helped by a very swollen lip) and she understood that he hated them seeing him vulnerable. (He once told Elizabeth he'd seen a TED Talk about how business leaders were more successful if they revealed their vulnerabilities but in his view, he told her, it really only applied to Americans, who liked to wail in public.) She and Lola had left the house after just ten minutes and Elizabeth, in a rush of affection, had kissed him goodbye on the cheek and assured him that everything in the office was falling apart.

Lola picked up the tray of teas and wobbled dangerously down the open-plan office in her vertiginous heels. The researchers swiped mugs as she tottered past so that by the time she got to the writers' room at the end of the general office, only two cups were left on the tray and both were sitting in a brown puddle. She knocked loudly and marched in.

'Well… I think the police are getting the hang of how we operate here.' Matthew appeared at Elizabeth's elbow, staring after Lola. 'My assistant was going to bring down the china cups and saucers from the boardroom. I think that would've created a slightly better impression.'

'I'm not sure those cups are still there. I think they got, um, damaged. Ricky had us playing a game of drinking ping pong with them.'

Matthew gave a short ironic laugh. He moved uncertainly towards the coffee machine and Elizabeth noticed his left leg still dragged behind the other. He fiddled with the switches for a bit until she said brightly, 'Shall I make us some coffee?' and he leaned back against the counter in relief. 'Elizabeth, you're a star.'

'Yes, thank you, Matthew. I am a star. But not at making coffee. However, the good thing is that this machine does it for us.' She filled up the flask with water and attached it to the machine. 'I see the *Evening Standard* is saying the death is unexplained – so everyone knows now, right?'

'Yes. That's all the police are saying to anyone, But Kev's spoken to someone whose cousin works in the hospital labs and we're trying to find out more – you know, what exactly it was.'

'The police said very specifically to me that he'd been poisoned. Poisoned! Matthew, can you believe it, that he was p…'

'I know, I know.' Matthew stopped her from saying the word out loud again. It felt obscene.

'By the way, Lorna's asked to see me this evening.'

'Ah. She called you, did she? Hmm.' Matthew looked down

at his coffee. 'I phoned her myself this morning. We've put some guys down there to help with the paps. She can't get her head round it, of course. Like the rest of us.'

Elizabeth wondered why, if Lorna had already spoken to Matthew on the phone that morning, she still wanted to see her.

'She's okay, Lorna. You could never tell how much she knew and turned a blind eye to. She was happy enough in Surrey with her horses – and they say, with the stable boys.'

He looked over at Elizabeth as if expecting a rebuttal, but she said nothing. She'd heard this gossip before – that Lorna Clough was content to ride her horses over the South Downs while her husband partied in Soho with dancers the age she was when they first met. And that she might have found further solace in the hay with the stable boys employed to shovel it. Elizabeth suspected it was a story put about by Ricky to make himself feel better.

'You know, I was at their wedding.' Matthew leaned heavily against the counter with his coffee. 'Sat between the Prime Minister and the editor of the *Sun*. He was good at collecting people, old Ricky. He boasted that McCartney was supposed to put in an appearance – he didn't show, of course. But Cilla was there, which had Liverpool sorted. He could really dance, you know – in his day. And play the piano. He had many talents, did Ricky. You don't get many of them like that any more...'

Cilla. Suddenly it came to Elizabeth. The poem. *You're my world, you're every breath I take, you're my world, you're every move I make*. It was a bloody Cilla Black song! Hutch had even been humming it in his kitchen, damn him! Elizabeth was momentarily mortified by her intellectual snobbery, but was far more exercised by the realisation that Hutch had managed to expose it with his lyrical joke.

She tried hard to concentrate. 'So, do you have any theories, Matthew?'

'I think he took some stuff that made him ill. I'm sure that's what they'll conclude.'

'Maybe. That's what Kev thinks. But Ricky was still enough of a pro not to overdo it before a show. We're talking about him as if he'd given up. But I always thought, in a way, the problem was that Ricky cared *too much* about the shows. He wanted perfection, all the time. But this week was good. He was firing on all cylinders. I didn't think he was off his head. At all.'

Matthew was still looking at her closely. 'But what are you saying, Elizabeth? I mean, what's the alternative? That someone wanted to hurt him – kill him, possibly?'

She stared miserably at her Ricky Clough mug. 'I know. It seems incredible.'

'Have you spoken to Lola yet? About what the police think?'

Elizabeth was alarmed by his questioning stare. 'Um, no, not yet.'

'They were close, weren't they? Lola and Ricky? But of course, he was close in that way to a lot of women... But Lola? Well, you've got to admit, she's headstrong and she's, you know, very feisty.'

Elizabeth hated that word feisty – when is a man ever feisty? She couldn't believe what Matthew was trying to say. 'You mean, you think she's a *suspect*? Lola?!'

'Well, Elizabeth, you've got to consider. Someone gave him something. I imagine the police will be looking for someone with a motive. That's all I'm saying.'

'Well, that's probably most of the team, Matthew. But Lola! That's absurd. She adored Ricky. Well, in her way.'

'Come into my meeting room for a minute.' Her boss turned and walked off to a small room that he had appropriated for himself. Six months ago, the company chairman had insisted that everyone move into open-plan offices after he'd read in an American business journal that it encouraged better communication and increased creativity. Matthew had then found himself in the unenviable position where arguing for the retention of his wood-panelled office with flat screen and drinks cabinet would also involve him arguing against better communication and increased creativity. And he hadn't got where he'd got to without understanding that those were two quite vital components for a thriving television network. He'd made do with appropriating one of the meeting rooms and was in it so often that it had become, effectively, his new office.

He sat down on the squashy too-large leather sofa he'd managed to salvage and which Elizabeth knew from cruel experience was impossible to sit on without feeling acutely aware of your crotch. There was one matching armchair, with equally fatal cushions, so she had no option but to choose this. She sank down into it as gracefully and discreetly as she could and then realised she hadn't put her knickers back on after leaving Hutch's flat. She decided to tuck one leg under the other and sit on it, hoping that it would bestow on her both height and dignity. The sick feeling in the back of her throat still wouldn't go away.

Matthew affected not to notice her fidgeting. He began in confidential tones and she felt again that the day was taking a highly unusual turn. 'Elizabeth, you know, I tried to get Ricky into rehab. I didn't call it that – I just suggested he take a break somewhere, away from the old demons. Take time out, I said. Take Lorna. I offered to pay for it too, which I have to say was pretty generous of me. But he said he didn't need it. Said it was nothing he couldn't deal with himself, maybe he'd just been overdoing it. I thought it was going to be okay. But then it got worse again and his demands became ridiculous. You saw how he was in that last showdown we had with him.'

Elizabeth shuddered at the memory of the last confrontation they'd had with Ricky, the Monday morning after the terrible episode of *Saturday Bonkers* with Hutch. It had been an unedifying spectacle, where she'd seen up close the hopeless consequence of two enormous male egos coming head to head. Matthew, whose professional smoothness and cunning she'd always rather admired, had abandoned all his managerial level-headedness when faced with a mocking Ricky Clough, and had squared up to his opponent with a red face and clenched teeth. She had not enjoyed witnessing her boss lose his cool. It had been alarming – like the very rare moments when her dad would lose his temper and thump the table so that the tea cups jittered against their saucers.

Matthew shifted in his seat and winced slightly as he did so. Elizabeth looked at him concerned, but he said quickly as if to deflect her, 'How's it going with Hutch?'

Elizabeth kept her gaze level. 'Okay, I think. Hutch wants to put some music numbers at the end of the show… It's not such a bad idea, but it's very close to *Bonkers*.'

'Oh, don't worry about that!' Matthew dismissed her sensitivities with an airy wave of his hand. 'You've got to do what's best for the show. And everyone will remember Hutch's dance routine with Ricky on *Bonkers*. Actually, that's good, we can get the marketing guys to push that.' He noticed Elizabeth's face. 'Well, you know what they say, the show must go on!' He shrugged at his own tasteless joke. 'But you're not having doubts about making the show with Hutch? I'm told you haven't signed the contract yet.'

Elizabeth bit her lip. The contract was lying on her kitchen table at home. She couldn't quite bring herself to sign on the dotted line, to commit herself to being in a professional partnership with Hutch. She was sure she knew how to make the show a hit. But could she – *should* she – work with Hutch, given where they were? And it would delay her secret plan to set up her own company. On many levels, she was conflicted.

Matthew misunderstood her hesitation. 'You'll get it right, Elizabeth, I know you will. It's a good idea.' (It was, of course, his idea.) 'By the way, any thoughts for a show my wife could appear on? Would be a great help, you know…'

This was a familiar refrain. Matthew was being pressed by his wife, the history don, to get her a television gig that would increase the sales of her impenetrable book. Elizabeth had seriously given it a very small amount of thought, but the entertainment world wasn't really awash with roles for an Oxbridge historian whose specialist subject was the dissolution of the monasteries. 'I've been thinking hard. Nothing so far!' she said brightly.

'Perhaps a history panel show?' Matthew pressed her. 'I'd put money behind it if you came up with a good enough idea. What with that and the Hutch show, you could set up a new comedy entertainment department. You could become a departmental head – and all that comes with it, you know, in terms of your package.'

Elizabeth had to admire once more the brazen chutzpah of her boss. 'Thank you.' She was studiedly non-committal. 'Very tempting.'

Matthew frowned, irritated at her lack of excitement. He spread his muscular legs wide and stretched both his arms along the back of the sofa so that she was forced to acknowledge both the breadth of his authority and the bulge of his groin.

'I'm going to issue an edict that we have at least one woman on every entertainment show from now on.' Matthew had recently been to a diversity awareness workshop. He'd found it less tiresome than he'd expected, although he'd skipped the second half, having by then easily mastered the gist of it. But he was now very alive to the dangers of having something called unconscious bias (quite a challenge, he frequently joked, it being unconscious). 'I'm not surprised my wife gets frustrated.' He said this with some feeling.

Elizabeth opened her mouth to talk about the inadvisability of insisting women appear in shows that were mostly made by men to reproduce schoolboy playgrounds, but her boss was already up and stretching. She understood that his sharing of confidences – and edicts – was over. As she struggled to her feet, she realised too late that the leg she'd been sitting on during his lecture had gone to sleep. Matthew paused, amused, as she leaned back unsteadily against the arm of the chair, like a drunk on stilts.

'Oh, and Elizabeth? Another thing. Don't let DI Watson catch you without any knickers on.'

He left the room, closing the door softly behind him. Elizabeth sank back down into the chair and put her head in her hands.

Back in the open-plan office, Zander and another junior researcher, Conor, had already completed their police interviews and were exchanging notes. Zander, who'd been in charge of the celebrity chef Paolo Culone, had been questioned closely about the food items he'd been asked to provide and to account for anyone who'd had access to them.

'I didn't have any.' Elizabeth sat on the corner of Zander's desk and looked at the photos pinned to his desk partition, showing him climbing Everest, aged 19, playing polo, and on a yacht with two other tall, good-looking boys. 'Why didn't I get any of the Culone titbits?'

'You were up in the gallery, I guess. And Robin was already having a major meltdown up there – we could hear it on the talkback. We didn't like to intrude on private grief.' They all looked across the office at Robin, who was wailing into his mobile phone. They listened for a moment, expecting hysterical accounts of how he'd had to ask the camera crew to train their lenses away from a dying man. But Robin was actually trying to book a British Airways flight using his Avios points.

They turned away from him with hoots of derision and

Zander picked up his army rucksack (two terms at Sandhurst), saying, 'Are we allowed to contact other people...? I mean, do we share information? I really ought to call Paolo – I think he's already been interviewed by the police.'

Elizabeth was impressed with his conscientiousness. 'Good question. I'll ask the legal bods here. But I don't see why not. That's sweet of you. I should contact all the show's guests.'

'Sure,' Zander said lightly. 'But it's just that I feel I owe Paolo. You know, I sort of talked him into it – Mummy gave me his mobile and he's so fond of her. I don't know that he'd have done it otherwise.'

She looked at him curiously. 'Your mum knows Paolo Culone? I'm not sure I knew that.'

Zander looked abashed. 'Well, I didn't say anything... you know, I didn't want to boast about my connections. I want to be a good researcher. But yes, he used to cook for Mummy's dinner parties.'

'You posh twat!' Conor, the other researcher, playfully knocked Zander's baseball cap off his head.

'Does it matter?' Zander looked at Elizabeth anxiously. 'I know I should've said something sooner.'

'Yes, you should have.' She slid off his desk. 'You should always be honest – to me, your producer, at least.'

'I told the police,' said Zander eagerly. 'I told them I'd known Paolo for years – he did a fabulous shepherd's pie and champagne thing for my eighteenth. I said, I can vouch for him – he's a great guy.'

Elizabeth had a momentary vision of girls in taffeta dresses, with peachy white shoulders and long glossy hair, and boys in white tie sitting at long candlelit tables in a baronial hall being served dollops of shepherd's pie. It was an image she suspected DI Watson had also enjoyed. 'Go home,' she said to Zander. 'And call Paolo out of courtesy but DO NOT repeat anything you might've overheard or that feels like pure speculation.'

She watched Lola trip her way towards the writers' meeting room and her own encounter with the imperturbable Ms Watson. Lola stopped to have a word with a harassed-looking head of Human Resources, and then turned hesitantly towards Elizabeth. 'Lizzie? Apparently, I can have a – what's it called? – a supporter in the room with me. Will you do it?' Elizabeth saw the HR woman imperceptibly nod her head. So she followed Lola into the room.

DI Watson was sitting on one of the plastic bubble seats, and had a notepad on the table in front of her. Her hair was out of its pink scrunchie, neatly combed, with a severe centre parting. The sleeves of her blue shirt were precisely rolled, her forearms revealing a dusting of pale blonde hairs. Ali Rafik was sitting beside her, awkward and out of place on the playful chair. They both smiled as Lola and Elizabeth took their seats on the other side of the table, side by side. Elizabeth was facing a new bit of graffiti she'd never noticed before that read 'Suck on my chocolate salty balls'. It was a line from a *South Park* song. She wondered if Watson and Rafik had carefully noted it down in their wire-bound notebooks, word for word. She pushed her chair a little closer to Lola and smiled reassuringly at her. She looked bright-eyed, eager, willing to help.

'Lola, hello. Thank you for helping us with our inquiries.' DI Watson was warm and gentle. She looked directly at Lola, her gaze not connecting with Elizabeth at all. 'Perhaps you could explain to me what your role is on *The Ricky Clough Show*? We don't know anything about how television programmes are made...' She smiled at Ali Rafik, who spread out his hands with a shrug as if to encompass the sum total of ignorance within the Metropolitan Police Force.

'I'm the production assistant.' Lola crossed her legs and sat back in her chair, squaring her shoulders, unconsciously adopting a more authoritative pose. 'I do the studio schedule and the camera scripts for the director, showing which camera takes which bit of script. So when we're in the gallery, I'm responsible for all the timings and count out the music beats, so that the director can call the shots. Ricky had open talkback...' DI Watson frowned, so Lola went on in a slightly more patronising tone, 'which means he had an invisible earpiece and could hear everything that went on in the gallery during the show. Most presenters only have switch talkback, so they just hear what they need to hear, like their own timings, but Ricky was very experienced and had done a lot of live telly so he liked to hear everything that was going on.' Lola said this rather proudly.

'So he could hear anything anyone said in the gallery? Even if it wasn't directed at him?' DI Watson asked.

'Yes, that's right.'

'And presumably, all the people equipped with live talkback could also hear everything that was being said in the gallery? So, all the cameramen?'

'Yes, and Sound. And Lighting.'

'And you'd worked with Ricky for a long time?'

'I suppose so. I did *Bonkers* with him, too.'

'Ah yes. But that was a live show, I believe? So your job looking after the timings was even more crucial?'

'Yes, we had to come off air to the exact second.'

DI Watson glanced at her notes. 'But I've heard, sometimes, Ricky didn't like that? He wanted to keep going, even though time was up?'

'Yes, well sometimes while we were live on air he liked to say to the audience stuff like, "The bosses want us to come off air, but shall we keep going?" And they'd all cheer, so he'd say to the cameras, "Let's keep going, guys!" But actually, mostly, it was all rehearsed. We'd agree with the network in advance if we could have an overrun, and then Ricky would just make out like it was spontaneous at the time.'

DI Watson looked over at Ali Rafik and said sarcastically, 'Already rehearsed? Really? I guess we mere mortals don't know a lot about the tricks of television.' She glanced down at her notes. Elizabeth twisted her head and tried to read them upside down.

'One of the cameramen from this week's show, what was his name, Phil. He would've been on live talkback, yes?'

'Of course. He's camera 5, Ricky's autocue camera.'

'Yes, so he said that he heard Ricky say a few things this week that he thought were – out of character?'

Elizabeth sat up and Lola leaned forward. 'Oh?'

'Did you think he said anything odd? Was he behaving differently?'

'No, not really.'

DI Watson looked again at her notes. 'Phil thought that, just before the show started, Ricky said something like, "Come on, guys, let's make this a show to remember". Did you hear him say that, Lola?'

'Well, maybe. Maybe he said that. I mean, I'm not sure why that would be unusual. He wanted to have a good show, that's all.'

'Phil seemed to think it was odd.' DI Watson's voice was light and even. 'He said that in previous weeks Ricky had been grumpy before and during a show. And,' she looked at her notes, as if checking her facts, 'sometimes even falling asleep?'

'He only did that once!' Elizabeth protested.

DI Watson was unmoved. She kept her eyes on Lola. 'I think you knew Ricky very well, Lola. Better, I think, than most people on the team? Would that be correct?'

Elizabeth stiffened, but Lola boldly returned the police-woman's stare. 'Yes, I knew him well. That is, I've known him for longer than some people on the team. But you know, he's a very sociable guy – we all used to go out together a lot, the researchers and the producers. Drinking. And so on.'

DI Watson nodded. 'Yes. Drinking.' She laid heavy emphasis on the word. 'In your view, was Ricky drunk in the studio on Wednesday night?'

'Well, you have to remember that Ricky's a man who can take his drink. He functions quite well on quite a lot of booze. So, yes, I'd say he'd had a few. But I've seen him worse.' Lola sounded confident, very certain of her knowledge of Ricky.

'Did you go out drinking with Ricky the night before the recording on Tuesday night? I believe a few members of the team did.'

This was news to Elizabeth. She thought back over the

events on Tuesday. They'd had their production meeting, as usual, in the afternoon – the one Ricky had missed – and then the writers had gone back into their room to make changes to the script and Elizabeth had left them to it. She was seeing Hutch that night and for once he was coming to her flat. This time, she was going to try and cook supper. Most of the team were dispersing as she'd left the office, apart from Zander, whose job it was to sort out the food props for Paolo Culone's slot. And Lola, who was finishing the camera script.

'No,' Lola said, but her voice was suddenly quiet.

'I see. So you weren't in the party that went to the King's Head and met Harry Hutchinson?' DI Watson's gaze lifted from her pad, fixed on Lola, and then travelled slowly across to Elizabeth, where it rested, penetratingly. Elizabeth's heart began to pound painfully. She was hot and uncomfortable.

'No. I didn't know anything about a meeting with Hutch. Are you sure? Ricky met him? Who else went?' Lola looked at Elizabeth, astonished. DI Watson closed her pad. 'Some other members of the team, I believe. Are you surprised, Lola, that Ricky might have met Harry Hutchinson?'

'Yes. I didn't think Ricky liked him,' Lola said flatly. Elizabeth winced slightly on behalf of Hutch but tried to keep her eyes straight ahead.

'Oh? Had he said so to you?'

'Well, no, not exactly.' Lola faltered and she glanced guiltily at Elizabeth, as if worrying she'd overstepped a mark. 'And actually, I think their wives knew each other quite well. But you know, Ricky had said general things to the team: unpleasant bitchy things about the Channel 4 show Hutch was doing and stuff. And then Hutch came on a *Bonkers* show a month or so ago and well, Ricky wasn't very nice…' Lola was suddenly reflective. 'You know, in many ways Hutch was a bit similar to Ricky…'

The new secret show with Hutch was one of the few programmes Elizabeth had ever considered making without the support of Lola and now more than ever she felt bad about it. Her head was all over the place. Was it possible that Hutch had met Ricky for a drink in the King's Head before coming to her flat for supper? But why on earth hadn't he mentioned it? She tried to remember what time he'd arrived at the flat and recalled that she'd had time to change her outfit twice, finally settling for a pair of boyfriend Levis and a black T-shirt with 'Made in Hackney' written in large white letters across her chest. And that she'd still had time to drink half a bottle of wine before he got there. Elizabeth had a sudden vision of her spaghetti Bolognese congealing uneaten in the pan. When Hutch finally arrived, he'd swept into her tiny sitting room, kissed her long and hard on the mouth and lifted her T-shirt over her head, murmuring, 'Okay, let's get this off, my little pearly queen.' There hadn't been a lot of conversation. Or even eating. Hutch had seemed more than usually excited and also in a hurry. He couldn't stay the night – they'd never made it to her bed – and in the end, he'd left his jumper on her chair. But he'd told her, over and over, that he loved her. She remembered that.

'Elizabeth?' Lola nudged her. She was looking at her strangely. Elizabeth jumped out of her skin. 'DI Watson was asking if you knew about the King's Head?'

Elizabeth knew her face was red. She shook her head. 'No…
no, I didn't. Who else went? From the team?'

'Well, we don't need to discuss that now. We'll need to talk
to you later in any case.' DI Watson was brisk and had folded
over the cover of her notebook. Lola was scrabbling thankfully
to her feet. But then the policewoman put up her hand as if
she'd just thought of something. Automatically, Elizabeth and
Lola froze.

'Tell me, who had access to Ricky Clough's dressing room?'

'There's a key card, like in hotels. Only Ricky has it.'

'But he could give it to someone else? If someone wanted
to get in while he was in the studio, for example?'

'Yes, he could…' Lola looked anxiously at Elizabeth. 'His
mates sometimes hung out there during the show – Deniz
Pegasus, his manager, often does. He was there. I guess Ricky
might sometimes give him the key card.'

DI Watson leaned forward, as if about to lower her voice
and exchange a confidence, but in fact she spoke out clearly
and unambiguously. 'We've discovered that someone deleted
all recent activity on Ricky's laptop at 6.30 on Wednesday
evening. His internet history, all his recent emails.'

Lola glanced again at Elizabeth but then shrugged. 'Well,
we were on the crew supper break by 6.30. We called everyone
back to the studio at 7.15. Ricky was probably in his dressing
room himself, going through his script. It wouldn't surprise
me if he had stuff on the internet he wanted to delete. Most
middle-aged men do, don't they?' Lola looked scornfully at
the policewoman, who simply sat still in her chair, steadily
returning her gaze.

Elizabeth got up to move towards the door. 'Did you say you want to see me again? The thing is, I've agreed to drive down to Surrey to see Ricky's wife later today.' She felt Lola stiffen beside her. 'What time will you want to see me?'

DI Watson looked at her shrewdly. 'You're seeing Lorna Clough?'

'Yes,' said Elizabeth defiantly. 'I'm sure she needs some support.' She almost blushed at the shamefulness of what she'd said. After all, she hadn't volunteered to support Lorna or even really thought about it until Lorna had called. Lola turned away from her.

'Well, we can meet in the morning, first thing. After you've seen Lorna Clough.' DI Watson nodded at Ali Rafik, who dutifully made a note. 'Would you prefer us to come to your home or here to the office?'

Elizabeth thought about her small Islington flat, with its red-painted bedroom and the mantelpiece with her National TV Award on it, over which Hutch had tossed her Agent Provocateur bra on Tuesday night. No, she didn't want DI Watson with those sharp weasel eyes in her personal space, thank you.

'The office will be fine.'

Lola was halfway out the door but DI Watson coughed and she turned automatically, her foot propping open the door.

'And Lola, if there's anything else you'd like to add – anything at all…' DI Watson paused. 'Please don't hesitate to call me. Here, take my card.' She passed a white calling card to Lola, and Elizabeth marvelled at the modernity of a police force that issued its staff with business cards as well as stab vests.

Outside the writers' room, the Head of HR was waiting anxiously at a desk. 'How did it go?' she hissed at Elizabeth as Lola ran past. Elizabeth wondered if this high level of anxiety around Lola's police interview suggested that there was widespread knowledge about her late-night visits to Ricky.

'She did very well. There's nothing to be worried about.'

Elizabeth picked up her bag and phone from her desk and debated about whether or not to call Hutch, but decided that particular confrontation could wait until later. She looked around the office for Lola – she wanted to give her a hug – but she'd vanished. Elizabeth left a Post-it note on her desk saying, '*Babe, you were great. Call u later* xxx'. She then retrieved her Beetle with its annoying parking ticket, lowered the sunroof to get a big blast of fume-filled London air and put her foot down towards the M3 and Lorna Clough.

Chapter Eight

The Clough mansion was on one of those winding tree-lined B roads, where the houses sit invisibly at the end of long leafy drives. Fields with sleek chestnut horses lazily grazing at the fences stretched away into the distance. Elizabeth remembered reading somewhere that Surrey is the most wooded county in England, as well as being the wealthiest – and by some way, she thought, as she peered down yet another unending driveway and a virtual car park of supercars. She smiled to herself as she passed a sign to Box Hill, the setting for her favourite-ever episode in a Jane Austen novel and also the subject of her Year Two dissertation 'Jane Austen and the Nastiness of Women' (referred to forever afterwards by her sister as 'Jane Austen's Bitches').

Thoughts of university made her think of Jamie, and Elizabeth wondered if he'd yet heard about Ricky – if he'd perhaps resisted calling her, texting her. She hadn't heard from him for so long, she wondered if she could properly remember the sound of his voice. Two days after the wedding that wasn't, Jamie removed several things from the flat they had bought jointly and which were no more his than hers: a beautiful blue vase, a casserole dish, an antique mirror. And he took his grandmother's wing-backed chair, the chair he sat in every night, his knees bobbing up and down, tilting his book towards the reading lamp. Even now, there were four faint footmarks on the carpet where his chair had been. They never spoke about the things he'd taken and why. They'd never spoken since. While he was moving out, she went to stay with her sister Vic, where she was served strong sweet tea and a piece of her own wedding cake ('Waste not, want not,' Vic said, wielding a long silver blade) and Elizabeth had wept bitter tears into the white icing.

A few weeks after he'd left and to signal her independence, she re-painted their bedroom a dark brothel red. Miserable though she was, she felt she needed to change the scenery in preparation for the string of exciting new lovers she would bring home to increase her woeful tally. 'How many is a good number?' she'd asked Vic, who was helping her paint, wearing a pair of their dad's old pyjamas. 'Well, if you must persist with this, I'd say ten.' Vic slapped on the scarlet paint. 'Twenty is slutty. Fifteen sounds like you can't hang on to them for long.'

'Interesting that you've gone for round numbers. Are you meant to just stop when you get to a common factor? I think I might go for twelve.'

But there were no new lovers. She learned that she was very bad at one-night stands and the only real action her brothel-red bedroom got to see was Elizabeth attempting to do the plank every morning, alone. Three months after the wedding that wasn't, she bumped into Hutch again at a book launch in a fashionable club. They'd both arrived alone (Lola had abandoned Elizabeth for a night in with Ricky) and he quickly made a beeline for her. They were very soon huddled together alone in a dark corner, where they ate rosemary-coated chips from a tin flowerpot and drank a red wine that Hutch promised would change her life. He knew a lot about food and wine; he knew even more about football, he was surprisingly knowledgeable about politics and, Elizabeth was astonished to learn, described himself as right-leaning rather than left. (She knew no one like this. She wasn't sure anyone who declared themselves Conservative was allowed to work in television, or live in the bits of London she frequented.) She hadn't realised before that it was even possible to talk about the welfare state without being earnest. At the end of a long and hilarious night in which all her beliefs were severely and outrageously challenged, Hutch offered to teach her more about benefits, back in his flat. Bed and breakfast was what he offered and although Elizabeth very much liked the bed bit, the breakfast was sensational: a tray of fresh strawberries with a dusting of icing sugar, thick creamy Greek yogurt, homemade granola, Colombian coffee brewed to perfection in a stove pot, steaming hot milk. She allowed herself to be spoon-fed and she also allowed herself to forget that he was married.

It took Elizabeth several U-turns to find the Clough house, Tetherdown (she did think one-word house names were very classy). The name was carved into a piece of cedar wood, which sat low on the grass as the drive swept in and off to the right. A motorbike was parked on the grassy verge, technically, Elizabeth supposed, still on the public road but virtually on the Clough property. Several men in leather jackets were leaning against it and as she turned in, they quickly pointed their camera rifles at Elizabeth, firing flashes in rapid succession and she instinctively put up her hand to shield her face as she swung past them and then out of sight, into the gloom of the overhanging oak trees.

Elizabeth circled the lawn and parked up behind a creamy Jag with tinted windows. The imposing stone house had ground-floor bay windows with looped curtains of swathed silk and soft lamps with crimson shades sitting on occasional tables. All the other windows were dark. As she walked towards the porch, automatic lights drenched her in white light and the door opened before she could ring the bell. The last time she had been to the house, just three short weeks ago, they'd partied in large marquees crowned with chandeliers and had danced on the lawn festooned with fairy lights. Now the house seemed silent and shut down. Everything had changed.

The Help, a Filipina in a black dress, gestured her in without smiling. She guided her into the room on the left, which stretched the length of the house, in which there were at least five white and beige sofas with soft padded cushions, surely recently plumped. Scented candles burned on almost every surface and a fake fire was blazing in the fireplace. The room was insufferably hot. There was a large portrait over the mantelpiece of the Clough boys; Elizabeth was fairly sure it had been painted by Jonathan Yeo. She also noted a Banksy and a signed Hockney. There was a pile of post on a console table beside a ticking clock and Elizabeth spotted a thick creamy envelope half hidden under a bank letter. She gave a small start. The distinctive bold, sloping, handwritten address written in black ink ('*Tetherdown, Maple Lane...*') was unmistakable: the handwriting belonged to Ricky. Over the years, Elizabeth had received several hand-penned notes from Ricky, nearly all of them nice. He liked writing letters. He liked the indelible effect of ink on paper. He liked his thoughts immortalised, not easily deleted with one press of the keypad. She wondered if it was on the table because it had arrived in today's post. But she couldn't imagine why Ricky would be sending letters to his own home. Somewhere in the back of the house, she could hear furiously yapping dogs and remembered Hiss and Boo. It seemed they'd managed to find their way safely back to Surrey.

'Tea?' offered The Help with a big sigh.

'Um...' Elizabeth hesitated, thinking that she would find this encounter quite hard without the lubricating assistance of some fine wine, many bottles of which she knew were held in the temperature-controlled cellar beneath her feet.

'I'm sure Elizabeth would prefer some wine, yes?' Lorna Clough strode into the sitting room with a wriggling Pomeranian tucked under one arm and she bent over to kiss Elizabeth lightly on both cheeks. She had a dancer's grace, she was tall and willowy and was dressed head to toe in taupe, with a tight-fitting cashmere jumper and fine wool tapered trousers. 'Let's open a bottle of the Merlot, thank you, Pearl.'

Lorna sank on to one of the sofas and held either Hiss or Boo on her lap. 'Thanks for coming,' she said heavily, gesturing for Elizabeth to sit opposite her.

'No, no, I'm sorry – I should've called earlier to see if there was anything I could do. You know, in situations like this, you never know quite what to say or do...'

'Have you been in a situation like this before? Because I haven't.'

Elizabeth blushed at her stupidity. 'No, of course not. Not like this.' Pearl arrived with a bottle and two elegant long-stemmed red wine glasses. 'But um, when my dad died, you know – it was very sudden. So I know what my mum went through.' She reached gratefully for a gulp of wine.

'How old was your mum?' Lorna asked curiously.

'She was fifty. My dad was only fifty-four.'

'I'm forty-two.' said Lorna. 'I'm a widow at forty-two. I can't get my head round it.'

Elizabeth felt there was nothing she could say. A silence fell between them. Lorna gazed down at the small lump of fur on her lap and her blonde hair fell over her face, obscuring her expression. 'The police rang me this evening. They say there's no update. They're still doing the tests on what it could be. It seems to be taking a long time.' She looked up with tear-rimmed eyes. 'Elizabeth, please tell me. How was he? Was he drunk?' She swallowed. 'Was he high? Did it seem to you that he might've taken something?'

'Honestly, no.' Elizabeth put down her glass and leaned forward as if to emphasise her certainty. 'He seemed completely normal. On form, in fact. I went through his notes and cue cards with him in the dressing room and he was concentrating, contributing – on top of it. I mean, he'd had a drink or two but I suspected far less than usual. He seemed very professional.'

Lorna nodded gratefully, her chest heaved and a small sound

escaped, half sigh, half gulp. She sat for a moment, seeming to consider what to say next, looking all the while down at the dog in her lap. She then said softly, 'And of course, he'd been out to lunch with Matthew the day before.'

'Yes, I believe so.'

'Do you know what they talked about?' Lorna twisted her head to reach for her glass and again Elizabeth couldn't see her face.

'I'm not sure... I wasn't there.'

'Of course I heard about Matthew's mugging the other week. It must've been horrible for him. It was just a week or so after our party, I think. Is he still limping?'

'Yes, he is. I think it will heal, but they say it'll take time. The bruising's mostly gone now. He had a very bad black eye. It was right outside his house, close to Hampstead Heath. He was out walking his dog, I think it was about 10.30. He had nothing on him except his phone.' Elizabeth thought about Matthew's dragging leg, the result of his hip being stamped on as he curled up, defenceless, on the pavement. 'It's hard to know what he's feeling – you know, he finds it hard to talk about personal things.' Elizabeth looked carefully at Lorna to see how well she might know these facts about Matthew, but once again Lorna's head was turned away.

'Yes, like all men.' Lorna looked up with a pale smile. 'Rick went to see him in hospital, the day after it happened. I was down here but I know Rick went, when he was in town.'

'Really?' Elizabeth hadn't known this. Matthew's wife had told her very definitely that he didn't want any visitors in hospital.

'Don't suppose they'll catch whoever did it. They never do.' Lorna swilled the wine around her glass.

'Matthew was able to give reasonably good descriptions. They produced some photofits, you know. There were three of them. He says he remembers a smell – like really strong spicy aftershave. His wife told me the police brought him lots of samples and he got distressed when he couldn't place it.'

Lorna shuddered. 'Terrible, living in London. No chance of that sort of thing happening down here.' She gave a short bitter laugh. 'Truth is, nothing happens down here.' She put down her glass and Elizabeth noticed her hand shaking. She drained her own glass and Lorna sat for a moment staring out of the window at the gathering gloom. Finally, she turned slowly to look at her. 'Rick thought that maybe you, Elizabeth, were planning to do another show? That you were planning to leave him?'

'Wha... what do you mean? Leaving him?'

'He thought you might be thinking of producing a pilot with someone else? Perhaps a show to replace his?'

Elizabeth sank back into her chair. How long had Ricky suspected? Had he in fact already known something when Matthew had told him about the Hutch pilot over lunch on Tuesday?

'Lorna, I'm not sure I can talk about this...' Elizabeth said helplessly.

'Oh, this is just between us.' Lorna's face was so very pale, her eyes so watery, it was almost, Elizabeth felt, as if she was dissolving in front of her. Her voice had become a whisper. 'I'm just trying to catch up, you know, on everything that was going on with Rick. In London.' She paused. 'I always wanted to live in the country, have horses and fresh air, especially when the boys were born. I grew up in Yorkshire, I had ponies, I was used to big open spaces. Rick wanted that for us, too. You know, he'd grown up on a council estate in East Ham and he wanted the boys to have all the things he'd never had. And he loved coming down at weekends. To begin with. But it did mean we led, well, quite separate lives during the week. He'd phone home every evening, but often he was tired and, well, not always full of detail about how his day had gone...'

Lorna glanced up self-consciously at Elizabeth, who nodded sympathetically. 'And so I ended up talking about the boys and school and Pony Club and what they'd had for tea... and after a while I felt I was always boring him. Of course, I knew what was really going on.' Lorna looked away and her white hand gripped the arm of the chair. 'Well, how could I avoid it? The tabloids used to ring me up and let me know... "*Hi, Lorna, just checking that it was you with Ricky last night in The Wolseley, yes?*" or "*Loved the way you ran into that taxi last night with Ricky's jacket over your head!*" So many times! Can you *imagine*?'

Elizabeth couldn't. She felt terrible.

'I was the one who had to ring my husband and tell him they were on his trail. His own wife! I was the one who had to tell him to keep it in his fucking pants!' Lorna almost spat out this last, suddenly very animated, and Elizabeth jumped, slopping wine over her hands.

'So I knew all about the other women – what am I saying? – the other *girls*.' Lorna's voice dropped again to a level of hopelessness and Elizabeth had to lean forward to hear her.

'But Rick kept saying he would stop and like a fool, I believed him. But then I got another call from a newspaper... So a week ago, I asked him for a divorce.'

Elizabeth swallowed hard. She hadn't realised how bad it had all become. Of course, she knew he fell for every sassy young woman that deceived him with her wide star-struck eyes, but then he'd talk with enthusiasm each Monday morning about weekends spent at home in Surrey with Lorna, fishing trips with his sons, watching them play rugby, playing FIFA with them. Had it all been a lie?

She felt for Lorna, sitting there so wax-like, her words betraying such a profound sense of hurt and desperation. 'Lorna, look, I'm really sorry, but honestly, I want you to know, I wasn't really a part of that – that other side of Ricky's life. Well, definitely not in the last few years. I worked with him, sure. But I didn't really go out with him on the town anymore. Although it's true other people on the team did...' She thought guiltily of Lola and her sleepovers with Ricky but pressed on. 'I guessed that Ricky was, well, not always on his best behaviour, but I just didn't want to know. It was easier to work with him if I kept all that at a distance.' Elizabeth felt that on balance what she had said was more true than not.

Lorna nodded slowly. Her eyes were still brimming with tears, but they fixed unwaveringly on Elizabeth. 'But were you planning to produce another show? A replacement show?'

Elizabeth couldn't face that imploring gaze. 'Yes. I'm supposed to be producing a new show. But we don't know whether or not the network will go with it. It's only a pilot.'

Lorna sat silently for a minute. 'Who's it with?'

'It's with Hutch… Harry Hutchinson.'

Lorna's face fell. Unconsciously, she raised her hand to her mouth and Elizabeth saw that it was trembling. 'Hutch?' she said in a voice full of incredulity. 'The new show's with *Hutch*?'

'Yes.' She couldn't understand why Lorna was so shocked. After all, there were only a handful of people ready to take on a network show of this sort, a list of maybe three or four.

'So, Matthew knew?' Lorna was speaking slowly, trying to put the puzzling pieces together. 'Matthew has commissioned a show – this pilot show – with Hutch? Behind Rick's back?'

'I'm sorry, Lorna. I can see how disloyal it looks. But you must understand, Matthew has to look after the whole network. He commissions lots of pilot shows. We didn't know if this one was going to work so we didn't want to tell everyone in advance. And it might not have replaced Ricky's show. It might've gone into another slot. We just didn't know.' Elizabeth bit her lip.

'I know how television works, thank you. God knows, I've been around it for long enough!' Lorna said with some force and then muttered, 'Sorry, Elizabeth, I don't mean to be rude… But he knew! He knew all along and he didn't say! It's such a betrayal!'

Elizabeth wasn't sure if Lorna was still referring to Matthew. It seemed Lorna had been betrayed by several men – not least, her own husband. After a long pregnant pause, Lorna unwrapped her long legs so that the sleeping dog slid off her lap and on to the floor. She lifted herself from the sofa and Elizabeth realised it was a signal so she also stood.

'Lorna, is there anything I – anything we – can do for you

and the boys? Do you need help with the arrangements, or anything?'

Elizabeth had a sudden memory of being with her mother and sister in what was laughingly called the funeral parlour, looking with bewilderment through a catalogue of coffins, where a weasel in a tie served them yet more sweet tea, murmuring, 'This one's most suitable, this one's also very popular, very nice wood, silk inlay you see, there, there; how about willow? Basket caskets are very popular. Take a tissue, let me leave you to it for a moment...' until Vic had cried out, 'Oh, for God's sake, what does it matter? What does dad know or care about it? Let's just take the cheapest!' and had run from the room.

Lorna now held out her soft white hand. It was trembling. 'Thank you, but Deniz – of course you know Deniz Pegasus? He's a very old friend of Rick's and he's been here today. I guess he'll come back later. He's been really helpful.' Lorna shivered slightly. Elizabeth looked at her quickly but she went smoothly on, 'And Kevin from your press office is taking care of the newspapers, of course.' She paused. 'But thank you, Elizabeth, for your honesty. And thank you for coming. Will you be okay to drive back?'

Lorna's voice was hesitant again and Elizabeth had a sudden urge to embrace her. She felt for this publicly spurned wife, now inexplicably a widow. Something about Lorna's coolness and poise had caused Elizabeth to shrink from her in the past, but there was no mistaking the courage it had taken to have the conversation they'd just had. Lorna's confession that she knew she'd been cheated on, together with the suspicion that her husband's work colleagues were plotting against him, must've been an agonising one to make, especially to Elizabeth, who had been complicit in both elements of the deceit. And yet, for some reason, Lorna had been determined to have this conversation. It seemed to Elizabeth that she'd been invited down to Surrey for this express purpose; the whole conversation had been pre-planned.

She made her way to the door, tripping over the dog and the rug, for they were impossible to tell apart. Lorna stood waiting, very still, in the large stone-flagged hall and opened her mouth as if to speak, then appeared to change her mind. Elizabeth stood also uncertainly, wondering whether she ought to have said more to reassure, or at least to explain. But then Lorna seemed to gather herself and took her once more by surprise. 'Just one thing… I presume you've kept the police up to speed? I think Detective Watson is coming here tomorrow. Just so you know.' She didn't meet Elizabeth's startled look, but simply opened the front door. Elizabeth could do nothing but kiss her awkwardly on the cheek and walk back to her car. As she reversed around the circular lawn she saw Lorna, who'd been standing very straight in the porch, reach out her arm to the wall as if for support, her long elegant neck wilting and her head drooping. She went limp like a rag doll. Elizabeth hesitated, her foot on the brake, but then Lorna, with an apparent effort of will, straightened, turned away and closed the front door behind her.

Chapter Nine

Elizabeth drove back home along the M3 and the suburbs of south London, her eyes glazed against the onslaught of white headlights and her neck aching. Her head felt stuffed with information she couldn't seem to process. She felt bad about rushing out of the office after Lola's police interview that afternoon, and without talking to her. She knew how hurt Lola would be that she'd gone to see Ricky's wife. Lola lived in a basement flat near Battersea Bridge. Elizabeth decided it wouldn't be much of a diversion – she would drop by on her way home with a bottle of vodka.

Lola opened the door wearing a pale pink chiffon peignoir, her hair was piled untidily on her head, her face was white with face cream. She took the bottle from Elizabeth without speaking and led the way into her sitting room. Lola spent her weekends trawling flea markets and had recreated in her small flat the look and feel of a bungalow at the Chateau Marmont in Hollywood: art-deco lamps on every surface, a mid-century couch and chairs, Adderley bone china tea sets crowding the shelves and in the corner, a padded vinyl cocktail cabinet. She took two glasses and expertly mixed them each a Bloody Mary.

She handed Elizabeth a glass, and raised her own: 'To Ricky!' Elizabeth clinked her glass, took one sip and handed it back to Lola. 'I'm not staying, hon, and I'm driving. You have this. I just wanted to check in on you.'

Lola shrugged and curled up on the sofa.

'I'm sorry I rushed off this afternoon. How did you feel after your interrogation?'

Lola swirled her drink, the ice cubes chinking in the glass. 'I think I did okay. Mind you, that Watson woman's no slouch. She talks to you like she can see right through you. But I don't care, I've got nothing to hide. How was Lorna Clough?'

'Sad. A bit weird. She can't believe it, like the rest of us.'

'Yeah, well, Ricky said she'd stopped giving out years ago. Busy making hay with her stable hands apparently.'

Elizabeth said gently, 'Lola, I'm not sure you can rely on Ricky to give you an accurate account of his marriage.' She wondered, though, if Lola had any idea about Lorna asking for a divorce. According to Lola, Ricky hadn't wanted to see her over the last few weeks, so she guessed he hadn't told her.

Lola looked at her sharply. 'Did she know what was going on?'

'With you? No, I don't think so. She knew that he wasn't faithful.'

'Yeah, well, you don't have to be a detective to work that out.' Lorna began to wipe off her face cream with a tissue. 'I feel so bad, Lizzie. I'm going to miss him so much.' She covered her face completely with the tissue, her shoulders heaved. 'Do you think I should've told the police? About sleeping with him? Does it matter?'

'I don't know.' Elizabeth had wondered whether or not she was going to have to confess her own secret to the police. She held Lola's hand. 'I'm not sure it matters, hon. Maybe wait to see if they ask any more questions. Are you going to be okay tonight?'

Lola sniffed. 'Yeah, I'm fine. I'm used to being alone. What about you?'

Elizabeth stood up. 'I'm hoping tonight will be better than last night. It was so weird – I kept thinking about Jamie. I haven't thought about him like that for weeks. And then I kept thinking about my dad. All the men who are missing from my life: husband, father.' She pulled a face and Lola smiled. It was a relief to see.

'C'mon, Lizzie, stop that! You're the feminist we all look up to. We don't need men to define us, you said. You didn't want to be married, remember? I'm certainly never going to ask a man to put a ring on it. No way. Sex without strings, that's what I'm up for.' Her sudden attempt at bravado failed, her bottom lip wobbled and her eyes filled with tears. 'But fuck, I'll miss him, Lizzie.'

'We'll all miss him.'

Lola stared into her glass. 'You know, the first time I realised Ricky was completely out of control was during that episode of *Bonkers* with Hutch.'

'Yes, me too.'

'What happened afterwards? You know, when you and Ricky had to go and see Matthew on the Monday morning? Ricky didn't talk about it. But he was different with me from then on.'

'Different how?'

'Oh, you know, more demanding. Moody. More controlling. He'd ring me up and expect me to jump. And if I jumped, it was all wham bam, thank you, ma'am.'

'Oh, Lola, I'm sorry...' Elizabeth sat down heavily. 'I don't know what happened really. The plan was that Matthew was going to read him the riot act that morning. You know, final warning and all that. But, like so many things to do with Ricky, it didn't quite go to plan... It was a complete balls-up.'

★

Elizabeth had sat waiting for Ricky that Monday morning in the coffee shop underneath the network's offices. The ratings had come in for the *Bonkers* show with Hutch the previous Friday, and they had lost two million viewers. Ricky finally arrived three minutes before nine, wearing a black suit and some shades and looking, she had thought, very like the Terminator. He was also carrying a large black holdall.

'Leave the talking to me,' he'd said, ordering a double expresso. His early morning breath was sour. 'I'll sort it.'

'Really?' Elizabeth said coolly. 'I very much doubt that.'

'Bad weekend?'

'You saw the ratings, I take it?'

'Yeah, well. Our ratings are still better than anything Matthew's getting for that egg-on-face disaster, his new breakfast show! Did you see him in *Private Eye*?'

She had. Matthew had recently introduced an innovative new item on his breakfast show, where the newspapers were reviewed each morning by two teddy bears. The *Private Eye* piece had referred to him as Daddy Bear and Lola had told her that last week, along with his post, Matthew had been delivered two bowls of cold porridge. But Elizabeth wasn't prepared to side with Ricky on this one. 'Yeah, well, I wouldn't mention that this morning if I were you, Ricky.'

The Controller called them up to his lair, where he was masterfully on the phone and at the same time prowling around his meeting room like a caged tiger. He'd practised the art of restless motion, which he felt suggested the sort of simmering creative energy entirely appropriate for a man who had commissioned both *Bears at Breakfast* as well as *Bonkers*. He gestured grandly for the two of them to sit on his leather sofa, under a framed photograph of the blonde hostess of the network's lunchtime consumer show. Elizabeth couldn't help noticing that the place on the wall where a framed photograph of Ricky Clough used to hang was now occupied by a picture of two fat teddy bears sitting on a breakfast bar.

Ricky looked irritable. He hadn't put down his holdall. He seemed very big in the room, and menacing. Elizabeth tried to gesture to the seat beside her but he frowned and ignored her. Matthew moved to pour some coffee, standing ready on a side table. Ricky was looking at the framed picture of the teddy bears.

'Ah, I see you've spotted our two new stars: Beatrice and Benedick Bear.' Matthew allowed himself a knowing chuckle and looked up quickly to see if either of them got the joke. Ricky was still staring at the bears.

To humour her boss, Elizabeth said merrily, 'Wow! What

would Shakespeare say?' and Matthew looked pleased. 'We've put them on the breakfast show. To review the papers. They're big up north. They're really going to appeal to our younger viewers.'

Ricky said nothing but carefully unzipped his holdall and pulled out an enormous black, double-barrelled water pistol. He tucked the drum under one arm and pointed its extended nozzle at Matthew, who had stopped stock-still and was open-mouthed. Ricky smiled.

'Got it from an army mate. Handheld water cannon. Rapid fire. Thirty-five kilos. Potentially deadly within three metres. What do you think?' He was still pointing it at Matthew. Elizabeth looked from one to the other, still holding her coffee.

'Ricky,' said Matthew, as if speaking to a small child. 'Put it down. It's making Elizabeth uncomfortable.'

Ricky laughed. Then he suddenly spun on his heels and pulled the trigger. A short, fierce torrent of water shot across the room, knocking Beatrice and Benedick Bear off the wall and on to the floor in a splintering, glass-shattering smash. It also knocked several trophies off a sideboard and toppled a table lamp. Rivers of water began running down the wall and pooled in puddles on the carpet, beside the broken glass.

Ricky calmly put the water gun back in his bag and sat down on the sofa beside Elizabeth. 'Whoops,' he said, winking at her. 'More powerful than I thought.'

Matthew flushed an angry red. The veins in his scalp and forehead pulsed with anger. He leaned into Ricky's face. 'That damage will need paying for. And it'll be coming out of your pay packet. I'm going to be picking it up with your agent.'

'I haven't got an agent!' Ricky said with a small air of triumph. 'I fired her.'

Elizabeth turned to him in surprise. 'You fired Janey? But you've been with her for years! She's been with you since you were doing the radio show. How could you fire her?'

'She hasn't got me any new work for years,' Ricky said flatly. 'She doesn't do anything for her twenty percent. Deniz Pegasus is looking after me now.'

Elizabeth thought with despair about the encounters she'd had so far with Deniz Pegasus, none of them pleasant. She couldn't see Matthew going along with the idea that he might need to discuss the future of his network's programmes with Bob the Builder. She thought of all the late-night phone calls over the last twenty years fielded by Janey from an hysterical Ricky; the trips she'd made to various bars and clubs to rescue her client; the press calls she'd had to take and make, the wheedling, the cajoling, the cover-ups and the lies. This was a new level of treachery.

'Look, Ricky.' Matthew was very angry. His body was quivering with tension. Elizabeth had never seen him so out of control and she didn't like to see him rising to Ricky's level of fury. 'There's a reason you're not getting any new work. And it's right there.' He nodded in the direction of the mini flood. 'Your behaviour's becoming completely unacceptable. People are finding you too unpredictable. I cannot have a loose cannon live on my network every Saturday night. I think this series of *Bonkers* should be your last. The ratings are dropping and you're out of control.'

'Really?' Ricky said sarcastically. 'Who else is going to get you seven million viewers on a Saturday night?'

Elizabeth froze, her cup trembling in her hand. But Matthew hadn't got where he'd got to without being effortlessly disingenuous. He was right in Ricky's face. Elizabeth had a sudden vision of two rhinos locking horns.

'Ricky, let me be clear. No one, however talented, is bigger than this network. If we have to, we'll find another Saturday night show, believe me. And we'll find another star. That's what we do: we find and we make stars. Shows come and shows go.'

Ricky said quickly, 'The ratings are dropping because we're not being ambitious enough. That's what I was trying to do last Saturday night – liven it up a bit. But booking Harry Hutchinson isn't going to do it.'

Matthew looked across at Elizabeth. 'Actually, and under the circumstances, I thought Hutch did rather well. I don't know many other celebrities who could've dealt with those antics.'

She couldn't help it, she glowed with pride. Ricky shot her a quick, piercing look. 'Hutch isn't a big enough name for our show. We need bigger names – and a bigger budget.'

Elizabeth looked at him with amazement. Matthew was on the verge of exploding. 'Let me get this right? You're actually asking for extra money? When I've brought you here to give you a formal warning? Ricky, you cannot do what you did on Saturday night – get out bloody sex toys and wave them around on a family show.'

'Ah, but I didn't get it out!' interrupted Ricky with a smirk.

'You cannot do it, Ricky. Full stop. You have to listen to Elizabeth. You have to do the show that's been planned and rehearsed or you can't be trusted to do live programmes. Take this as a final warning.'

Ricky jumped up and began pacing around the room, fizzing with impatience – probably, Elizabeth thought, with chemical energy.

'Listen, mate, this network needs me. I've got two shows on and you've got to admit it, they're bringing in the dosh as well as the audiences. The chat show's okay but what I'm really good at is live Saturday night shows. There's no one better. You just need to cut me some slack. I know what I'm doing.' He picked up his holdall. 'I'll get my boys round to fix your wall this afternoon. And I promise, no more rabbits on set. I've been loyal to you, mate. I said to Sky when they came knocking, thank you, but these guys have been with me from the beginning. They've stuck with me, and I'm going to stick with them. So thank you, Sky, for doubling my package – but no, I'll pass. I know about loyalty, believe you me. I've got mates from way back, from school – and you know what? That's what it's all about. Sticking together. Me and Lorna, we've known you for years, Matthew. You've been a friend. To both of us. And I give as good as I get, Matthew. No one could ever say otherwise.'

Elizabeth thought there was an odd emphasis on the words 'to both of us'. Matthew looked startled. Ricky stood for a moment with narrowed eyes that she knew only too well, but then with a dangerously brilliant smile, he left the room, taking his water rifle with him,

After a stunned moment, Matthew tiptoed to his desk through the small ocean Ricky had left in his wake. 'Well, that didn't go quite the way I expected.' He looked at Elizabeth with a pained expression. 'But I mean what I say about cancelling the show. He can threaten us all he wants.'

Elizabeth thought the meeting largely a disaster but she didn't say so. Instead, she nodded at the soaking floors and said, 'Well, I suppose it's one version of being carpeted… By the way, I didn't know you were such good friends with Ricky's wife?'

'Well, I offered Ricky his first TV show. I've known them for years. He was still doing his radio breakfast show at the time. I think he sees me – used to see me – as a sort of mentor. Those were the days when he listened to me! And Lorna,' he looked down at the papers on his desk, 'well, she rings me from time to time, asking advice about how to handle Ricky – you know, when he's on one of his benders. I know Janey's been his agent, but Lorna's really acted like his manager for the last couple of years. She's got a lot of good sense, has Lorna. She had a lot of say over what goes into his diary; you know, personal appearances and stuff. God knows what it'll be like with Deniz Pegasus running the bloody shop now. Have you seen those ghastly little boxes he slaps up? The man's got no taste.'

'Yes, dealing with Deniz won't be fun. I dare say it'll go badly and you'll end up with a horse's head in your bed.' Elizabeth was preoccupied with the revelation that Lorna Clough, whom she'd always found a little haughty, had a lot of good sense, as well as a hotline to Matthew. She didn't think her boss had ever mentioned it before.

'Actually,' Matthew went on musingly, 'I might give Lorna a call, try and meet up with her. See what she thinks is going on with Ricky.'

Elizabeth stood up, kicking over her cup of coffee which she'd left on the floor. 'I don't know. Maybe Ricky's getting too much attention. Perhaps we should all ignore him for a bit and he might stop it. Like a toddler having a tantrum. Sorry about this stain – add it to Ricky's cleaning bill.'

'Elizabeth, are the team okay? Anyone complaining – you know, about Ricky? About, er, inappropriate behaviour? Or anything?'

'No, they all seem in thrall.' It was true. They'd all found ways of dealing with Ricky Clough, figuring that the rewards of working on one of the nation's most popular shows were worth the occasional humiliation and lewd comment. And worse. Matthew had always known that Ricky's behaviour was dangerously extreme, he was in the camp that thought it explained why he was so brilliant on screen. But he hadn't – until now – called him out on it. That of course had made it very difficult for anyone else to make a formal complaint, since it would inevitably end up on Matthew's desk. And no one wanted to be the party pooper. No one wanted to get a reputation for not being part of the gang, for telling tales out of school. They might never get another job as good. That was the bind. Ricky had them all sewn up, trussed and bound.

'Good.' Matthew was relieved. 'You know, I meant what I said about Hutch. He was really good on the show. And I've been reading his football columns.' He gestured to a pile of papers marked up by his assistant with Post-it notes. 'He's funny, you know.'

'Yes, I do know.' Elizabeth was amused, but also felt a secret thrill on behalf of Hutch.

'Good. Let's make this new show as soon as we can. Do the budget for a one-off pilot and get it to me this afternoon. I'll send you the contract. Hand-pick your team. I think best not to take Lola, but anyone else you want. I don't want Ricky getting wind of it before the end of this series. We need him on his best behaviour from now on.'

Elizabeth opened her mouth to speak and then shut it again. Could she possibly make this show in secret? Without Lola? And with Hutch! It would be exciting and she was sure she could create a hit, but she felt compromised. She wanted to confess. She looked over at her boss, hoping that he would invite her to speak. But he was fidgeting with his mobile phone and her courage failed her. 'Yes, okay. Actually, I'm seeing Hutch tomorrow night to talk it through. I'll get the budget to you after that.'

She paused but Matthew didn't look up, didn't notice her hesitation, didn't register the date with Hutch.

'Well, I'll paddle my way out, then,' she said lightly, and her feet made a satisfyingly smutty sound as she squelched her way across the soaking carpet.

Chapter Ten

By the time Elizabeth had finished telling Lola the story of the showdown, it was past midnight. She drove back home along the Embankment, the river glistening darkly and the long straight road glassy in the late evening drizzle. The brutalist buildings across the water loomed malevolently out of the hazy mist. Her head ached badly and her back hurt from the long drive to Surrey and back. When she finally got home, she ran a hot bath and tipped in some lavender salts but as she lay back gingerly in the steaming water, she felt a terrible sense of panic. The world, her small universe, which two days ago she'd understood so well, now felt as if it had been built on foundations of quicksand. An image of Ricky contorted in pain on the studio floor, his eyes wide and bloodshot, gripping her hand, caused her to sit up suddenly and cry out loud in grief.

She closed her eyes and tried to remember everything about that night: sitting with Ricky in his dressing room during the crew supper break, rehearsing his cues and his jokes; the wine bottle beside him, open but largely untasted; the basket of fruit sweating under its plastic wrapping; the Hollywood make-up lights blazing in a circle around the mirror; his laptop open on the shelf. He was concentrating, listening, making notes on his script with a fountain pen while she perched on the velvet stool beside him. He'd made her laugh with a joke about Paolo Culone and she'd suggested putting it in the script. He'd smiled at her wistfully, as if to say, '*You see, I'm still good at this...*'

She hugged her knees, burying her head in her arms. None of it made sense to her any more. She tried to work through everything that had been said in the last forty-eight hours. She couldn't understand why Hutch hadn't told her about meeting Ricky in the pub before he came to her flat to have supper/sex on Tuesday night. It was just about conceivable that having clapped eyes on her in her 'Made in Hackney' T-shirt, he was so overcome with desire to take her (she seemed to remember, on all fours) that it had driven everything else out of his head. She'd certainly been struck by how little they'd talked about anything much that night. He definitely hadn't said what she'd been wanting him to say these last few months: that his right moment had come. But then why hadn't he mentioned meeting Ricky when he rang her yesterday, once he'd heard about his death? And why had Lorna called her down to Surrey to ask about the new show – and to let her know that Ricky had known about it, possibly all along?

Elizabeth stretched out in the bath and let her arms float up to the surface of the water as she tipped back her head. There was too much she still didn't know about Hutch. She knew every inch of his chest, the freckles here and there, the rise of his stomach, the muscular swell of his thighs. In the early days they would talk of nothing but their feelings, lying side by side on his bed, Hutch's hand slowly tracing the line downwards from her navel, the tickle of it making her legs twitch and jump. They were in love, they were drunk with it, they couldn't stop talking about how in love they were. She'd nestle into the strong sweet-smelling curve of his armpit and they'd murmur about living together in their loft and how they'd eat meals cooked by Hutch, barely dressed, at their kitchen table. (Elizabeth sometimes silently added into these scenes a baby sleeping angelically in a Moses basket; she'd understood from hints Hutch let drop that there had been some kind of issue with Sue being able to have kids and that it was one of the things that had taken its toll on their marriage.) She knew from starting to work with him on the pilot that he was funny and full of ideas. She knew that he liked her reading poetry to him, preferably naked. She knew that he thought football was a religion and that Manchester City's manager, Guardiola, was a God.

But what he did when he wasn't with her? She didn't know that. He told her again and again that he loved her and she found it thrilling. But Jamie had said he loved her, and it turned out he didn't love her *enough*. She thought she'd known Jamie inside out and yet she hadn't known he was unhappy. She was not prepared to have another relationship where things were not said out loud.

She slipped under the water completely and let it run over her face. She'd felt for some months now that Hutch was waiting for someone else to make a decision, someone to give him an ultimatum. She suspected that he was in fact weak, whereas she had thought him strong. She'd tried to end it after the *Bonkers* episode – and they'd lasted two days. But then he'd sent her a list of all the reasons why he missed her. Top of the list was the fact that in the nine months he'd known her, she'd spilt coffee on him five times and that he was missing the stains. Second was that he missed watching her bump into furniture. Third, that he missed her eating his pudding as well as her own. Along with the list was a black and white postcard of Montmartre in the mist and on the back he'd written out one of her favourite poems:

See the mountains kiss high heaven
And the waves clasp one another;...
And the sunlight clasps the earth
And the moonbeams kiss the sea:
What is all this sweet work worth
If thou kiss not me?

(Good ol' Percy. As taught by you to me in bed.)

That evening, she went to his flat in a purple velvet skirt and they had sex without undressing in front of a full-length mirror, where he watched over her shoulder the reflection of her legs in their black stockings, her ruched skirt, her exposed buttocks.

She got out of the bath and into an old brushed cotton gardening shirt of her dad's, now very frayed. It was late, but she knew sleep would evade her. Even as a small child, Elizabeth had found sleeping hard. She had begun to think of sleep as a skill some people had and others didn't. It was a test for her every night, simply to close her eyes and let go. ('Lie on the edge of the bed and you'll soon drop off,' her dad used to tell her.) These days, her bed seemed cavernous, she could never quite get comfortable. In recent weeks, when she did sleep, she had vivid dreams of being at the wheel of a huge lorry hurtling down the fast lane of a motorway, like some hyper-real version of the movie *Speed*, trying desperately to dodge obstacles in her way, and beside her in the passenger seat, a maniacally laughing Ricky Clough would try to grab the steering wheel, or reach impulsively for the handbrake. Not even Keanu Reeves could cope with that. And Elizabeth would wake and sit bolt upright, sweating, her hair damp and stinking of lavender.

And of course, there had been the phone calls. Late at night, just as she was working hard at feeling sleepy, her mobile would vibrate and chirrup and it would be Ricky. She remembered the last late-night phone call he'd made. It was way past midnight but Elizabeth was awake, lying in bed eating custard and watching a re-run of *Butch Cassidy*. The sudden ring of the phone had made her sit bolt upright, her heart pounding, her eyes wide open to terror. It was her mum, it was Vic, oh God, there was something wrong with one of her nephews… She had grabbed the phone. It was 12.45 a.m. and the caller was Ricky.

'Hello?' She'd been trembling.

'Elizabeth, I've been thinking…' he'd said without any introduction or apology. 'We should do an extra sugar item on *Bonkers* this week. I think we should drop the other guests and do some real people stories. Like that kid Kieron's.' His voice was breathy and fast.

'Okay. Do you know what time it is, Ricky? Where are you?'

'I think we should get a few more sportsmen on — you know, we're live on Saturday nights, most people spend their weekends doing some kind of sporting activity. Me and Deniz were just talking about it.' He seemed to be pacing about. 'Let's try and get Beckham again. Put the team on it tomorrow. They need to push harder on booking these guests. Get Zander to do it. He's got the gift of the gab. And I saw Jose Mourinho on a show the other week — he was great. Let's get him.'

Elizabeth sat up, now more alert. 'You saw Jose Mourinho on a show? You mean, on Hutch's show? I saw him too — it was on the other week.'

Ricky was silent for a minute. 'I dunno,' he drawled. 'Maybe Deniz mentioned it. Maybe that was the show. Anyway, I want to push this sports thing, okay?'

'Ricky, let's talk about this tomorrow. Please?'

'We need to keep an eye on that new show the BBC are making. I heard they're copying our song and dance finales. Do you think they're trying to poach any of our team?'

'Maybe.' Elizabeth yawned.

'We've got to stop them!' Ricky's voice was suddenly urgent. 'We should feed something to the press. To the ShowBiz column—something about them not having any of their own ideas. I'll get Deniz on to it. You mustn't let it happen, Elizabeth, you hear me?' She didn't like the rising hysteria nor the threat in his voice.

'You okay, Ricky? I mean, are you alone? What's going on?'

'I've got a new idea for a show. I don't want to tell anyone about it but you and Deniz. I can't trust anyone. But it's going to be big – I mean, huge. I'm so excited about it. This is the next move for me, for sure.'

'That sounds great, Ricky. Let's talk about it tomorrow.'

'It'll take big bucks. I might sell it to America first, then bring it here. It's time I broke America. Or maybe Indonesia. They need someone like me.'

Elizabeth restrained herself from saying that of all the things Indonesia might need to import, a paranoid light entertainment clown from East Ham, famous for dumping green gunk on people's heads, was probably quite low down the list.

'Ricky, let's talk in the morning, yes?'

'You, me and Deniz should meet – not in the office, it's too leaky. At The Dorchester or somewhere.'

Elizabeth thought this a new level of madness. The idea that she might have to meet Ricky clandestinely in a London hotel and then sit and listen to programme ideas from Deniz Pegasus was very irritating.

'I can't sleep.'

'Well, I don't suppose I'll be able to now, either,' Elizabeth hit back. 'Have a bowl of custard. Take some Xanax. Read some poetry.'

Ricky let out a snort. 'Talking of Xanax, I hear Matthew's getting better… Have you seen him yet?'

'Yes, Lola and I went to see him at home yesterday. God, Ricky, he looks bad! Really beaten up.'

'Yeah? Did he know who they were? Did he say?'

'He didn't want to talk about it. But no, he didn't know them. He gave pretty good descriptions to the police, I think. He could smell something, too – like aftershave. Such a pointless random act of violence! It's horrible.' Elizabeth shivered. 'Can I go to sleep now? I'll probably have nightmares now, thanks for that.'

Ricky gave a short, mirthless laugh. 'I really like working with you – you know that, right? We're a good team. We need to stick together, you and me against the world.'

Elizabeth said softly, 'I don't think the world is against us, Ricky.'

'Goodnight, Elizabeth.'

She couldn't get back to sleep after that call. She watched the end of *Butch Cassidy* and wept like a child, wrapped in her dad's gardening shirt.

The next morning a package was waiting for her when she walked into the office. It was wrapped in brown paper and string. 'Where did this come from?' she asked Lola.

'Oh? Weren't you expecting it? Ricky's driver dropped it off. I assumed it was for the show.'

Elizabeth untied the parcel string. Inside, was a hard-backed leather-bound first edition of the poems of WB Yeats. And on its title page an inscription, handwritten in black ink: *Dearest E, Found this in that bookshop on Charing Cross Road we once went to together. I was going to sell it, but I'd like it to be yours because 'I have spread my dreams under your feet.' Yours, Ricky.* Elizabeth sat down on the chair, gently turning the beautiful pages. She knew only too well how that line continued: *I have spread my dreams under your feet/Tread softly because you tread on my dreams.*

Elizabeth remembered the trip to the bookshop. She'd taken Ricky there after a long lunch at The Ivy. While she'd browsed the shelves, Ricky had studied every price label and engaged the bookshop dealer in a detailed analysis of the ups and downs of the secondhand book market. He bought five or six books from the dealer there and then, including Graham Greene's *A Life in Letters*, since letter-writing was one of his few literary pursuits. He'd spoken excitedly to Elizabeth on the way home about adding the collecting of books to his other magpie activities (the collecting of vinyl, comics, heraldic tableware). But afterwards she heard no more about this giddy plan to enter the antiquarian book market and assumed like much else in his life, he'd very quickly tired of it.

She texted him to say thank you, but Ricky didn't turn up in the office until after three, and when he did, there was no more talk of meeting up to talk about a secret new show and he brushed aside her attempts to thank him more fulsomely. The late-night incident seemed to have been forgotten, or at least, Ricky had no desire to return to it.

Now, as she lay in bed, alone in her flat, growing colder and colder, she wished that she'd listened to him more.

After a restless night, she woke to face her second interview with DI Watson. Elizabeth was more nervous than ever of facing those narrowed, penetrating eyes, that lithe, taut body, ready to pounce. Ricky Clough was still the top news story on all outlets. The *Daily Mail* front page had a large photo of Ricky looking half-cut, taken at his party, and the headline said: DID SOMEONE KILL RICKY CLOUGH?

She felt her whole body shaking with nerves. She couldn't

decide if she ought to volunteer the information to DI Watson about the secret show with Hutch. She felt guilty for not telling her the whole story. In the end, she got to the office early and was surprised to see her researcher, Zander, already at his desk.

'Hi, hon,' she said, dumping her bag on her desk and wandering over to his. 'You didn't have to come in, you know? You can stay at home.'

Zander smiled shyly at her. When he joined the Ricky Clough team he'd quickly won friends for being deliciously self-deprecating about his background, as well as for being the source of many sensational stories about how the other half live. Ricky Clough in particular had championed Zander early on and taken him under his wing. Elizabeth, innately suspicious of the upper classes, had been ready to dismiss Zander for being too privileged to be clever but she'd had to acknowledge quite quickly that she was wrong.

'Oh, it's okay. Couldn't really bear to be in that shoebox.' Zander lived in the garden flat of an Edwardian villa owned by his family in Fulham – his sitting room was twice the size of Elizabeth's. 'Thought I'd clear up a few things here. But I'm going to go home this afternoon, if that's okay? I can catch the lunchtime train.' Home was the family castle.

'Of course. How are you feeling?'

Zander smiled sadly. 'I still can't quite believe it. Mummy's upset too – you know, that Paolo was there as well – and of course he's very cut up, anxious, you know, about all the tests. But Ricky seemed so full of life! On such good form.'

Elizabeth thought how many times over the last couple of days they'd all said that out loud: *Ricky seemed on such good form.*

She suddenly recalled a moment a few weeks ago when Ricky had sharply rebuked Zander in the production meeting for suggesting a guest for the show he thought unworthy. Later that day, when she was in a meeting with the Controller, Ricky had returned to the office with a toy crown and a sash saying 'Lord Snooty' and had made Zander wear both, which he'd done with bashful good humour, even parading around the office with his nose in the air. Lola told her later that Zander had dismissed the incident by saying, 'It's no worse than fagging.' Elizabeth shuddered: how *had* they let Ricky get away with it?

'I can't believe it either,' she said softly, glancing unconsciously towards the little glass-walled room where Ricky had his desk and a Z-bed (napping was the declared function of this unlikely piece of office furniture and Ricky did indeed retire for an hour after lunch, pulling down the blinds and telling anyone who'd listen that Winston Churchill always said it was napping that got him through the Battle of Britain). But these days the springs were straining at their leashes and the mattress was horribly stained. His coat was still hanging from a peg on the wall.

Elizabeth turned back and with fake casualness said, 'Oh, I gather you guys were all at the pub with Ricky on Tuesday night?'

Zander looked at her quickly, then turned away. 'Oh yes,' he said. 'I did talk to the police about that, you know. I did tell them.'

'I know you did. It's not a problem, I was just curious. Who was there?'

Zander named two other male researchers on the team. 'Actually, you know,' he said, 'it was very much like the old days. You know, the good old days on *Bonkers*. Ricky was very hospitable, very jolly. Life and soul, really.'

'Yes, but…' Elizabeth became aware fractionally too late that she probably sounded pompous. 'But the night before a studio recording? Helping the star of the show get drunk? Maybe not such a good idea.'

Zander looked at her sadly. 'Yes, I know. But he was awfully persuasive. Determined, really. I mean, I said I had a lot to do, sorting out the Culone dishes, etc. for the next day. But he suggested I brought some of the tasting stuff to the pub, once I'd picked it up from Paolo at the restaurant. He'd missed the production meeting that afternoon, so I thought maybe it would be useful. He said we could work out which dishes we would definitely use over a pint.' He shrugged apologetically. 'It didn't seem such a bad idea. I thought it might help the next day – if he'd had a jolly evening, then he might also be in a good mood for the studio.'

Elizabeth could see the logic. She perched on the edge of his desk and said nonchalantly, 'And Hutch was there too, right?'

Zander shot her another look. 'Er, yes. I don't know if Ricky invited him or whether he just happened to be there. I've seen him in there before.'

So. That was one of the other things about Hutch that she didn't know: he *often* went to the King's Head.

'But he joined you – Hutch, I mean?'

'Yes, well, he and Ricky were already sitting together by the time I got there.'

Elizabeth bit her nail, imagining the scene, and Zander said after a short pause, 'Actually, you know, Hutch was really quite useful. He knows Paolo Culone awfully well. I mean, almost as well as Mummy. He was rather good at helping us choose the dishes.'

Here was another blow. Hutch had also contributed opinions about what they should do on the show – on the show Elizabeth herself was producing! Yet one more thing he'd failed to mention when she saw him later. She found this unbearably irritating. She got up quickly and Zander looked anxious again. 'I'm sorry if I did a wrong thing.'

'It's okay,' she said tersely.

'They've got all the Culone food, you know. The police, I mean. They took everything. Well, what was left. You don't think Ricky had a reaction to something I gave him, do you? I mean, I asked him about allergies. He said he didn't have any. There wasn't any seafood... Maybe nuts? Do you think he was allergic and didn't know?'

Elizabeth took a deep breath. 'I don't think the police think it was an allergic reaction,' she said carefully.

'I've been ever so worried.'

Elizabeth smiled at him and then on impulse leaned forward and gave him a hug. 'You're good at your job, Zander. Please don't let any of this put you off. People dying on you, I mean. One day – if you don't end up running the castle – you'll be a shit-hot producer.'

Zander smiled bashfully. 'All I hope is that one day, I'll be as good at it as you,' he said and somehow, with his beautiful-sounding vowels and his sincere gaze, it didn't sound as corny as it might have done.

Her head still reeling, Elizabeth went to greet DI Watson and DS Rafik, who'd arrived at 10 a.m. on the dot. The Detective was wearing navy wool trousers, and a blazer with shiny brass buttons. Her blonde hair was scraped back into a tortoiseshell clip and Elizabeth was disappointed to note the absence of the pink scrunchie. Karen Watson seemed to be glowing with health, as if she'd just arrived from a workout. Lola, who'd also arrived in the office, happily offered to make everyone coffee. (DI Watson declined; she produced from her bag a plastic beaker of greenish liquid and it appeared that she'd taken time before work to liquidise some kale and broccoli.) Lola was looking much better than she had the day before: she'd twisted her hair into plaits and was wearing a figure-hugging knitted dress that looked as if it had been sprayed on. It did more than ample justice to her assets; indeed, everything about Lola today appeared to have acquired some extra bounce.

Elizabeth led the police into the Controller's meeting room. DI Watson took one look at the deep cushiony leather sofa and opted for the only hard-backed chair. Sergeant Rafik sank on to the sofa and spent half a minute trying to lever himself into a more formal sitting position – his belly unfortunately anchoring him – eventually clinging with both hands to the armrest. Elizabeth asked Lola to bring in another upright chair and so she sat, directly facing DI Watson, to all intents and purposes on her level. Sergeant Rafik was trying to balance his coffee mug on his knee, which was now unfortunately level with his chin.

'How was Lorna Clough?' DI Watson smiled at Elizabeth, who had momentarily forgotten about her meeting the night before in Surrey.

'Oh, well, you know – upset. Bewildered.'

DI Watson nodded. She crossed a trousered leg. 'I'm going down there myself later today.' Elizabeth remembered that Lorna had told her she would be seeing the detective. She also remembered that it had sounded like a threat.

'What can I help you with today?' Elizabeth said brightly. She'd rehearsed the line. This time, she wanted to try and be in control. Karen Watson looked entirely unruffled and unsurprised. She said nothing and just when Elizabeth was foolishly feeling the need to fill the silence, the DI answered.

'Tell me about your new show. The one you're making with Harry Hutchinson.'

Elizabeth took a quick intake of breath. She tried to keep her voice neutral. 'Well, it's meant to be a pilot – a try-out. We'll never broadcast it. We're trying to work out if Hutch – Harry – could reach a more mainstream audience. You know, he has a late-night show on Channel 4...' DI Watson looked blank and Elizabeth couldn't resist adding, 'You should watch it. It's mostly about football, but he sometimes covers other sport. Not sure he's done netball, but you never know.' Elizabeth smiled at her and was pleased to receive a smile in return. 'We can always hope,' said DI Watson unexpectedly.

'So, this is capitalising on that show and Hutch's skills...

It's a talent show to find all-round sports stars. We're going to call it *Shoot for the Moon*. I think Hutch will be good, you know, he's probably ready for it…' Elizabeth trailed to a halt. She was sure her hot face would give her away.

'But it's being thought of as a replacement for *Bonkers*, right?' DI Watson's eyebrows were slightly raised.

'Well, that would be Matthew's decision, not mine,' Elizabeth said primly.

'But would I be right in saying that you'd had enough of producing Ricky Clough?'

Elizabeth looked up quickly at DI Watson, who was staring back at her. Her heart began to thump. She could see how this might seem to the policewoman, who had no time for subtleties and shades of grey and wanted only cold, hard facts. Elizabeth felt desperate and her eyes filled with tears. But she simply said in a small voice, 'Yes. Yes, I suppose I had.'

DI Watson said nothing. The moment's silence felt like a lifetime to Elizabeth. Finally, in a sudden rush to explain herself, she said, 'I've been thinking for a while now – you know, before this happened – that I might set up my own production company. Do it by myself. I've got some good ideas, more serious shows actually, and I know how to produce them. If I can find some backers, then I know how to do the rest. I think I might have outgrown tipping green gunk on people's heads.'

DI Watson raised her eyebrows and asked coolly, 'So what's stopping you?'

Elizabeth opened her mouth to speak and then closed it. What *was* stopping her? She realised that every time she'd thought about leaving, Matthew had offered her another show. And now she'd got excited about producing a new hit show with Hutch – but this one was so much more complicated than the rest. 'You're right.' Elizabeth shrugged. 'There's nothing really stopping me.'

'But at the moment you're still doing both – producing the shows with Ricky as well as the pilot show with Hutch?'

'Yes.'

'So I suppose it's been like leading a double life? A bit like those men who manage to keep second families in another house a few streets away.' Karen Watson looked across at Sergeant Rafik, who nodded appreciatively at the aptness of the comparison. Elizabeth looked down at her feet.

'And tell me, did Ricky Clough know about the plans for a new show with Harry Hutchinson?'

'Well, I only found out after he'd died that he'd been told about it. By Matthew, the day they went out to lunch. But actually, something Lorna said last night made me feel he'd probably known about it before. We thought it was the best-kept secret.' She shrugged in despair. 'But I suppose nothing much is a secret in television. It's an industry that thrives on gossip.' Elizabeth had always believed this to be the case, but she was now beginning to wonder if in fact everyone had very well-kept secrets and that the whole enterprise might be built on smoke and mirrors.

'And how would Ricky have felt, do you think, knowing that you were perhaps leaving him to produce a show with Harry Hutchinson? They knew each other quite well, I think?'

'I'm not sure how well they knew each other,' Elizabeth said, since this turned out to be the truth – she seemed to know nothing much for certain, any more. 'But yes, they definitely moved in the same circles. Hutch came to Ricky's party the other week. And no, of course, Ricky wouldn't have liked the idea. No one wants to be replaced.' Her voice cracked.

DI Watson nodded sympathetically and Elizabeth wondered if she'd struck a chord. She and Karen Watson were roughly the same age, she reckoned, and had probably both fought to get to where they'd got to, and were both fighting to stay there still. They might have much to share, if only circumstances were different.

'But they were together in the pub the night before, Ricky and Harry Hutchinson? By all accounts they seemed to be getting on very well.'

'So I hear.'

Sergeant Rafik spoke from his semi-submerged position in the depths of the leather sofa. 'I've been watching a recording of the show.' Elizabeth turned to him in surprise. Of course the police had got hold of the programme file. She'd completely forgotten that some of Ricky's dying moments were on record. His first convulsions were filmed, before Robin had stopped the cameras. 'The recording starts before Ricky walks on set. So you can hear him on his microphone before you see him – when he's backstage, I guess.'

'Yes, he'd be behind the set. Waiting for the warm-up guy to announce him.'

'Yes, you can hear the warm-up on one microphone. The audience are cheering too, so it's quite hard to hear, but it sounds like Ricky has been checking on where the food props are for when Paolo Culone comes on.' Ali Rafik frowned at his notebook. 'Ricky's halfway through a sentence when his microphone is switched on, but it sounds to me like he says, "*the dishes Hutch chose*". Or something like that?' He looked up at Elizabeth earnestly.

Elizabeth responded coolly. 'Yes, well, apparently and unbeknownst to me, Hutch helped Ricky choose which of Paolo's dishes to taste on the show. It was discussed in the pub the night before. Hutch knows Culone well and I guess Ricky thought his advice would be useful, as he was there. By the way, I'm sure we can isolate Ricky's microphone for you – put it on one track so that you can hear it more clearly – if that would help.'

'Thank you,' said Sergeant Rafik, looking pleased with the results of his sleuthing. DI Watson seemed to be staring into the middle distance. Then she turned slowly and her new tack took Elizabeth by surprise.

'So you were working with Matthew Grayling when he was mugged?'

'Yes, of course. Well, I mean, we heard about it the day after it happened. He hadn't come into the office and I think his wife rang that afternoon. He was in hospital. It was very shocking. He was quite badly hurt.' Elizabeth paused, remembering something else Lorna had said last night. 'We were told he didn't want any visitors in the hospital. But, um…' Elizabeth hesitated and DI Watson looked at her quickly. 'Well, Lorna told me last night that in fact Ricky *did* go and visit him in hospital. I hadn't known that – Ricky never mentioned it.

Maybe we should've just shown up – that's probably what Ricky did.'

DI Watson was sitting very straight-backed in her chair. Elizabeth wondered whether, along with netball, yoga also occupied the detective's days. She found herself slumping further into her own chair, exhausted at just the thought of DI Watson winding down after a bout on the netball court by standing perfectly still on one leg. She felt stupidly tired.

'It's strange that nothing was taken from Mr Grayling during the attack, don't you think?' DI Watson's Essex accent meant she leant on the word 'straaaaange'.

'Yes, I suppose... but he does live in Hampstead. Maybe they just assumed he would have something on him – a Rolex watch or a wad of cash? It must be a pretty good bet round there. Have you talked to Matthew himself about it?'

'No, not yet. It came up yesterday. Our colleagues at Camden CID investigated. I've given them a call and I'm seeing Matthew Grayling later. It seems he rang asking to speak to the detective in charge of his case on Wednesday afternoon – the day Ricky Clough died – but the detective was on holiday. Did he mention anything to you?'

'Matthew? No, nothing. He doesn't like talking about it.'

'You saw the photofits they issued?'

'Yes. Of course.'

DI Watson looked at her penetratingly.

'Oh, you mean, did I recognise any of them? Of course I didn't! I don't generally socialise with thugs and goons.' And how true is that, Elizabeth found herself wondering.

'It seems odd, though, doesn't it? Matthew was badly beaten

up, ten days ago – for no apparent reason – and now Ricky Clough has died. I'm a detective, Elizabeth, I don't really believe in coincidence. I think, more often than not, things are connected for a reason.'

Elizabeth's head felt full of treacle. She wasn't sure she understood what the policewoman was getting at. 'I've told you, I didn't recognise anyone from the photofits,' she said weakly.

DI Watson leaned forward, resting her arms on her knees. 'You know, often our cases are solved by the flimsiest of clues, the barest recollection from people. We once had a case of an assault in a park in Dagenham.' Elizabeth looked up, surprised by the new conversational tone. 'Months later, an eyewitness we'd already spoken to came forward to say she'd spotted a sweatshirt in a local shop with a distinctive logo on it and she'd realised that the assailant's coat had the same logo on its sleeve. Turned out Sergeant Rafik here was able to date the peak of sales of this coat and we traced all local purchases. And that led us to our man – or at least to his wife, who'd bought the coat for him with a credit card!' DI Watson grinned at Sergeant Rafik, who looked chuffed.

Elizabeth shrugged helplessly. 'I'm sorry. I'll keep thinking.'

'Yes, please do. Any little detail. Any small fact, anything about that night might help us – you just never know.'

This was another subtle tactic of the detective's, Elizabeth felt, to suggest that she might well hold the key to unlocking the whole sorry story if she could only think straight. That she might know the one crucial fact about that night that would explain the unexplained death of Ricky Clough. But she simply shook her head and the detectives both got up. Before she had a chance to react, DI Watson had already moved to the door but in passing she touched Elizabeth lightly, almost imperceptibly, on the shoulder. She looked up quickly, gratefully, but the detective had turned her back and was already sailing through the open door.

Chapter Eleven

Elizabeth and Lola watched the police leave the network's warehouse offices later that morning. They were sitting on top of their desks talking about pulling together a Ricky Clough tribute programme, which was allowing them the luxury of reminding each other of all the good bits. Lola was demurely sipping something from a flask; when pressed by Elizabeth, she admitted to it being the remains of the vodka. They were also sharing a giant chocolate teddy bear Ricky had bought them a few days ago: he'd been delivered to the office with a notice round his neck which said, *'Please look after this bear. Abuse of bears is rife at this network'*.

'Will you include that episode of *Saturday Bonkers* with Hutch in the tribute programme?'

'No. I'm not sure it shows off Ricky at his best,' Elizabeth said neutrally.

'I don't want Hutch anywhere near a tribute programme to Ricky, that's all.' Lola was looking at her defiantly and Elizabeth bridled slightly. It wasn't Lola's job to decide what went into the tribute programme and she felt with some force the unspoken criticism of Hutch himself. She returned Lola's penetrating look as levelly as she could, saying smoothly, 'Well, let's book an edit for Monday. I'll put the tribute together on paper over the weekend. I'll email you the running order.'

Lola gave her one more questioning glance, but then went off to make the edit booking. Elizabeth reached down and picked up her mobile. She'd left two messages for Hutch asking him to call. They didn't usually speak during the weekend but she wasn't sure she could wait until Monday to have it out with him. There was nothing from Hutch, but there was a text from Vic.

Hey little sis. Run away with me to Frinton! So much to talk about! And you're not the only one with NEWS!

Elizabeth chewed her nail and gazed out of the window. She wasn't sure how she'd get through the weekend in her flat, alone. It was very unlikely that Hutch would be available for the confrontation she planned to have with him. She thought maybe a fresh perspective – even the sort delivered by the weirdly brown North Sea and the windswept estuaries of Essex – was exactly what she needed. She explained her plan to a surprised Lola, and headed out of town in the Beetle, slogging down the A12 and through the bleak industrial suburbs of Dagenham and Romford.

All through Elizabeth's childhood, her mum and dad had been restlessly, upwardly mobile, moving every five years, one stop at a time down the Central Line. Her dad's real ambition had been to get to the Essex coast, fancying himself as the sort of man who might tinker about with boats in his retirement, despite having grown up in Hackney Wick, where the closest he ever got to tinkering with water was to pee quite regularly into the Regent's Canal. So Eric had persuaded the family to move to Frinton-on-Sea – still in Essex, but as he liked to say, 'a cut above'. Frinton was devotedly attached to preserving itself as a genteel enclave, sandwiched as it was between the much more rowdy, frolicking seaside towns of Clacton-on-Sea and Walton-on-the-Naze. Its exclusivity was helped by the fact that it was enclosed at one end by the North Sea and at the other by a railway line and the gates of a level crossing. Whenever a train went through (roughly every thirty minutes) and the gates came down, Frinton became an impregnable fortress. Every half an hour, it satisfied itself that it was indeed an island, a deterrent to any delinquents.

But six months after moving in, Eric was warned by his doctor that he had dangerously high cholesterol and Maureen had set about producing entirely new meals with cottage cheese and cold turkey, even though it wasn't Boxing Day and Eric couldn't have it with a nice bit of piccalilli. It made no difference. A year later and no closer to his dream of owning a little wooden clipper, Elizabeth's dad died of a heart attack. She was seventeen, her sister twenty-one.

Elizabeth arrived in Frinton in time for tea which, as it had every Friday evening in her childhood, consisted of freshly peeled prawns, brown bread and butter, and a bowl of watercress. Her dad's family had long ties to the watercress beds of Hackney Wick and as children, Elizabeth and Vic had dutifully grown it on their bedroom window-sills from seeds on wet flannels. The table, with its neatly laundered tablecloth, was groaning under the weight of a very large brown earthenware teapot and a cake stand displaying a big fat fruit loaf. There was no evidence of any alcohol. Elizabeth's stomach churned at the sight of the cake and for a moment she thought she might actually be sick. It was an unusual sensation and she sat rather suddenly on a chair, her mum shooting her an anxious look. Maureen, small and very thin like a bird, handed her a brimming cup of tea. Resigned, Elizabeth ladled two spoonfuls of sugar into it.

'Tell us everything.' Vic sat her youngest son on her knee. 'Don't miss out a single detail.'

Elizabeth told them everything about that night. She took them through what had happened in The Ricky Clough Show studio, and in the long days since. Vic was transfixed; Maureen left her tea largely untasted. When Elizabeth got to the meeting with DI Watson and mentioned the word 'poison', Vic let out a small shriek and exclaimed, 'Murder?! You're fucking kidding me!' and then sat open-mouthed for the remainder.

'But do they know who dunnit?' she said when Elizabeth finished.

'No. Or at least if they do, they haven't told me. All they've told me is that they found poison in his bloodstream.'

'Bloody hell, Elizabeth! Wait. It's not you, is it? You didn't finally reach breaking point? I mean, let's face it, no one could blame you. But if you want me to be your lawyer, don't say anything now you may regret later. And also, I should point out, I really only do divorce cases. But – did you do it?'

'No, Vic, I didn't do it.'

'Oh, that's a relief. I didn't fancy bringing the boys to visit you in prison. Well, who do you think did do it?'

'I just don't know. I keep going over it all in my head. Was it someone I know? Maybe. Was it someone on my team? Could be. God knows, we've had enough provocation! And he knew some pretty seedy people – he had a sort of morbid fascination for that sort of underbelly world. And of course, there were the drugs. There was definitely a dark side. We all saw glimpses of it. He had a foul temper. But I wonder if it went wrong – if someone just meant to scare him. I can't believe someone wanted him dead.'

'Oh, Elizabeth, it must've been so upsetting for you.' Her mum looked nervously at her younger daughter, who was now rummaging feverishly in the sideboard for some form of alcoholic drink. She finally produced a dusty bottle of Rioja with a flourish: 'Hurrah! Majorca 1990, I reckon.'

'Yes!' cried Vic, reaching for a corkscrew. 'The holiday when Mum threw up out of a coach window! God, that dreadful all-inclusive banquet. Do you remember, those young waiters were literally pouring wine from a watering can straight down Mum's throat? What were they thinking?' She uncorked the bottle with a satisfying pop. 'I was sitting behind you on the coach, Mum, and I remember the vomit streaming along the window pane towards me. I couldn't see out. Do you know how damaging those episodes are in a child's life? That's years of therapy right there.'

'Don't be ridiculous, darling. You were fourteen.'

Elizabeth threw her arms around Maureen. 'Poor mum! You never could take your drink. Actually, I don't think you even thought drinking was for people like you – not wine drinking, anyway. That was for posh people, wasn't it?'

Maureen rather pointedly sipped her cup of tea. She worried that her girls seemed to require alcohol to power them through their complicated lives, that having choices had somehow driven her daughters to drink. She'd been determined they shouldn't have to settle for drudgery and housework, as she'd had to, despite being clever. So she'd taught them to read before they went to school and coached them in fractions using segments of orange, but the older she got, the more she wondered if giving her girls choices had complicated their lives too much. It bothered her that Elizabeth was still single at thirty-five and had been dumped at the altar. She would tell her younger daughter very firmly that in her view, professional success was not worth achieving at the cost of being childless. She'd always suspected Elizabeth's commitment to her job had driven Jamie away. Elizabeth would became a petulant teenager when having these conversations with her mother: *'Mum, it wasn't like that! There was fault on both sides.'* But her mother would purse her lips as if to say Mums know best – an argument Elizabeth was patently not qualified to challenge.

'Wasn't Ricky Clough married? Aren't there some kids?' Vic handed Billy to his granny and leaned back in her chair to savour the luxury of drinking a compete glass of wine without a wriggling child to upset it.

'Yes. He's been married to Lorna for years and years but they've been leading very separate lives. She lives in this gilded cage down in Surrey – you know, gorgeous house, horses, fields, lots of money. But I went down to see her yesterday and she told me she'd asked him for a divorce. And she was a bit hostile. I think she blames us all for his lifestyle – but of course, that lifestyle also furnished her with an estate in Surrey and a stableful of thoroughbreds.'

'Nice.' Vic drained her glass. 'How long can they keep it quiet – that he was actually poisoned?'

'Not for much longer, I wouldn't have thought. It's been two days, now.' Elizabeth paused. 'The thing is, Vic, Ricky's wife knew I was working on a new show. That seemed to be why she asked me down there. I felt really bad about it. She said that Ricky had suspected all along that I was planning to leave him to make another show – you know, the one I told you about. With Hutch.' They both glanced over at their mum, but she was very busy illicitly feeding her grandson chunks of sugar-coated fruit loaf. 'You know it's odd… Lorna's really quite close to Matthew, my boss. But she didn't ask him about it. I don't know why…'

'Maybe she found it easier to talk to you? Maybe she could say things to you she couldn't say to her husband's boss? Poor sis! How do you feel? About Ricky? You must've been working with him for about six years now, haven't you?'

Elizabeth sighed. 'Seven. I don't know, I just went into overdrive on the night. I was in charge, I had to do things right. I guess it might hit me much later. I was really fond of him – although God knows, he made it hard for us to love him.'

'You did put up with a lot, Lizzie. You were like the very definition of an abused wife, going back for more. You kept telling me you were going to resign, set up your own thing.'

'I know. But it could also be very rewarding. I mean, *Bonkers* was the show to work on, if you wanted to make it in Entertainment. We won an award for it just last year, remember? When he was on form, it was exhilarating. Anything was possible – we had crazy ideas, and just made them happen. It wasn't like work, it was fun.' Elizabeth found her eyes welling again. She shook her head. 'It just became a shared joke amongst the team how outrageous his behaviour had become. He dropped his trousers again in the production meeting last week. He'd got a tattoo on his arse with a "Permit Holders Only" sign. He showed it to the entire team.'

'Ugh! Lizzie, there are so many laws against that, I don't know where to begin.'

'He thought it was funny. He said we were all too uptight. He said the best entertainment will never be made by a bunch of tight-lipped do-gooders, but by madmen, people pushing the boundaries. People not wearing their pants.'

'Did no one on your team ever complain about being exposed to Ricky's arse when they were at work, in a place where they might have a reasonable expectation of not being mooned at?'

'No, no one. We all just found these elaborate ways of coping with it, of normalising it. He'd got us all believing his own motto, you know, if you can't take the heat, get out of the kitchen. But of course that was just an excuse for him to be as badly behaved as he liked. So no one really called him out.'

'Well, *you* could've done it.'

'God, I know! But, Vic, it felt so disloyal. I didn't want to be the turncoat that no one would ever really trust again. The team, it's like a family, it's really close-knit. That's what I mean about normalising; it was like we're all in the gang, and we were standing shoulder to shoulder, sharing the burden of his impossible tantrums. And he was generous. The team all went out partying with him. So then they'd forget that he'd been unforgivably rude to them a few hours earlier.'

'Hmm.' Vic was cynical. 'Buying off their silence, you could say. That's a classic bullying tactic: stroke them one day and beat them the next. Are you in the clique today or outside it? It's horrible. That reminds me, Lizzie, I wouldn't have told you this, but Ricky's name came up in a case I was dealing with a few weeks back.'

'Ricky? Really? What case?'

'A divorce case. But there was an allegation of intimidation. Ricky Clough apparently threatened the husband of my client. It all got quite nasty; he said he'd get him "seen to" if he pursued the case.'

'Who was your client?'

'Sarah McManus. She was married to the Manchester City player, Marcus McManus.'

Elizabeth knew very well who McManus was; she'd been coached in bed by Hutch to learn the names and positions of every Manchester City footballer. She also remembered that he'd told her Ricky had mouthed something in his ear about McManus when he'd appeared on *Saturday Bonkers*.

'McManus was divorcing his wife because he said she was unfaithful. It was a joke really. He'd hardly been a good boy himself. Do you remember that horrible roasting incident when he was younger? But anyway, he accused her of having an affair.'

'With Ricky?'

'No. He'd been photographed with her in various clubs, but she was really tied up with someone he introduced her to. A friend of his. The guy who owns Pegasus Construction.'

'Oh yes, Deniz Pegasus.' Elizabeth groaned. 'He's an old schoolfriend. He went everywhere with Ricky. He acted like his enforcer. Wait. Yes – Sarah! I'm sure I met her at Ricky's party a couple of weeks ago – she was with Deniz Pegasus then.'

'Yeah? Well, I'm not impressed with him.' Vic lifted her youngest out of his chair. 'Mark's had dealings with Pegasus too – they got done for using illegal immigrants on their workforce and paying them a pittance. Mark got involved in a case of a vicious assault on one of the building sites and discovered that both men involved were here illegally and seemed to have by-passed UK immigration checks. God knows what Sarah McManus sees in him.'

'Ricky Clough did look like he had a temper on him,' her mum added feelingly.

Vic kicked her sister under the table and mouthed, 'How's it going with Hutch?'

Their mum knew very little of Elizabeth's continuing relationship with Hutch. It was not something of which she would approve – an affair with a married man. She'd always told her daughters that she knew from the day she met him that their dad was the only man for her. They were married within the year – Maureen in a homemade lace dress that showed to great advantage her narrow ankles and tiny waist – and she would tell her spellbound little girls as she sat brushing their hair before bed it was the happiest day of her life. Oh, she smiled so much her cheeks ached with it. And along with this persuasive tale of her own, Maureen also set about making sure her daughters read every book they could lay their hands on – from *The Blue Book of Fairytales* to *Little Women* and Mabel Esther Allan with her poised, elegant adventuresses who all found their heroes in books with titles like 'It Happened in Arles'. And so Elizabeth and Vic grew up convinced that *real* love was only ever an arrow, straight and true, and that it would pierce you so precisely that there could be no mistake and no doubting. You would see him across a room, maybe on a train, and you would know *for sure* and *instantly* that he was The One.

Vic looked at Elizabeth and signalled silently to the front door. 'Mum, Lizzie and I are going to go for a walk. You can watch *Pointless* in peace. We'll take the boys.'

They shrugged on coats and strode down the Frinton Esplanade, the youngest in his buggy, dropping down the zig-zag path through the blowsy hydrangeas to the long, sandy beach. They sat on one of the old wooden groynes as Billy dug excitedly in the sand, his face pink in the blast of the north-east sea wind. The days were getting longer; the arms of the steel giants in the wind farm far out at sea were gracefully slicing the still-clear blue skies. Elizabeth pushed her hands deep into the pockets of her parka and gazed out at the gulls sweeping low and menacing over the waves.

'So now tell me about your sex life,' Vic said, once they were settled.

Elizabeth smiled at her. 'What do you want to know?'

'Well, which position, obviously. Doh! I want to know how it's going, fuckwit! When am I going to meet him?'

'Well… We've been seeing each other a fair bit now we're working together as well. But I don't know, I'm not sure I really understand him, Vic. I mean, he's funny and clever – well, he's never read any poetry but I'm teaching him – and he's a bit right-wing.' Vic pulled a face. 'But all that feels so different to Jamie. And Hutch and I have lots of laughs. He's like Dad – you know, no joke's too corny. I love that about him.' She bit her lip. 'Jamie was, well, quite serious, I s'pose. Or maybe we'd forgotten how to have a laugh. But then I think, that's the real attraction: Hutch is just so unlike Jamie.'

'I don't suppose he's any closer to ending his marriage? I thought he told you it was on the verge of ending months ago?'

'Yes, he did. He did. He says his marriage is very unhappy. But nothing's happened and it's got to the point where I can't bear to talk to him about it.' She sighed. 'Oh, Vic, I'd love you to meet him. You'll like him, I know you will. You know, he lost his dad when he was young, too – that's another thing that ties us together.' Vic nodded but a frown threatened to cloud her expression.

Elizabeth clocked it and went on, 'But I've been thinking, when something terrible happens, completely out of the blue, it makes you examine how well you know someone. I'm wondering, now, after all that's happened, if I really knew Ricky at all. And that's made me think about Hutch – and I just don't know how well I know him, either. I mean, I'd been with Jamie for ten years and I *still* didn't realise he was about to end things. How can you ever be sure? Sure enough to have a baby with someone? It feels like such a leap of faith.'

'Well done, Lizzie. That's exactly what commitment is. That's why they say, for better or worse.'

'Ricky said this weird thing a few weeks ago; he told me he'd seen Hutch out with someone he shouldn't have been. I mean, who on earth was that? I don't always know what he does or where he goes. Apparently, he met Ricky in the pub this week, the night before my show, and he didn't even tell me that!'

'I didn't know they were mates?'

'Me neither.' Elizabeth watched a gull pick at a shell, shake it violently from side to side, and toss it away. 'I mean, I never really see Hutch when he's bored or frustrated or depressed. I only ever see him when he's…'

'Horny?'

'Thank you.' Elizabeth kicked at some pebbles. 'We never have any normal times. It's always so furtive and frenzied, snatching hours here and there. Do you ever really know someone until you've lived with them?'

She had thought about this a lot in the year since the wedding that wasn't. How would you know the regular smell of their morning breath? Whether they nuzzle your neck when they come home, even though they did it yesterday and the day before? Jamie had talked in his sleep and picked his nose in front of her. He sang 'Bohemian Rhapsody' from beginning to end when he did the hoovering. He gave up nuzzling her neck years ago. He got annoyed that Elizabeth regarded his morning poo as the ideal moment to get his full attention, and once he started locking the bathroom door she knew that other bits of him would be closed to her forever. But Hutch? She knew none of these telling things.

'I know you must be clever enough to work this out for yourself, Elizabeth, but of course the sex with Hutch is great – it's secretive and naughty. But imagine doing it with him every night, or in the morning when you really just fancy a cup of tea, or with the lights on, or once it starts taking longer and longer? What would you feel for him then?'

'I said to Hutch, the trouble is we only ever see the best of each other and do you know what he said? "Or maybe we bring out the best in each other, have you thought of that?"'

'Oh, please!' Vic rolled her eyes. 'You think it's the first time he's ever said that?'

Elizabeth blushed. 'I know. Oh, but Vic, I think I love him! And he says he loves me. But I'm scared now that it's a rebound thing – that I just needed someone to make me feel better about myself. And Hutch loves my job and makes me feel clever and good at it, whereas Jamie seemed to hate it. Hutch makes me feel good about just being me. But over these last few weeks, I've had so many doubts.'

'And your boss still doesn't know? About you and Hutch?'

'I don't think so. But I feel I should tell Matthew before signing the contract to do the show. It feels wrong. And in a funny kind of way, I want his approval. His permission.'

'Like a dad, you mean?' Vic smiled at her. 'Still... Be careful, Lizzie. You are your job. I mean, you live and breathe it. Don't let Hutch mess that up.'

'That's not entirely true, Vic. It makes me sound very one-dimensional. I have lots of other things in my life.'

'Yes? Like what?'

Elizabeth gazed out to sea. *Shit.*

'It doesn't matter, Lizzie. You love your job. That's fine. Maybe that's all you need. For now. Just don't wake up in five years' time and wonder where the years went.'

Good God, Vic was turning into their mother! And yet, as Elizabeth lifted her adorably sleepy nephew and he snuggled into the crook of her neck, his scalp smelling of sea salt, sand and something sweet, she felt her whole body ache for one of her own.

'So, what's your gossip, Vic? You said in your text you had news. I'd completely forgotten. Tell me.'

Vic bit her lip and frowned slightly. 'Oh, never mind. Let's get the boys home.'

'Oh no you don't, bitch. Come on, tell me!'

Vic's elfin face was suddenly pale; her grey eyes were cloudy with concern. 'It's about Jamie.'

Elizabeth's heart lurched and then began to thump. She settled her nephew back into his buggy and then straightened up. 'What about Jamie?'

Vic reached for her hand. She looked anguished. Elizabeth momentarily closed her eyes.

'I don't know for sure if it's true, Lizzie. But Mark's been representing the charity in Leeds that Jamie was involved in – the one working with refugees. He's been helping them with a deportation case. And… well, the woman Mark's been dealing with at the charity said that… she said that Jamie's got married.'

The shock sliced through Elizabeth like an ice-cold blade. Jamie? Married? In less than a year? 'But I thought he was living abroad?' she whispered. Vic had not let go of her hand.

'Yes. I don't know if he still is. He married a girl who worked at the Leeds charity. That's how this woman knew.'

Elizabeth suddenly remembered a night before the wedding when Jamie had stayed the night in Leeds. Was it then that he'd met her? Had he in fact met this girl *before* their wedding? He'd certainly been up and down a few times to Leeds those last few months. At the time, she'd scarcely thought about it. Like so much else to do with Jamie. She'd been too completely wrapped up in her own life to notice what was going on in his.

'Oh God, Vic! Do you think it was going on before the wedding? Was he fucking her and planning to marry me? How can you meet and decide to marry someone in less than a year? For God's sake! Was he unfaithful to me?'

'Whoa, Lizzie! I think you're jumping to conclusions here. Lots of people do impulsive things after the breakdown of long-term relationships. I think it's really common. I'm sorry… I… um… there's something else.' Vic looked at her anxiously.

Elizabeth froze. She knew. She nodded slightly, unable to speak. Vic said very quickly, 'They're having a baby. She's pregnant. I'm sorry, Lizzie. Really. I'm so sorry.'

Elizabeth sat down on the sand, winded. Jamie was going to be a dad! She knew of course that he wanted kids. His proposal had been more or less, 'Let's have one of our own', not 'Let's get married'. Although it's true they'd never really talked about it in any kind of practical way. Perhaps he'd doubted that she would? Perhaps her mum was right – he thought her job was all-consuming. God! What *had* they talked about for all those years? Seemingly, nothing that mattered.

She caught Vic looking nervously at her. 'Elizabeth, I know this is horrible news. But I'm going to say something. I've been thinking about saying it for a while now. I think we were all so overwhelmed with the shock. You know, Jamie was our loss too, a loss to the family. But actually, I think he did the right thing on your wedding day. And I think you know it, in your heart of hearts. I thought that whatever spark you and Jamie might have had, years ago, had long since gone out. You seemed more and more unsuited to each other the longer it went on. And to be honest, Lizzie, I thought you deserved someone who loved you for who you were, not who they wanted you to be.'

Elizabeth's eyes filled with tears. 'Thank you,' she said simply. She wiped her eyes and took a moment to recover. 'I know it was the right thing. Honestly, I do. I've come to terms with it over these last few months. We'd just stopped communicating – on any level, really. When I'm alone, when I really think about it, I know I wouldn't have been happy with Jamie.'

Vic hugged her. 'Oh, Lizzie, I wish you and Mum lived nearer to me. We need each other. Well, I could certainly do with some family support – could do with Mum's steady hand. I don't think I'll ever not feel tired – the boys wear me out. I feel I'm dragging my body around, like my shoes are full of glue. The juggling's so hard, believe me. They say you can have it all but actually, it's just one compromise after another… I feel like an old hag most of the time. Come on, we'd better get them back for bedtime, before I get one of Mum's disapproving glances.'

On the way back, arm in arm, Elizabeth leaned her head on her sister's shoulder and said, 'Do you know what, Vic? I realise I'm happy for Jamie. Honestly, I am. I'm jealous of what he's found, but I don't begrudge him for finding it.'

Vic kissed her.

'But Vic, I really want to get on with the next chapter of my life. I've been treading water for months – at work, as well. I keep talking about setting up this production company. Why haven't I done anything about it? And I'm not waiting for Hutch any more. I'm done with trusting him. I'm going to take things into my own hands.'

'Good girl! You know what, Lizzie? Maybe something good might come out of this dreadful thing with Ricky? For you, I mean?'

Elizabeth wondered about this as she drove back home later that night, through the arid, flat Essex countryside. She knew about trauma. She knew that as you tiptoe down the weeks and months and years thinking, this feels a bit safer, this feels more secure, a crack might suddenly appear and threaten to tear apart the whole facade. There would be consequences from Ricky's death, of that she was sure. And not knowing what they might be made her feel scared, uneasy and sick.

That night when she finally went to sleep, she dreamed that everyone she met had a face like Ricky. And all these Rickys were holding babies, cradling infants wrapped in soft shawls. Babies with hideous grown-up faces, just like Ricky. The world was suddenly full of Ricky. He was omnipresent, like a god. When she woke, sweating, at 4 a.m., she lay for a moment, shaken. And then she realised. She'd been in a real world where there were many faces of Ricky. It wasn't just a dream. It had been at his own decadent, hedonistic, self-indulgent party, just three weeks before he died.

Chapter Twelve

Three weeks earlier

Elizabeth twirled around and around in front of her full-length mirror. The flimsy, floaty Paule Ka shift dress rippled with a satisfying rustle of silk over her hips and thighs and fell to a frivolous hem just above her knees. Ricky's annual summer party was always the event of the year. Anyone who hadn't received the black and gold embossed invitation by March was in social purgatory. Prime ministers had been seen there alongside tabloid barons and newspaper editors, captains of industry, rock stars and models. But this year, she'd detected a greater anxiety from Ricky about his RSVPs and had over-heard him in the office chasing people to check whether they were coming. Would the fact that he seemed to be losing his popularity on television have any effect on his party's pulling power? In a year's time, she had no doubt, *Saturday Bonkers* would be off the air and so probably would Ricky Clough. Would there even be a party?

Robin, Lola and Zander were picking her up. Robin had agreed to drive. Hutch was also going. He'd told her that despite his own feelings about Ricky, it would look odd if he didn't attend, with his wife, who was of course friends with Lorna Clough. At the time, Elizabeth had received this as another blow. Tonight, as she skipped down the stairs, carrying her silver sandals by their straps, she wondered how much she really cared.

'Elizabeth! Get your arse down here! It's time to PARTAAAY!' Lola was leaning out of the car window, waving a bottle of champagne by its neck. She was channelling Jayne Mansfield and wearing a long fishtail dress with tiny diamante straps. Her breasts were ballooning out from the corseted bustier and her hair had been blow-dried into a glorious 1940s blonde tumble of curls. Ricky's wife Lorna would have a hard job competing with that, Elizabeth thought to herself.

Zander handed her a plastic beaker full of champagne. 'Did you see the guest list?' he said excitedly. 'It was in the *Daily Mail* today: they're expecting the Home Secretary, a Kardashian no less, the entire cast of *The Real Housewives*, someone off *Game of Thrones*, the Mayor of London, that woman who does those archaeology programmes with the wild frizzy hair...'

Elizabeth laughed. 'Stop! How could those two have possibly ever met? Ricky is a dark horse. Who knew?'

'On a radio show,' said Lola, passing her a tray of chocolate truffles. 'Ricky took her out for lunch afterwards. Apparently, they talked for hours about Pompeii – you know he loves all that Roman stuff.' That Roman stuff, as far as Elizabeth knew, amounted to several secret nights away with Lola to a discreet little hotel close to the Spanish Steps, where Ricky had presumably demonstrated his gladiatorial skills.

The end of the Clough driveway in Surrey thronged with

paparazzi. A long queue of luxury cars were waiting to get through a security barrier. It took them half an hour to be signed in, despite having displayed the requisite VIP car parking sign on their windscreen.

Robin was finding it hard to sit still. Ordinarily, he found it hard to sit still and when directing cameras in the gallery was more often out of his chair than in it. The driver's car seat presented him with a more than usually restrictive challenge: his knee jerked up and down and he drummed his fingers irritably on the steering wheel. 'Darlings, in the time it's taken us to get through this gate, I could've got through US immigration at JFK. Even with a Class A drug offence.'

They were finally directed to a field by a handsome boy in a Barbour and green wellies and they parked up between a Range Rover and a Bentley. Many other brightly coloured peacocks were being set free from their traps and were tottering about on their Manolas as if finding their sea legs. There was much preening to be done: the shaking out of embroidered jackets and the fluttering of patterned pashminas; the smoothing down of expensive, terribly creased dresses; the raising of fascinators and tiaras. The plumage was flamboyant and fabulous. Everyone was pirouetting on their heels, checking out the latest arrival, searching for a suitable mate, even though the one they'd arrived with had until that moment seemed more than passable. Every alpha male was puffing out his chest, every woman was wishing she was a bit less cold. Like all good mating rituals, what no one was doing was keeping their eyes firmly on the ground and so in consequence, roughly one-third of the party arrived with their feet covered in cow dung. Lola's tight, fishtailed dress allowed her only to teeter across the fields in the manner of a geisha and Elizabeth decided to go barefoot, although Zander rather gamely offered to carry her over his shoulder, and by the time they arrived at the marquee, the party was in full swing.

The waiting staff were all wearing Ricky Clough face masks. The name Ricky Clough was projected in laser beams across the front of the imposing grey-stone manor house (unfortunately, one of the lights was faulty and it read 'icky Clough'). Everywhere Elizabeth looked, she saw Ricky Cloughs: all male, all in white shirt sleeves, taller or shorter, all incredibly fit. It was very like being at a Ricky Clough convention. The Ricky Cloughs were carrying trays laden with garishly coloured cocktails, complete with candy striped umbrellas. The drinks were as lethal as their names; Elizabeth took her Slow Comfortable Screw With Ricky and sipped it demurely as she strolled across the lawn towards the marquee. She spotted one of the ageing rock stars walking stiffly in tight leather trousers and someone mentioned he was performing later. A Victoria's Secret model stood talking to the frizzy-haired archaelogist, who was inhaling deeply from a long, elegant cigarette holder. She and Lola went to find their table on the seating plan. They were table number 32, right on the top-left of the plan, close to the edge of the paper. There was no table 33. She spotted that Hutch – and his wife – were on table 4, right at the front, with a leading actor from the Royal Shakespeare Company, two Arsenal footballers (Ricky's joke, surely) and a celebrity hypnotist. Elizabeth was seated with Lola, Robin, Zander, some other members of the former *Saturday Bonkers* team and Matthew, with his hard-work wife, the academic. On the neighbouring table was the Home Secretary, a Chinese cellist and an American acrobat. A media mogul was talking earnestly to a very pretty, plainly bored Ukranian pop star, and a Booker prize-winning novelist was pouring wine into the glass of a defected Russian spy.

Matthew was wearing a Versace embroidered tuxedo that reminded Elizabeth of her mum's lounge curtains. His wife was wearing a knee-length black lace dress with some sensible flat pumps. She was attractive in a bookish way and had youthfully unblemished pale skin that Elizabeth assumed came from spending a lot of time inside libraries. Her grey hair was streaked with blonde highlights and had been expensively blow-dried. The lace dress was couture, Elizabeth reckoned, and was unlikely to have been financed by her latest book on the Tudors.

'It seems I've been demoted,' said Matthew grimly as he sat at their table, which was on the very edge of the marquee, next to the flap where the waiting staff marched in and out, carrying trays.

'Thank you.' Elizabeth reached over to kiss his wife's cheek.

'No offence, but back in the day, I would've been on the top table.' Her boss went on heedlessly. 'I bet it's because I've turned down all his latest ideas. Do you know what the latest is from Deniz Pegasus? A celebrity golf show! Really? Men in stupid trousers in primetime on my network? No thank you very much.' Matthew's wife looked extremely pained at the indignities he had to suffer. 'He was so mad at me – called me a twat. You should've been there.'

Elizabeth was rather glad she hadn't. His wife reached into her bag for a pair of reading glasses. She studied the menu with some disdain, as if it were an academic text in need of some deciphering. In fact, as far as Elizabeth could tell, they were to be served school food: fish and chips or sausages and mash, steamed pudding and custard.

A jazz quartet was playing on the stage, although Elizabeth could barely see them through the rainforest of foliage on each table. Tall branches of forsythia, cherry blossom and long stem roses adorned every available surface and effectively blocked every guest from being able to see their plus one on the opposite side of the table. Elizabeth had worked out from the map where table 4 was located and by half standing on her chair she could spot Hutch talking animatedly to the TV critic. She strained to get a glimpse of Mrs Hutchinson, but all she could see was a blonde head and satiny blue shoulders. Elizabeth hoped very much that Sue Hutchinson was wearing taffeta.

The ageing rock star in the tight trousers jumped on to the stage in the extravagantly athletic way that only seventy-two-year-old rock stars wearing restrictive leather can, and pausing only for a good few minutes to catch his breath, asked everyone to welcome their host and hostess for the night. The band played a version of 'You Make Me Feel So Young' and from the back of the marquee came Ricky and Lorna, strolling between the tables, as if down the aisle, accepting the cheers and claps. They were both in white: Ricky in a white dinner jacket and trousers, with a white T-shirt on which his name was written in sequins, and Lorna in an off-the-shoulder

Versace white beaded cocktail dress. She was wearing a red sash printed with the slogan 'Mrs Clough'. Elizabeth looked anxiously across at Lola to see how she was taking it, but Lola had a fixed glassy smile on her face and was pouring herself another glass of champagne.

Ricky took the mic: 'Thank you. Thank you all for coming this eve. And thanks for all the presents. What? You didn't bring me a present? Go and get one, now! The petrol station down the road does a very good box of Quality Street. Do me a favour and take out the green triangles. Seriously, though, I'm not going to take up a lot of your time' (calls of 'No, please, Rick, take your time!' from the floor), 'but I couldn't let this evening go without thanking a few people. My wife, Lovely Lorna, of course.' (Huge cheers from the floor.) 'Of course this party is all her doing. I don't have her good taste. And I'd never have chosen those good-looking waiters.' (Much laughter from the floor.) 'My sons, who are cowering somewhere at the back, hoping I don't mention them. My mum, who's here on my table, still going strong at eighty-seven.' (Many more cheers and stamps from the floor.) 'Love you, Mum. And all of you who've stuck by me over the years. I don't mean those hangers-on who've just known me for five minutes – yes, Home Secretary, I'm looking at you! No, I mean my mates. My real mates – Deniz, Paul and Lee – all the boys who've known me since I was a kid. One thing I've learned over the years: you can't buy loyalty. So thanks, guys. And as for the rest of you – the bill's on me, so take your fill! Now, enough from me. We're in for a good night. Some of it's X-rated so Mum, please let's get you to off to bed before the cabaret. Okay! As Barry White would say – Let The Music Play!'

The band struck up. Ricky kissed his wife, and then left the stage to join his mum at the top table. Lola got up and tottered to the loo. Elizabeth watched her go and wondered whether to follow, but Matthew tapped her on the arm.

'Typical Ricky speech. Doesn't bother to mention any of the people who've helped him make all this...' He waved his arm about to encompass the glittering estate.

'Well, I've learned never to expect thanks. In fact, I think you taught me that, Matthew.'

'Listen, I'm really not happy with the way *Bonkers* is going. You're doing the best you can, but Ricky has lost his sparkle. It's got to come off air. I'm meeting him and Pegasus on Monday to tell him. That Hutch pilot can't come along fast enough. We need another talent show.'

Before Elizabeth could mention her continuing doubts about the Hutch show, Matthew's wife, the history professor, said quite loudly, 'I think talent shows are finished.'

Elizabeth paused, her glass halfway to her mouth.

'It's all too predictable,' went on the Professor as if predictability was somehow a crime. 'When is television going to come up with something truly original?'

By television, Elizabeth understood she meant her husband. She understood the dynamic of Matthew's marriage; she'd seen it played out in public before. In private, it seemed to Elizabeth, Matthew's wife enjoyed all the material benefits of her husband's job while going out of her way in public to belittle him and his industry. They'd been together since Oxford where – slightly to his mystification – Matthew had won her hand, the cleverest girl in his year. While she'd stayed in the library to write a lengthy PhD entitled 'Feminism and The Virgin Queen', he'd landed a job booking Elton Johns and Rod Stewarts for a singing lookalikes show. Of course, the job was beneath him (it was certainly beneath her), but having progressed through the challenging foothills of daytime quiz shows, he had finally summited with his own gameshow format: *Who Dunnit?* This thrilling format was eventually sold around the world and had made him a small fortune, causing his wife to moderate her disdain, for it turned out she was not so preoccupied with the Elizabethans that she couldn't enjoy frequent holidays to the Maldives.

They were thankfully saved from any further professorial analysis of television talent shows by the arrival on stage of the cabaret. It began with a burlesque act and two girls in sparkly bustiers, suspenders and stockings who did 'some weird shit' with balloons, as Zander described it later. The climax of this act involved a Thai female (probably, in fact, as Elizabeth learned afterwards, a Thai male), who proceeded to take off her bustier, sit on a high stool, and by lifting one beautifully stockinged leg, appeared to ejaculate ping pong balls from her (his?) vagina into the crowd.

'But I haven't had my pudding yet!' cried Robin theatrically, covering his eyes. Elizabeth tried to spot what the BBC archaeologist was making of it but she appeared to have left the table and instead Elizabeth caught Hutch's eye, who slowly winked at her.

Lola, on Elizabeth's other side, grabbed her wrist, her eyes shining. 'Have you been to the loo?' she hissed. 'There are photos of Ricky on the backs of the doors, so you have to take a piss with him smiling at you. And there's free make-up – and girls offering you trays of condoms and Viagra!' She sank down on to one of the chairs and fanned herself with a menu.

'You okay?' Elizabeth asked her.

'Yes,' Lola breathed into her ear. 'I've had a text. I'm meeting Ricky in half an hour.' She smiled saucily and Elizabeth couldn't help looking over at Lorna, who was standing, her back perfectly straight from hours of dance training, coolly chatting to a heavyweight boxer. Lola lifted herself out of her chair and wandered off, stumbling through the forest of chair legs. Elizabeth made her excuses and slipped away from the Professor's hostile glare. She came across Ricky sitting with a group of people, amongst whom she recognised his old schoolfriends.

'Hey babe, come and sit down!' Ricky kissed her. 'Now then, Trouble, do you need anything?' He looked at Elizabeth with an incriminating smile. 'This man can help you out, you know, if you want some…' He gestured to Deniz Pegasus, who stared back at her, cigar between his lips, his eyes twinkling in an over-fleshy face. He'd eschewed black tie, and was wearing a loud checked jacket, in bright greens and blues. He had a long-legged girl on his lap, in a tiny sequinned dress. She smiled at Elizabeth with glassy eyes.

'I don't, but thank you.' Cocaine had never done it for her. She'd tried it plenty in her twenties, but she felt she always ended up babbling like an overexcited small child. And she'd never been one to keep going all night. She quite liked getting up in the mornings.

Deniz Pegasus shifted his legs, so that his girlfriend had

no choice but to slide on to the nearest other vacant seat. He turned his whole body to face Elizabeth and for a wild, hilarious moment she wondered if he was going to invite her to take the vacant place on his lap. But instead he said low and conspiratorially, 'Ricky trusts you, Elizabeth. Not many he trusts in your crazy world – but he trusts you, babe. It's a shame we didn't get those ideas off the ground. Personally, I think there was a hit show in there.'

'Well, it's a tough thing, coming up with a hit TV show,' Elizabeth said lightly. 'Everyone in the world thinks they have one, but they're actually few and far between. You need all the right ingredients and you need to be in the right place at the right time. It's like a secret alchemy.'

Deniz Pegasus thought for a moment about alchemy and what it might mean, and then stood so that he leered over Elizabeth. 'You're smart. Ricardo always said you're smart. Tell you what – let me talk to Rick – but I've got an idea.' Her heart sank. 'What we need to do, right, is set up a company: me, you and Ricky. We should make the programmes ourselves, control the merchandising, the licensing – all of that. I can do the commercial stuff, you can do the producing – Ricky'll come up with the ideas. We need to go global. Ricky could be huge in Indonesia, Malaysia, all the Asias. I can make you rich. Very rich. Give me the name of your lawyer and I'll send him over a proposal.'

Elizabeth laughed. 'I don't have a lawyer.'

'Even better. Let's do the deal now. My word is my bond. Anyone who's had dealings with me will vouch for that. Tell you what...' His chest was puffed with a powerful can-do

214

energy that made Elizabeth want to giggle. 'What are you doing next weekend? Ricardo's coming on the boat – we're going to be in Cannes. We'll fly you down, spend the weekend on the boat. We can get it all sorted.'

Elizabeth of course had nothing to do next weekend. For a tempting moment she thought about crystal blue waters, a polished deck and fit young guys in beige shorts and crisp white polo shirts handing her towels and cocktails. But then she thought about parading about in front of Deniz Pegasus in a swimsuit, or even in her cut-off denim shorts, and she pulled herself together.

'Oh, let's not talk business now. It's such a lovely evening,' she said sweetly.

Deniz looked startled and she realised that as far as he was concerned, any time was right for business. She kissed him lightly but dismissively on the cheek, smiled at his girlfriend who was swaying to the music in her chair and then wandered out to the lake, where beautiful people were lingering in the late silvery dusk, hourglass silhouettes, tall men in dinner jackets, couples embracing. She stood perfectly still, watching, until a voice close behind her said in her ear, 'Elizabeth, you're not wearing any knickers.'

Hutch's hand took hers, where it was resting at her side and she didn't turn round. His fingers drew a circle on her palm and then he moved closer, still behind her, softly kissing the back of her neck and her bare shoulders, his other hand caressing her hips. Elizabeth was very aware that only one flimsy layer separated his hand from her bare flesh. She stayed motionless for a minute and then as one they stepped apart and stood side by side, gazing at the lake, like regular friends.

'How did you enjoy the vaginal tennis match?' she asked.

'I was virtually umpiring it,' said Hutch. 'If it hadn't ended when it did, I was going to be the one shouting "You cannot be serious!" I couldn't wait for it to be over.'

'Typical Ricky.' Elizabeth shrugged. 'There's such a bizarre collection of people here. It's like a scene from *The Great Gatsby*.'

'It makes me think of Versailles and the Sun King. The dying days of Versailles.'

'Why dying?' She turned to face him.

He shrugged and put his hands in his pockets. 'Ricky can't go on like this. All this excess. All this self-indulgence. He's on the slide, you know he is. He can't possibly keep it up.' He looked around the garden, as if searching for something, and then suddenly reached in to kiss her on the lips. She reached up to his shoulders, but he gently lowered her arms. 'Not here,' he sighed. They stepped apart again, both breathing more heavily. Another couple began strolling towards them.

'I've just been offered some cocaine,' said Elizabeth.

'Yeah? Well, no surprises there.' Hutch was wearing a white dress shirt with Manchester City FC cufflinks and he started fiddling with one of them. 'Who offered it to you?'

'Ricky. Well, he said his friend had some. You know, that friend of his who owns the building firm, Deniz Pegasus.'

'Yeah, I know him.' Before Elizabeth had time to register this unlikely fact, he went on, quickly, breathlessly. 'I can't bear to be this close to you, dressed like that, and not touch you.'

'But what can we do? Your wife's here.' She smiled innocently at him. He stared at her.

'Meet me in the summerhouse, in half an hour. I'll find a way. It's the other side of the lake.' He spun on his heel and Elizabeth heard him say behind her, 'George! Antonia! Hi, how are you?' as he smoothly led away the couple who'd been advancing on them.

She wandered back to the dance floor and threw off her silver instruments of torture. Barefoot, she danced without stopping, first with Robin, who'd cultivated a dancing style that was part ballet, part ballroom, part YMCA – and then with Zander, who could do proper Scottish reeling. Matthew was dancing with Lorna, their heads touching, his hand on the small of her back. The girl who'd been sitting with Deniz was moving in a louche, dreamy way completely on her own, and after a while Elizabeth asked her if she wanted a drink. The girl said she'd go with her and they ended up leaning against the pop-up bar, sharing mojitos.

'I'm Sarah.' Her voice was slow and slurred. 'Sarah McManus.'

'Hi, I'm Elizabeth. I work with Ricky Clough.'

'Oh, you work in television? That's nice. I've been asked to do a reality show actually,' Sarah drawled. 'About my charity work.'

'Really?' Elizabeth drank deeply to hide her smirk.

'Yeah, I do a lot of lunches, you know, raising money and stuff. And I have good contacts ... I know a lot of footballers.'

Elizabeth laughed but Sarah McManus turned very big doleful eyes on her.

'I'm sorry,' Elizabeth said more kindly, 'they'll tell you it's about your charity work, but actually they'll cut all that out in the edit. They just want access to you – and your life, your friends. Who's been talking to you?'

'Oh.' Sarah turned and looked lazily around the room. 'Well, he's here actually… That's him over there.' She pointed to Matthew.

'Aha,' said Elizabeth and ordered another mojito. She had to give her boss credit for having his fingers in an awful lot of pies. Sarah took a drink too. She slid her arm lazily along the bar so that she was half lying down.

'Do you know everyone here?' she asked Elizabeth languidly from her semi-recumbent position.

'A few. Not that many. Do you?'

'No. I'm here with Deniz, you know, he went to school with Ricky. It's funny, we were just saying, there are so many people here who hate each other.'

Elizabeth looked around the fabulous lawn. An MP stood talking to a newspaper editor. She saw a married cabinet minister stroke the back of a model whose husband, a film producer, was sitting only yards away talking to an Indian Bollywood star. Hutch was standing across the lawn, talking to a group of people that included England's football manager. Hutch's wife had looped her arm round his waist. Sarah followed her gaze.

'Deniz says that's what Ricky does. He keeps his enemies close. And, he says, there are always secrets that bind people together – especially well-known people, you know what I mean?' Sarah smiled a vacant wide-eyed smile and slid back up to a standing position, using Elizabeth's shoulder to steady herself. Then she smiled, kissed her on the lips and sashayed away.

It had been more than half an hour since Elizabeth had spoken to Hutch. As she left the marquee to cross the lawn to the summerhouse, she spotted Deniz Pegasus striding quite fast across the terrace and disappearing around the corner of the house. Something about the angry thrust of his shoulders and the urgency of his movements caused Elizabeth to pause. She turned and tiptoed slowly, barefoot and silent, towards the edge of the building. Behind the bay window, almost obscured by it, stood Pegasus, face to face with Ricky. Both seemed furious. Ricky's body was strained, his arms by his sides seemed poised, his fists very ready to make contact. Pegasus, bigger and heavier, leaned in and said something quietly in his ear. Elizabeth saw Ricky reel backwards, his face full of shock. Then his hand came up, the fist clenched, but Pegasus swiftly reached out and caught it, mid-air. The two of them seemed to freeze in this unexpected grip, as if caught in the spotlight during a slow-motion dance. Ricky glanced over his shoulder, then to his left and before he could clock her, Elizabeth darted back around the corner.

Her heart pounding, she went running across the grass to the summerhouse and peered in through the windows. Embroidered Indian cushions were scattered across the floor as well as some gaudy throws and cashmere blankets. It was empty. But then she saw Hutch across the stream that led to the small lake. He was pacing back and forth. Before she could signal to him she spotted another man, his back to her, not in black tie but wearing jeans and trainers. He emerged from a path lined with rhododendrons, nodded briefly at Hutch and slipped silently away across the lawn. As she turned to watch him go, she clocked Matthew, also standing alone, watching, in the shade of a large oak tree on the lawn, close to the stream. Matthew hadn't noticed her and he soon turned and walked slowly back up towards the marquees.

Once Hutch saw her, he came half running along the path, his eyes shining like pin pricks in the dusk, his arms open. Their mouths met and with one hand he opened the door of the summerhouse and with the other, pushed Elizabeth down on to the cushions so that she found her mouth suddenly full of sequins. His breathing was quick and urgent and he had his flies undone before she could get back up on to her knees. One of Hutch's pet hates was wearing condoms. Early on, he'd told her he couldn't bear not to feel her, didn't want to wear a rubber glove like a housewife in an ad for liquid detergent. She'd laughed at the time but couldn't help thinking of Jamie, carefully opening the bedside drawer, expertly peeling the wrapper with one hand, fastidiously inspecting it afterwards for rips and tears. Hutch simply relied on her to sort all that out and she kept forgetting. At least twice, she'd had to go and get the morning-after pill. But now, as carelessly as ever, he lifted her dress up around her hips as she knelt there in the garden house and she felt an overwhelming urge to giggle, thinking it had all gone a bit Lady Chatterley. It was hard to feel the usual thrill, the breathless excitement. The whole affair seemed suddenly ridiculous. What was she doing, creeping around the garden bushes late at night, like some dopey teenager? The sequins were digging into her knees and she couldn't maintain her balance as he began thrusting. He put his hand over her mouth and she bit his finger. He took this to be a sign of passion and gripped her hips harder, rocking her backwards and forwards against him, murmuring, 'I so love fucking you, Elizabeth Place' into her hair. She was almost collapsing with suppressed laughter. But then suddenly it was over and he stood and did up his flies. She smoothed down her crumpled silk and tried to get up from all fours as gracefully as someone aged thirty-five with grazed knees can do. She turned round to face him and pulled him to her by the lapels of his jacket and buried her face in his chest so that he couldn't see her expression. 'Whoa, that was quick!' she said eventually.

'Sorry.' He stroked her hair absently and seeming entirely satisfied himself, failed to register her own sense of anticlimax. Looking round anxiously, he then said, 'I'll go first, okay?' His breathing was still short and fast; he was panting, Elizabeth thought, in a wholly unsexy way and his eyes were still burning with excitement. 'You follow after me – yes?' Elizabeth nodded, thinking that above all else, she wanted to go and find Lola and Robin on the dance floor, to be with her friends. He made to kiss her, but she turned her head at the last minute. She waited five long minutes, staring out at the lake, and then wandered slowly back up the garden. Pegasus was standing on the terrace, alone, smoking and watching her. Elizabeth self-consciously smoothed down her dress with shaking hands. Her hair, she realised, was a mess.

'Ah, Elizabeth. Enjoying the party? Making full use of the facilities?'

'Yes, actually, I've just been down to the summerhouse,' she answered over-brightly. 'It's lovely.'

'Ricardo keeps a good place here, that's for sure. Let's hope he can keep it up, eh?' Deniz took a step closer to her and she felt suddenly wary. 'Let's hope he stays at the top of his game, know what I mean? That someone doesn't try and take it all from him. That's why we need to all stick together, Elizabeth.'

She was puzzled. Take what away? An hour ago he'd offered to cut her in on a deal with Ricky! Did he mean Lorna? She'd just witnessed him having some sort of fight with Ricky, and yet here he was apparently acting as his protector. She couldn't tell if it was the wine or the bad sex, but she felt unsteady. Nothing seemed quite right. It was if she was taking part in an elegant costume drama that had somehow spun out of control: someone had put the film on the wrong speed; it had all got out of sync, people disappearing in and out of bushes, descending into bare-knuckle fighting, getting drunk or high and making no sense.

She turned away and said, 'Well, my many dancing partners are lining up. Excuse me, I must go.' With relief, she found her way back to the dance floor, where Lola and Robin were dancing slowly, round and round, to Rod Stewart's 'Sailing'. Lola looked post-coital, half asleep, her head on Robin's chest. Across the floor, Elizabeth saw Hutch slowly smooching, also post-coital, but with his wife. She *was* wearing taffeta, although that didn't make it any easier. Elizabeth turned away, biting her lip, and found her waist suddenly clasped from behind by Ricky Clough.

'Dance with me, Elizabeth Place.'

They began to sway. Ricky was an excellent dancer. He showed no sign of his earlier fury. 'That's a very good dress,' he murmured in her ear. She saw both Hutch and Matthew looking across at her and she felt suddenly very tired. She rested her head on Ricky's shoulder.

'Thank you for a lovely party.'

Ricky didn't answer, but swung her out with his arms, expertly controlling her spin, and then pulled her back into him. He held her close. 'Stay with me, Elizabeth. I'm no good without you. Stay with me. Please.'

Elizabeth turned her face on his shoulder and let her body move with the music, in time with his. The moon was blood-orange, heavy and bloated, and the strings of fairy lights were combining with the stars to bring the lake sparklingly alive. She closed her eyes as he led her, round and round in ever-widening circles on the dance floor until the music stopped.

★

Two days after Ricky's party, Elizabeth opened her front door to find an enormous bouquet of white lilies standing apparently without assistance on her doorstep. 'Miss Elizabeth Place?' said the bouquet in a breathless voice. Two small feet suddenly appeared beneath the flowers, tottering slightly, and then the entire edifice began to keel. She grabbed at the stems and a red sweating face ducked out from behind them to say, 'This is literally the biggest bunch of flowers I've ever delivered. Someone loves you. Sign here, please.'

Elizabeth struggled back into her flat with the flowers, edging in sideways through the sitting-room door. It took her a few moments searching through the white blowsy blooms to find a card but eventually she located a small brown envelope pinned to the cellophane. She hadn't heard from Hutch since the party and although she'd allowed him one day's grace, she thought two days of silence unacceptable. But flowers, especially big flowers, would do. She tore open the envelope. The card read:

You're the only person I trust, Elizabeth Place. All love, Ricky.

She turned the card over and over in her hands as she sat looking at the flowers. Of course, only Ricky would send the entire contents of a florist's shop. But Elizabeth didn't like that note. It was, she felt, more evidence of his creeping paranoia.

As she was searching her cupboards for enough vases to accommodate the flowers, Lola called. 'Have you seen what he's done now?'

'Oh God! I suppose you mean Ricky?'

'Yeah. It's in the papers. I bought them to look at the photos from the party. By the way, did you know Prince Edward was there? I didn't spot him. But I mean, Ricky even had royalty there, babe!'

'Well, steady on, Lola. He had Prince Edward.'

'Anyway, it seems Ricky went to some fashionable restaurant the night after his party and Geordie Burns from the *Mail* was in there – you know, he wrote that stinking review about *Bonkers* – and well, it came to blows, apparently. Ricky broke the man's glasses. He literally punched him!'

Elizabeth stared at the mountain of flowers on her kitchen floor.

'Will you speak to him, Lizzie? I think you should. He listens to you. He's getting out of hand – more than ever before. He thinks he can control everything. Even me.'

'Oh God, Lola! Really?'

'Oh, it's nothing I can't handle. But speak to him, Lizzie. He listens to you. Tell him he can't behave like this. I'm worried something really bad will happen.'

After Lola had hung up Elizabeth wandered to the window, wondering if she should call Ricky and what she could say. She was surprised to see a fat navy blue Bentley parked outside her house with its engine softly purring. The tall narrow Georgian houses on her Islington street were mostly converted into flats and stretched across two postcodes: N1 at the top end of the street and less desirably, E8 at the bottom end. Elizabeth lived at the bottom end, with the Turkish corner shop, the Vietnamese laundry and the greasy spoon café, where black cab drivers had their bacon butty breakfasts on their way into town from Essex. A Mercedes at the wrong end of the street was a rare sight. She wondered if her downstairs neighbour, a nocturnal IT consultant with a penchant for playing Pink Floyd at 2 a.m., had unexpectedly landed the Apple servicing contract for east London.

Five minutes later, she glanced out of the window again and saw the car was still there. She could make out the bulky shape of a large man with sleek black hair sitting in the driving seat. There was something familiar about the set of his shoulders, the odd square shape of his head. Elizabeth ran quickly down the stairs and out into the street. She glanced in the passenger window: the man inside the car waved a large fleshy hand at her. The car window slipped open silkily.

'Hello, Elizabeth.'

'Mr Pegasus! What are you doing here? Are you looking for me?'

Pegasus shrugged. 'Just passing. Thought I'd check in on you. Make sure everything's okay, you know.'

'How did you know I lived here?'

'Ricky told me. Did you get the flowers?'

Elizabeth nodded, speechless.

'That's good.' Pegasus stretched his arm along the back of the passenger seat. 'Come in for a minute. Sit down.'

'Wait. Are you stalking me?' She was half angry, half fearful.

'Told you, I'm just passing. C'mon, take a seat.' The door swung open and Elizabeth found herself sliding on to the leather seat. The car smelt strongly of spicy aftershave and classical music was softly playing from the car speakers. Elizabeth recognised the Bruch violin concerto that her dad had always loved. She turned to look at Deniz Pegasus with new interest. 'Pegasus? It's an unusual name. Like the horse with wings, you know?'

Deniz frowned. 'It's Turkish.'

Of course. She remembered Ricky telling her that the Pegasus family had opened the first kebab shop in East Ham when he was a boy and he'd gone in there every single day after school for his tea.

'Listen, Elizabeth. Rick's a good guy – he likes to look after those close to him. Like I said the other night, it'd be a shame if he lost it all, if his friends turned against him.' Deniz turned his narrow eyes on her. 'You know, like that boss of yours. He's no good.'

'Well, I guess that's a point of view... I mean, Matthew's running a pretty successful network. Actually, overall, our ratings are up. I know Ricky's been having a hard time with him, but...'

'He's too close to Lorna,' Deniz said suddenly.

Elizabeth looked at him in surprise. 'Matthew? You mean, Matthew's too close to Lorna?'

He looked at her bitterly. 'Yeah. He talks to her these days more than he talks to Rick, that's for sure. He needs to keep his hands off her.' Elizabeth tried to gather her thoughts, but she couldn't get rid of the image that had been playing on her mind: her boss turning slowly round and round in time to the music, his head touching Lorna's, his hand very low on the small of her back.

'He thinks no one knows. But we're watching, we know what he's up to. That's why we need a plan, Elizabeth. An exit plan. For Rick. He should be on the air more. He needs another big show. On another network. They're threatening to cancel *Bonkers* – do you know that? Rick needs another show. So do you, babe.' He looked at her cynically. 'I mean, Rick's the best there is. You wouldn't want to waste your time with any other crap. With any other tossers who think they're the next big thing. Would you now?'

Elizabeth's heart sank. She couldn't look at him.

'Rick wants you to find a new show for him. There's money in it for you, babe. Big money.'

The violins were swelling to a mournful crescendo and Deniz sat still for a moment, his head slightly tipped to one side, as if lost in the music. Elizabeth's head was throbbing at the thought of the layers of intrigue and deception that threatened to complicate her life. And now Pegasus was effectively offering her a bribe. She fumbled at the passenger door, feeling panicky and sick. 'Yes, well look, I'll talk to Ricky. Maybe we can find a show to do together.' She managed to open the door and paused, one leg on the pavement. 'I do like working with Ricky. I'm sorry that he's having a tough time. I'll do what I can, I promise.' She got out and Deniz leaned over the seat to speak to her through the window.

'Thank you, Elizabeth. And in the meantime, let me know if you need anything. Anything at all. I know you live on your own.' He looked at her meaningfully. Then he closed the window and the car slipped away from the kerb with a low growl.

Once upstairs in her flat, Elizabeth realised she was shaking. She poured herself a glass of wine and stood by the window, the sweet sticky smell of the lilies pressingly close. She downed the wine and poured another. Then, after a deep breath, she phoned Ricky. He answered almost immediately.

'Elizabeth, he's not returning my calls.' Ricky's voice was high and she found herself saying, 'Who's not returning your calls?'

'The Controller of Fucking Up Programmes. The moron who holds all our futures in his tiny hands. I've left three voicemails now. It's just fucking rude, that's what it is.'

She took a deep breath. 'Well, perhaps Matthew heard about the incident in the restaurant last night?'

Ricky let out a short laugh. 'Come on, Elizabeth. I've done everyone who works in television a favour there. Let's hope he can't write without his bloody glasses. Those who can, do, and those who can't become a critic. Jumped-up son of a bitch.' She heard a rustle and Ricky began reading aloud: '*Ricky Clough has become a parody of himself. The King Midas of Entertainment has become the desperate court jester, clutching at a game of straws. The format of* Bonkers *has truly lived up to its unfortunate name: empty of content, simply mad. Ricky Clough has become a whirligig of maniacal energy, spinning round and round, going nowhere, the furious pace of his presentation failing to compensate for its lack of substance. Remember, this is the once-great genius of television who one night persuaded us all to stand in the street and look for shooting stars. Well, now Ricky Clough truly does need some supernatural help. Because nothing on earth can save this show.'* Ricky snorted. 'Yeah, he had it coming alright.'

'Well, that's only one review and one critic's opinion.' She found herself inexplicably trying to placate him.

'Yeah, that's right. And I've got other ideas. New shows. That's what I want to talk to you about.'

'Ricky, thank you for the flowers. But did you know Deniz has just been here? To my flat?'

'Yeah?'

'Did you send him, Ricky? To check up on me?'

'Course not! He's got a mind of his own. He looks after my interests, that's all. I bet he was just passing.'

'Yes. Funny – that's exactly what he said.'

'Elizabeth, you're going to produce my next big thing, right? You said you would, at the party.'

Elizabeth wasn't sure she had, exactly, but she said, 'I'm only going to talk to you about that, Ricky. Not Deniz, okay? I just want to be clear.'

'Alright, alright, keep your knickers on! But I need you, Elizabeth. Don't forget it.'

She hung up, drained her glass, and stared at the flowers, still on the floor. Their scent was overwhelming her small flat. She felt it was creeping up the walls, curling like smoke into the corners, through the hall, down the stairs. She suddenly felt she couldn't breathe. She threw open a window and gulped in the fresh air as if surfacing from a deep dive. Then she grabbed the flowers and stumbled down the stairs with them, their heavy heads and yellow stamens leaving a jaundiced smear on the walls. She lifted the lid of her dustbin and threw in the flowers, shoving them down with her hands, the stalks all torn, the blowsy heads all crushed.

Chapter Thirteen

The morning after she got back from seeing Vic and her mum in Frinton, Elizabeth woke to a text from Hutch, so surprising that she had to check twice that it was actually Saturday. It said simply, 'I'm on my own. Meet at the flat? Don't dress up.' Elizabeth chewed her nail. She didn't really want to have her confrontation with Hutch in his bachelor flat, sitting on his bachelor sofa where he'd once spoon-fed her oysters, naked and blindfold. On the other hand, Elizabeth didn't much fancy the horrible pastries at Café Cecile, nor the thought of shouting at him in public. She was also annoyed with his assumption that she had nothing better to do. But, on the other hand, she had nothing better to do.

They met at lunchtime. Hutch buzzed her through the main entrance and was waiting at his open front door, dressed barefoot, in baggy sweatpants and an oversized black T-shirt. His hair was damp and Elizabeth had a sudden recollection of seeing him semi-naked in his dressing room after the *Bonkers* show, wrapped in a towel, dripping green gunge and wrath. This time, he seemed pumped, full of fizzing excitement, and his eyes, fixed on her, were glittering with anticipation.

He pulled her to him quickly to kiss her on the mouth but she turned her head and he bruised her cheek with his lips instead. Elizabeth was wearing a shapeless striped shirt over some skinny jeans. She'd washed her hair but not dried it properly and it was curling in all the wrong places. She wore no make-up. The strange, sick feeling she'd had all week still lingered. She'd even found herself wondering that morning if she too had somehow been affected by the Culone dishes in the studio. Could the same thing have slightly touched her, as it touched Ricky?

Hutch followed her into the kitchen. He offered her a drink and as he juggled the stove-top coffeepot and steamed some milk, she caught him looking at her, testing the temperature of their meeting. He handed her a coffee but she noticed, unusually, he didn't have one himself. There were some dirty plates in the sink; she assumed he must've had a large breakfast. He gestured for her to sit at the breakfast bar (good move, upright stools) and he took a seat on the opposite side. She didn't want her coffee.

'It's Saturday,' Elizabeth said flatly.

'Yes, Sue's gone to do some PR for a golf thing.' Hearing her name out loud always gave Elizabeth a jolt. It was like having someone bang a loud drum next to your ear. Or like someone shouting an obscenity in the middle of a classical concert.

'So, what's up?' He had a very slight note of irritation in his voice. Elizabeth was quick to detect it and even quicker to be riled by it.

'Why didn't you tell me about Tuesday night? The night you went to the pub with Ricky? The night before he died.

The night you also came to my flat?' She glared at him. He looked taken aback.

'Well, I don't know… I guess I was distracted. You jumped on me before I'd even got through your front door!' He smiled insinuatingly and she burned with fury.

'Well, I'd waited long enough – you were so late! And now I know why. You preferred to linger in the pub with Ricky Clough and half MY production team – talking about MY show, discussing which of Culone's dishes to use in MY studio – and all without telling me!'

Hutch rubbed his nose, distractedly. 'I'm sorry. I think I just lost track of the time.'

'Oh? So not that keen to come and see me, then?'

He tried to take her hand across the breakfast bar, but she quickly withdrew it. 'Always keen, Elizabeth. More than keen. Desperate, a lot of the time. You have no idea how often I think about you. How hard it is…'

'Okay. So you were overcome with the need to take me from behind when you got to my flat. Or, in your telling of it, I jumped on you and had your clothes off before you could get through the door. But why didn't you mention it once you'd found out that Ricky had died? When you phoned me first thing on Thursday morning? For God's sake, Hutch, you'd seen Ricky, had been out with him, only two nights before!'

He flung himself out of his seat and began pacing around the kitchen. His face had a new hard set to it and his eyes were glinting with an anger she'd never seen in him before. The sudden swing of his mood took her by surprise.

'Elizabeth! What is this? A fucking interrogation?' He

slammed his hand down on the counter and she jumped. 'I was gobsmacked that Ricky had died. And you were on your way to the police station! You were talking about how it had happened, in the studio, and I was listening. I was being fucking sympathetic, for God's sake! We didn't have much time to talk about me, or when I last saw Ricky.' He raised his hands helplessly. 'It didn't seem – in the scheme of things – all that important.'

'And when I met you after I'd seen the police? At Cecile's? And when we came back here? Why didn't you mention it then, either?'

Hutch looked at her for a long moment and when he replied, his voice was icy and unpleasant. 'Elizabeth, I don't know what this is all about. I can accept that it's all been horribly traumatic for you and that you're still very upset. I never understood your relationship with Ricky Clough, but I know that he had some sort of weird hold over you, that you kept going back for more, although fuck knows why. I'm assuming you've been honest when you say it was only ever professional.' Elizabeth glared at him but he glared back, now really furious. 'Honestly, I don't know how Jamie put up with it all those years.'

Hearing Hutch say Jamie's name out loud, and in sympathy with him, was so brutal, so offensive, it almost took her breath away. But Hutch was on a roll. 'Fuck, Elizabeth! Coming here like this, accusing me of – I don't know what, exactly, but so angry and hostile. What on earth have I done to deserve that?' He turned abruptly on his heel, stalked out, and she heard a door slam somewhere down the hall.

She'd been left alone. She was shaking. She felt tearful. The jibes about Ricky, about Jamie, had hit home. There was truth in it: Jamie had hated how she'd dropped everything to take a call from Ricky, even in the middle of the night. How she'd stayed late in the office, working to Ricky's peculiar timetable, ignoring the fact Jamie had cooked dinner for her. How she'd lain awake most nights of the week, grinding her teeth.

Elizabeth glanced around Hutch's sitting room with its black leather sofa, its shelf of vinyls, the framed photo of his wife. There was, she noticed, an empty beer bottle and an upturned wine glass beside a full ashtray on the glass coffee table. The mirrored top of the coffee table was smeared and slightly grimy, there was a discarded white T-shirt lying on the floor beside the sofa. Elizabeth couldn't remember the room looking quite so dishevelled, so apparently lived-in before. She'd assumed that Hutch really only used his flat for sex with her. After all, he had another home across town. A home with an Aga. But here was evidence of, well, what exactly? A night in, perhaps. An indulgent Friday night in his bachelor flat. With a curry to follow, perhaps, given the dirty dishes in the sink. Almost against her will, she moved quietly from her stool to the sofa and then stood very still. The overturned wine glass had the faintest smear of pink along its edge. She bent closer to check the glass and it was then she spotted, discarded, half underneath the sofa, two rolled-up notes, both fivers. She picked up one of the notes, ran her finger tentatively along its curled edges and licked it. Cocaine. She looked again at the smeared coffee-table top. She froze, the fiver in her hand, her mind racing, her heart pounding painfully in her ribcage. She remembered Hutch's text that morning: 'I'm on my own. Meet

at the flat?' She'd assumed he'd driven over this morning to meet her, but of course, he must have been here, in the flat, all night. And if so, who else had been here? Who had he entertained in his bachelor flat? And how had he entertained them? With wine, with beer, with drugs…? She looked again at the T-shirt. With sex?

Elizabeth heard another door slam in the hall and she dropped the fiver, moving quickly back to her stool. Hutch strode back into the kitchen, his eyes still blazing. She watched his furious movements with a new kind of despair. He slammed her cup down in the sink and turned towards her. They stared at each other across the room. She was full of dawning horror. She bit her lip. Please, Hutch, she thought, please tell me it isn't true. She opened her mouth to speak, but his face suddenly softened, his shoulders sagged and he more or less flung himself at her, seizing her hand.

'Elizabeth!' His voice was husky, desperate. 'Let's not behave like…' He trailed off and she looked up at him, sharply.

'Like a married couple? Is that what you were going to say?'

The silence between them was heavy. She wanted to talk about it but couldn't bring herself to ask him explicitly what she suspected.

'Were you here last night?' she finally asked.

Another look of anger swept over his features. He dropped her hand. 'Yes. I told you. Sue's gone to St Andrew's.'

'It looks like you had quite a party.' She nodded towards the coffee table. He stood very still, watching her carefully as if working out what he was going to say, but Elizabeth stopped him with her hand. 'Hutch, it's no good. I can't, I can't do this…'

He gently lifted up her chin. 'Don't, Elizabeth! Don't say it.' He kissed her softly on the lips.

She didn't return the kiss, but sat feeling numb. Maybe she wouldn't speak. Wouldn't life be easier if she didn't actually say anything? After all, she'd known what she was in for these last nine months: weekends spent wistfully alone in her flat, when he was at home with his wife, in his busy kitchen with the Aga, not looking at her texts, not reading her emails – not thinking about her. She had only herself to blame. She'd been shell-shocked and was reeling from not being loved, enough. She had run willingly into Hutch's arms; she'd waltzed into this affair as if dancing on air. She had trusted him blindly. And it was such a relief to be loved again. But her last relationship had foundered because of her blindness. Too many things had stayed below the surface, slowly rotting in a heap of unaired emotions. She couldn't let it happen again. But giving voice to secret feelings would have consequences. There would be no going back to the way they were. She might lose him. But was losing him worse than this constant state of un-knowing? She sighed. It felt like a pressure valve bursting. And then she said, 'Jamie's having a baby. He got married.'

Hutch's face softened. 'Oh, Elizabeth. When did you find out?'

'Vic told me yesterday. I'm actually pleased for him. I don't have any ill feelings towards him. I want him to be happy.' She looked at Hutch, who was standing, confused, helpless, not sure what to say or do. She would do it for him, then.

'But Hutch, I realise it's what I want, too. I don't want to be one of those women who leaves it too late. I want a baby. I've wanted a baby for a long time, even before Jamie and I broke up. So now I need to know where we stand.' She looked at him. 'I mean, you've told me you were leaving, over and over. And look what's happened to Ricky! Who knows what life's going to throw at you? I want to seize the moment, Hutch, I don't want to go on waiting, treading water, wasting my time...' She looked up at him. 'Feeling betrayed. Again.'

A bell rang. Hutch ignored it. He was wrestling with his reaction. He took her hand again. 'Of course you should have a baby, Elizabeth. You'd be a great mum.' The bell rang again, this time for longer. 'But do you think you might be feeling like this because you're all mixed up? Because of Ricky, I mean? And because of the news about Jamie?'

The bell rang without stopping for several seconds. Elizabeth looked at him questioningly. For a sudden wild moment, she wondered if it was his party guest from the night before, returning on impulse. It couldn't be Sue; she surely would have a key. As if reading her mind, Hutch said irritably, 'It's the intercom. It's a Saturday, it can't be anything important. I'm ignoring it.'

He bent down and kissed her again, more tenderly. She understood this to be his answer. She let him undo the top buttons of her shirt. He kissed her gently, on her neck, on her shoulders, on the fast, beating pulse of her chest. She rested her head on his shoulder. There was a thumping at the front door. Then an insistent knocking. He pulled back, now very irritated, and said, 'For fuck's sake!' and went into the hall. Elizabeth heard him open the door and there was an agonising pause. She sat, holding her breath. Then she heard a voice she recognised say, 'Hello, Mr Hutchinson. May we come in?'

And before Elizabeth had a chance to do up her buttons, into the kitchen strode DI Watson, tall and imposing, dressed in her navy blue trouser suit, with Sergeant Rafik tripping along behind her.

'Hello, Elizabeth.' DI Watson didn't seem in the least bit surprised to see her there, in Hutch's kitchen, and with her shirt undone. The detective turned to Hutch, who was now standing behind her, his hands shaking. His eyes were darting anxiously around the flat; there was a sheen of sweat on his forehead. Elizabeth realised that he was terrified.

'Mr Hutchinson, we did ring the intercom but maybe you didn't hear? You were, no doubt, preoccupied.' The police-woman glanced coolly at Elizabeth. 'Anyway, I'm DI Watson and this is DS Rafik. We'd like you to come to the station please to answer a few questions about the death of Ricky Clough.'

'What? Today?'

'Yes. Now.' DI Watson's voice was firm.

'But Elizabeth's here.' He gestured lamely as she clambered down from her stool, still fumbling with her buttons.

'Elizabeth, you're free to go home.' DI Watson barely looked at her.

'Look,' said Hutch, recovering his poise, his easy charm. 'Can't we talk here? In the flat? Of course, I'm happy to answer any questions you might have. Is a visit to the station really necessary? I could make us some coffee?'

DI Watson looked slowly around the flat. She took in the black leather sofa, the vinyls, the framed photograph of Hutch's wife. Elizabeth, barely knowing what she was doing, moved slightly to block the coffee table from that penetrating gaze. But DI Watson had already turned away.

'Yes. We'd like you to accompany us to the station.'

He burst out angrily, 'But why? Why can't you talk to me here? What's wrong with here?'

Elizabeth almost ran to him, to hold him, to stop the wrong words from tumbling out of his mouth. Sergeant Rafik took a warning step towards Hutch, which seemed to incense him even further. 'It's a fucking Saturday morning! I don't want to go to a police station. I want to be in my own home.'

DI Watson said sharply, 'But you're not really in your own home, Mr Hutchinson, are you? Not your *family* home?'

He looked at her furiously. 'I'm not sure that's any of your fucking business.'

Elizabeth felt dizzy, she thought she might faint. Why was he being so stupid? She reached out to the counter to steady herself and opened her mouth to save him. But DI Watson put her hand out to silence her. She looked coolly at an angry, sweating Hutch and then said slowly and clearly, 'Harry Hutchinson, I am arresting you for the murder of Ricky Clough.'

Chapter Fourteen

Elizabeth left Hutch's flat without being able to exchange another look with him. It was an effort even to breathe or swallow, once DI Watson had uttered those words. Everyone seemed to be moving slowly as if through a suffocating fog. DI Watson was standing with the front door open, ready to usher her out. Sergeant Rafik was in the kitchen, urging Hutch to put on his shoes. She tried to catch Hutch's eye as she left, but he was bent over his shoelaces with shaking hands. He hadn't once looked at her since DI Watson had accused him of murder. As she went, Elizabeth looked up at DI Watson, standing straight-backed, serene, by the front door. Her expression was frank, level, unwavering. Her eyes met Elizabeth's and she shook her head slightly. Elizabeth opened her mouth to speak but the policewoman said firmly, 'Go home. We'll be in touch.'

Outside, she stood on the pavement, buses gliding past, people weaving around her. It was Saturday. A normal weekend day. Mothers were holding on to small hands or jogging by in brightly coloured Lycra, girls were gabbling into mobile phones, boys were running past in football shirts. Everyone seemed to be shouting, the traffic noise was thundering in her ears. Her knees suddenly buckled and she groped her way to a bus shelter and sank on to the narrow plastic bench. As she sat there, she saw Hutch being led out on to the street by Sergeant Rafik and into a waiting car. His shoulders were hunched, his eyes were down. In his tracksuit and trainers, he could be any other Saturday morning fitness freak. Except he was getting into an unmarked police car. He was some other kind of freak.

Elizabeth watched the car move quickly away and down the road. She sat perfectly still in her shelter as buses came and went, loading and unloading the chattering crowds with their shopping bags. She tried to make sense of it all, but her head felt full of lead, she couldn't think straight. Hutch a murderer? The man she'd hoped might be the future father of her baby? None of it made sense. She'd always known there was something unfathomable about him, a bit of him she couldn't reach – but *this?* She thought about this morning in the flat, the evidence of cocaine, the lipstick-stained glass, his barely controlled rage and restlessness. She felt dizzy with it all, the ground shifting and sinking beneath her feet. It surely couldn't be true. She couldn't allow herself to believe it. She closed her eyes.

She couldn't face going back to her flat, with its red-walled brothel bedroom, her underwear still on display where Hutch had placed it on her mantelpiece last Tuesday night. All of it there to mock her. She began walking aimlessly, hope-lessly. She wondered about calling Vic (*'You know that man I think I love? The man I thought all my futures were bound up with? Well, you'll never guess what….'*) And then, suddenly, she realised she'd walked the length of Westbourne Park Road and was at Paddington Basin. And beyond the Basin, across the Westway, was the police station. And inside, by now, was Hutch. Elizabeth crossed the busy roads in a daze, lorries blaring at her, black cab drivers hurling obscenities, one so close he almost bruised her legs. She reached the other side, breathlessly, leaning on a lamp post. She wasn't even sure police stations had waiting rooms. It's not as if they were hospitals; they weren't saving lives, they were ruining them – and she assumed they didn't like having spectators.

She stumbled along the Edgware Road, finally finding an empty, souless café, where she drank a builder's tea, sitting on a stool at the window counter. Then she ordered another, and a third, spooning sugar heedlessly into the mug. Her heart was pounding. The hours ticked slowly by, the café filled, emptied, and filled again. She realised she hadn't eaten and bought a stale fruit scone but it stuck to the roof of her mouth, attached itself like toffee to the back of her throat so that she couldn't swallow properly. She kept thinking back over all her exchanges with Hutch since last Wednesday. She remembered, with a sick heavy feeling in her stomach, sitting in Cecile's on Thursday and him saying, '*I know plenty of people who've wanted to kill him… I've wanted to kill him… He'd become a jerk and a boor…*' These two men, with whom she'd worked so closely, apparently loathed each other and with an intensity she'd consistently managed not to notice. How much else had she so carelessly missed?

Someone had left a copy of the *Sun* on a vacant chair. There was a double-page spread with Deniz Pegasus, based as far as she could tell on a genuine interview with him, in which he talked about his generous, fun-loving, schoolmate, Ricky

Clough. He'd given them a mischievous school photo: Ricky pulling a face, in short trousers with knee-length grey socks, one up, one down. Deniz had supplied other photos: the two of them on a yacht with some bikini-clad women, none of them Lorna, although Elizabeth recognised Sarah McManus, the footballer's wife and another of them in black tie at a Bafta awards ceremony, arms around each other's shoulders.

She sat staring for a while at the newspaper's front page with its banner headline boasting an exclusive and a photo of Ricky on his own, winking at the camera. Elizabeth knew every crease of that face, its entire range of expressions, the way a mood could creep across his eyes and cause his mouth to become a straight, unyielding line. She'd stared at that face for hours and hours, close-up, on multiple television screens, looking at every possible angle. During a live show, with every sinew of her body tightly tuned to the possible vagaries of his moods, she'd learned to read his face, his body movements, the quirks and curiosities that made him essentially unique, essentially Ricky. She'd studied him as if he were a comprehension test. And yet, here she was, trying to read between the lines, trying to make sense of Ricky's death. And still, she had no clue.

Unbidden, a memory stole into her mind of Ricky arriving at the network's offices one brilliantly sunny day on a tandem. Characteristically, he'd bought it on impulse from a cycling shop on his way in. He'd phoned Elizabeth from the cobbled courtyard and she'd run to the window and laughingly looked down at him as he slowly wobbled his way in bicycling circles around the cobbles beneath her. 'Come down! Let's take a ride!'

She'd skipped down the stairs. They'd cycled up and down the courtyard, their feet pedalling wildly out of sync, Elizabeth laughing and hoisting her skirt high up around her thighs. Lola had leaned out of the window, smiling and cheering, filming them on her mobile phone. Finally, they'd worked out how to cycle in unison and with a childlike whoop, Ricky had steered them out into the road and all the way down Kensington High Street. Taxi drivers were hooting at them, people were waving, everyone was laughing. Ricky had pulled over at an ice cream van and Elizabeth had jumped off and bought them each a cone, and then they'd cycled on again, eating their ice creams, one-handedly steering the wobbling tandem. Ricky, in front, had begun to sing, *'Daisy, Daisy, Give me your answer do!'* They cycled down to Kensington Gardens, in through the gates, and circled Kensington Palace, tourists pausing from taking photographs, picnickers hastily scrabbling to their feet to get a better look. By the time they'd slowly pedalled back to the office, the day had clouded over and Ricky began to hum, *'Raindrops keep fallin' on my head.'*

Elizabeth, who'd been brought up never to be lazy, to strive constantly for some unseen goal, loved these moments when Ricky could seduce her into being frivolous, fanciful, free. She might seem outwardly ordinary, but in fact dangerously lovable men could seduce her into behaving badly. She could easily be persuaded, if handled right, to become an accomplice wearing a smart dress and hat and help rob a few banks.

When they finally shuddered to a halt, Elizabeth felt suddenly sad, as if there might not be a happy ending after all. She leaned her head against Ricky's back and whispered, 'Thank you for the ride.'

Thank you for the ride.

In the café, Elizabeth's eyes filled with tears. She toyed with her mobile, wondering if Lola still had the phone footage. She'd missed their girly after-office gossipy drinks over the last few months, when she'd been so preoccupied with Hutch. She had not been a good friend. Did Lola have any more answers, did she yet understand it? Yesterday morning she'd found Lola bent over her computer keyboard. She'd confessed that she was writing down everything she could remember about her time with Ricky, it was helping her to grieve. Elizabeth glanced at the *Sun* and couldn't help herself wondering how much a newspaper might offer for the sort of memories of Ricky that Lola could supply.

'Where are you?' said Lola immediately as she picked up Elizabeth's call.

'I'm sitting outside Paddington Police Station. Lola, they've got Hutch! They've taken him in – they're accusing him of… Oh God, I can't believe it.'

'I'm coming,' Lola said immediately. 'Where are you exactly?'

Within half an hour, Lola was tumbling out of a black cab, her blonde hair piled high, secured precariously by some multicoloured combs and wearing a pink, fitted, calf-length dress that showed to advantage her small waist and cushiony backside. She eased herself on to the stool next to Elizabeth, swinging both legs elegantly underneath the counter, and ordered a black coffee.

'Tell me everything,' she said breathlessly.

'I don't really know anything. The police – DI Watson – came to Hutch's flat this morning.' Elizabeth paused, then she shrugged. She'd had enough of deceit and secrecy. 'I was there. In his flat.' She looked shyly up at Lola, who looked back, narrow-eyed. 'I've been seeing him – Hutch.'

Lola nodded, slowly.

'But I… well, I realise I hardly know him. I mean, all sorts of things have come out since Ricky died that I had no idea about. But Hutch killing him! I just can't take it in.'

Lola stirred her coffee. 'That's what they kept asking me – the police – when they came to see me again yesterday. They kept asking about Ricky and Hutch. What did I think? Did they spend much time together? Were they friends?'

'The police came to see you yesterday?' Elizabeth cried. 'Were you alone?'

Lola crossed her legs and smoothed down her dress. 'Yes. They know, Lizzie. About me and Ricky. They know everything.' She shot her a quick look and Elizabeth blushed. 'No one's said it out loud. But you know that DI Watson, she just lets you know that she knows by a look, and a slight emphasis here and there: "Lola, you know Ricky better than anyone else on the team, I think?"' She caught perfectly DI Watson's Essex accent, her caustic tone and insinuation.

'My shirt was undone,' Elizabeth said, grimacing, 'when she came to arrest Hutch. She barely glanced at me. She certainly wasn't surprised. And I was sitting in his kitchen with my red bra showing! I mean, I might as well have been wearing a big letter A round my neck like the Scarlet Woman.'

'Yeah, I got the feeling Watson could see right through me, like I was transparent or something. It's a bit like she's reading your mind when she's asking you questions.' Lola shrugged. 'But I didn't care what I said. I was having sex with Ricky, not plotting to bump him off. I answered all her questions – as far as I could. I just want them to catch whoever did this to him...' Her voice caught.

Elizabeth reached over and squeezed her hand. 'So, what did you say? About Hutch and Ricky?'

Lola didn't answer at first. Then she said brusquely, 'Ricky hated him. With a passion. I assume it was mutual.'

Elizabeth looked at her in alarm.

'He knew, Ricky did. About you and Hutch.' Lola's voice was suddenly accusatory, the full force of her hurt slamming into the words. 'He knew you were sleeping with Hutch. And he knew about the pilot show. He discussed it with me. And, Lizzie, I defended you! I told Ricky it couldn't be true – because if it was, you would've talked to me about it!'

Elizabeth swallowed hard. 'Lola, I'm so sorry. I couldn't discuss it with you. Matthew had us all sign a non-disclosure. He was worried about Ricky finding out.'

Lola looked scornful. 'Yeah? Does an NDA these days cover sex? No, Lizzie, you could've told me. You just chose not to. We're meant to be best friends, remember?' She sniffed haughtily. 'And did you know Matthew had stopped taking Ricky's calls? It was driving him nuts. Ricky didn't know where he was with him. Like I didn't know where I was with you. Lizzie, it was such a betrayal – I'm meant to be your best friend!'

Elizabeth took the brunt of Lola's wounded pride head-on. She couldn't wonder at it. She lowered her head in a weary acknowledgement of her treachery. After a pause, she said, 'But you told me you hadn't been seeing Ricky – sleeping with him – for a few weeks. Had you?'

Lola shook her head. 'He seemed to have other obsessions. And Hutch was definitely one of them. God, it was so boring! He kept going on and on about how Hutch was a talentless jerk who was trying to steal his crown. He said he knew stuff about Hutch that would end his TV career in an instant – he was just biding his time before he let the whole world know. He told me then – about you and Hutch. I mean, I tried to deny it, but of course I realised it must be true. Then Deniz joined in. He seems to go everywhere with Ricky these days, he loves that life, red carpets and clubs and parties – he's such a sponger. Ricky seemed to be blind to it. And Deniz kept offering to 'sort him out' – Hutch, I mean. Acting like he's this big godfather figure! Stupid tosser.'

'It was a complicated friendship between Deniz and Ricky. I saw them having a huge row at the party – Ricky was ready to wallop him.'

'Really? Yeah, Deniz could wind him up, like no one else – especially about Lorna. I overheard him once goading Ricky about where she was, what she was up to in Surrey. It drove Ricky mad, he was in a complete funk all night. Mind you, Ricky was all over the place at the party, you know. He was in a foul mood, and then all bright and breezy. I thought he'd done way too much stuff.'

'What was it that Ricky knew about Hutch that he said would end his career?' Elizabeth asked, her heart beating fast.

'I didn't ask. I didn't want anything to do with it. But he and Deniz were convinced they had something on him. They were talking about blackmail.'

'Blackmail? Do you think…? Oh God!'

'So when did it start – you and Hutch?'

'About nine months ago.'

'So it was going on when he came on to *Bonkers*?' Lola turned to face her. 'Jesus, Lizzie! I'd never seen Ricky so rude, so unhinged. I couldn't work out what Hutch had done to enrage him so much.'

'Me neither. Lola, listen I'm sorry. Truly I am. How are *you* feeling?'

Lola reached for a cigarette and tapped it absently on the table top. 'The writing helps. We had some good times.' She looked at Elizabeth defiantly. 'I've had quite a big offer to publish.'

Elizabeth pushed the *Sun* with its exclusive banner towards her and Lola grimaced. 'You can't blame me. Everyone's made money out of Ricky, all his lackeys. I got some dirty weekends away, but Ricky never gave me anything else. He just seemed to take me for granted. And he was pretty demanding these last few weeks. I don't see why I shouldn't get some cash. I think he owes me.'

Elizabeth looked at her friend in surprise at the bitterness of her tone. It seemed unlike her. 'I'm not going to judge you, Lola. It's up to you. Just make sure you don't do it and then regret it. And make sure whoever takes the story pays you a fortune. I guess the only person who will judge you is Lorna.'

They both sat silently, Lola still playing with her unlit cigarette. 'Lizzie, what on earth do you see in Hutch? Really?'

Elizabeth flinched. 'I don't know. He's funny. He knows about things I don't – like football, and food. He's eager. Keen. I suppose that was it – he was just so interested in me. He seemed to hang on my every word. Jamie had stopped listening to me, talking to me even – he seemed to despise everything about my professional life. Hutch admired what I knew, what I could do. He wanted to learn how to be good on telly – and I guess, I wanted to teach him.'

'Yeah, he wanted to learn how to be like Ricky! And of course you were the best person to teach him! Lizzie, haven't you noticed how Hutch turns his head slightly to one side just before he says a funny line? Like he's almost throwing it away? Shrugging it off? That's Ricky! He's nicked that from watching Ricky!'

Elizabeth shook her head, but she felt herself grow warm with the white heat of recognition. She didn't trust herself to speak.

'But Lizzie, you could have anyone! You're so pretty – in your tomboy way – and so clever, so successful. Why did you need Hutch?'

'Thank you, that's sweet. But you know, Jamie was my first proper boyfriend after my dad died. And I think I probably clung to the idea that he was the one because I couldn't face losing someone else from my life. I just haven't had that many boyfriends. I'm not like you, hon, I'm terrible at the no-strings thing. I want men to find me irresistible. And Hutch was just so different from Jamie. He seemed to find me fascinating and it made me feel powerful. To begin with.'

'Different? Hmm, I'm not sure, Lizzie. Wrong, more like. He's a wrong-un, definitely. You shouldn't have gone there.'

Elizabeth bit her lip, hurt by the disdain. She took a deep breath. 'You know, Lola, I've just heard that Jamie got married. Like, so quickly! And.... And he's having a baby...' Lola's mouth dropped open and a small gasp escaped. 'But you know what, I don't mind... It's a big revelation, but I don't mind. Except...Lola, I realise it's what *I* want.'

'Jamie's got *married*? Really? Wow. Oh, Lizzie.' Lola reached out and hugged her, and with that one sympathetic gesture the floodgates opened and Elizabeth put her head on Lola's shoulder and sobbed. When she finally raised her face, her nose running with snot and her eyes red with rubbing, she couldn't work out if she was crying mostly for Jamie, for Hutch, or for Ricky. Perhaps, she realised, for the loss of all three of them. She looked through the café window at the police station beyond. But maybe, maybe, Hutch wasn't lost to her – yet.

Lola handed her a paper napkin. 'C'mon, Lizzie. I need a fag. Let's go outside.'

Elizabeth blew her nose noisily and then picked up her coat. 'No. I'm going to go to the police station. I'm going to wait for Hutch, if they'll let me. He must be feeling so scared, so lonely. I didn't even speak to him once they came into the flat! God knows where this leaves us, but I can't abandon him. I feel responsible.'

Lola looked at her sceptically for a moment, then whispered in her ear, 'You can do better, Lizzie. Honestly, you can.' They went outside and Lola lit her cigarette, taking a deep drag. 'I'm meeting someone from the *Mirror* later. You know, to see how interested they are. But call me – let me know what happens to Hutch. If they, you know, charge him.'

Elizabeth flinched at the word, spoken out loud, but kissed Lola lightly on the cheek and left her on the pavement, one hand on her hip, her head tipped up and sideways, blowing rings of smoke pensively into the clear spring sky. People who passed by bestowed on her the sort of admiring looks usually reserved for works of art, or images of Hollywood movie stars straddling air vents in billowing skirts. Lola was oblivious to the attention, lost in her own thoughts. Elizabeth stood watching her for a moment, an idea slowly forming itself in her head. She promised herself that she would do better by Lola in the future, that she would restore this friendship to the dear place, professional and personal, that it once had in her life.

Then she dug her hands determinedly in the pockets of her parka, crossed the road and slowly climbed the steps to the police station.

Chapter Fifteen

Elizabeth thought that the waiting area of Paddington Police Station could not be less welcoming for people who had to sit and wait in it. There were no sofas, no magazines, no aquariums stuffed with catfish. At her TV offices, in the banana warehouse, the reception boasted two giant-sized soft teddy bears, on whose laps you could sit and wait if that was the look you were after, as well as a table football game, should you be in need of an activity other than waiting. (The table football was frequently used because anyone waiting for a meeting in the network's offices was either extremely competitive or incapable of sitting still.) Paddington Green's reception area seemed to be there to repel rather than receive you. It had two rows of chipped blue plastic chairs, which were chained together (Elizabeth understood there were thieves about, but she very much doubted that there was much of a black market for blue plastic seating nicked from a police station.) A desk and a back office could be glimpsed behind a forbidding grill. A policeman was sitting at the desk, balancing a phone in the crook of his neck, taking notes. (Surely things were the wrong way round, she thought. The policemen appeared to be the ones behind bars.) Elizabeth hadn't paid much attention to the reception when she'd last visited the station but now she noticed that the walls were covered in posters telling her there were thieves about, exhorting her to pick up litter, and then, despite this, to join the police force. No one seemed to register her; there were no welcoming smiles behind the desk. She went and sat by herself on one of the plastic chairs. It was as if she was taking a seat in the audience and waiting for the strangest show in the world to begin.

The policeman at the desk eventually called over to her and she jumped up.

'Um, I'm, um, a friend of Hutch – of Harry Hutchinson. He's been brought here, er, for questioning. Can I wait for him?'

The policeman had ginger hair and a face of freckles. He was quite fat. She guessed the nature of his police work mostly involved sitting down. He looked at Elizabeth, now very interested. 'The guy from Channel 4? Are you in television too?'

'Yes, I am.'

'Ah. Bet that's good fun. I like his programme, it's funny. But not his team. He doesn't give Spurs the credit they deserve.' It felt very weirdly as if they were having a normal chat. 'Bet you know a lot of famous people, then?'

Elizabeth leaned weakly against the counter. 'I was Ricky Clough's producer.'

'Oh.' The policeman glanced guiltily over his shoulder, where other colleagues were standing around a coffee machine. 'Oh, I'm sorry. Take a seat.'

Elizabeth sat and picked up a leaflet on community policing.

A door opened and closed behind her and she got a strong whiff of disinfectant. Great, she'd positioned herself right by the loo. God only knows what those lavatories had seen in their time. She stood up to change her seat and in turning, came face to face with Matthew, her boss. He'd just emerged from the offending cubicles and was rubbing his hands together, over and over. The smell of disinfectant was ripe.

'Elizabeth!' He was equally startled, caught red-handed. He recovered more quickly than she did. 'God, these places make you feel dirty, don't they?'

'What are you doing here?' She wondered what she was going to say when he asked her the same question.

But Matthew didn't ask her. He sat down beside her. 'I've been doing an identity parade. Behind a two-way mirror. Just like on the telly.' He grimaced. Elizabeth's heart stopped. Had Matthew been brought here – already – to identify Hutch?

'Was… was Hutch in there?'

'Hutch? Harry Hutchinson? No! Why would he be in the line-up?' Matthew looked at her, confused.

Elizabeth took a deep breath. 'It's just that he's here. Hutch. The police have got him.'

He said sharply, 'Have they? They've got Hutch? Oh.' He sat silently for a moment, looking at his shoes. He took a deep breath. 'The thing is, Elizabeth, something odd happened at lunch with Ricky the day before he died.' She nodded, her eyes fixed on his face. 'He was talking about his party. He was making all sorts of comments about Hutch, which, Elizabeth, I can assure you I was taking with a pinch of salt.' Elizabeth looked away. 'But Ricky reminded me of something I'd seen.

Someone I'd seen. At the party. And suddenly I had this really strong recall of the night I was mugged. A smell. A look. A flash of a shoe. It was like I could taste the fear in my mouth all over again.'

Elizabeth reached for his hand but suddenly they heard a door bang loudly and a man's voice shouting, '*How much fucking longer?*'

Matthew looked up quickly. 'That's Deniz Pegasus! I'd know that voice anywhere.'

'*I SAID – how much fucking longer do I have to sit here and take this?*'

Elizabeth recognised the voice too. 'God, he gets every-where! What on earth is he doing here?' She had a sudden memory of Pegasus leaning into Ricky at the party, heavy and menacing.

'I think I know,' Matthew said grimly. But before he could explain, DI Watson came with her rapid strides through the biting teeth of the barrier that separated the police from the policed. She clocked the two of them with some surprise and quickly walked over. Her face was slightly flushed, her eyes were sharp and bright, she was in shirtsleeves and strands of blonde hair were slipping loose from their pink fastening.

'Thank you for that, Matthew. You've been very helpful. Hello again, Elizabeth.' She barely glanced at her, but Elizabeth couldn't help surreptitiously glancing down to check that her shirt buttons were all done up.

'I've been waiting a while, now.' Matthew had his I'm-really-a-very-busy-man voice on but DI Watson was looking down at him apparently unmoved. 'Do we have a result?' he asked.

Elizabeth was startled. It was as if they were in some weird kind of talent show: *Who's The Guilty Party?* She was almost expecting a drumroll and Dermot O'Leary to turn up and say to DI Watson, 'C'mon, I have to hurry you, we must have an answer. Who are you sending down?'

The detective stood for a minute coolly appraising the two of them. 'Yes, Matthew, as it happens, I can fill you in. Would you like to follow me?' She turned to walk back through the barrier and Elizabeth found herself saying in a ridiculously small voice, 'Can I come?' DI Watson spun on her heel, her face suddenly animated with an expression that was half amused, half outraged. But Matthew hadn't got where he'd got to without taking the initiative, even when it wasn't his to take. He said firmly, 'Yes, I'd like Elizabeth to come too,' and without waiting for DI Watson to demur, he ushered her ahead of him and through the barrier.

DI Watson took them down the corridor and into the office Elizabeth had visited the day after Ricky's death, the one with the desiccated cactus and sour-tasting tea. DI Watson moved towards the kettle but both Matthew and Elizabeth cried as one, 'No tea, thank you.' She shrugged, sniffed the milk and made herself a cup anyway. DS Rafik poked his sweating head through the door and said, 'Charge sheet just being drawn up, ma'am,' and she nodded as he quickly closed the door behind him. Elizabeth's heart was beating painfully in her chest. A charge sheet! Already! She thought of Hutch, as she'd last seen him, fiddling with his laces, damp patches appearing through his T-shirt, his face creased with panic. She winced.

DI Watson perched on the edge of her desk, stirring her tea.

'The man you identified this morning, Matthew, thank you, goes by the name of Zoltan, although that's not his real name. He's of Turkish descent and he's been employed on and off at the Pegasus building sites for two years. Zoltan means king in Turkish.' DI Watson seemed pleased with her additional facts. She was speaking slowly and carefully. 'But Zoltan's no king. He's a crook, a drug dealer, as you correctly guessed. And you're right – he was at Ricky's party three weeks ago. And yes, he's one of the men who attacked you.'

At this, Elizabeth let out a gasp. She turned impulsively to look at Matthew, whose face was white.

'Zoltan has now confessed to your mugging – perhaps with a little bit of pressure from us concerning his immigration status.' DI Watson allowed herself a small humourless smile. 'But he's a thug for hire. It wasn't his idea. He wasn't the mastermind behind it.'

Elizabeth's mouth was hanging open. DI Watson ignored her, fixing her eyes on Matthew, who was now shaking in his chair. Spots of perspiration appeared on his scalp and threatened to trickle down his creased forehead.

'So it... it was definitely a planned assault? My mugging?' Matthew's voice was thin like a small boy's. 'I was targeted? They were looking for me?'

'Yes, I'm afraid they were.'

'But, hang on... he worked for Pegasus?' Matthew said slowly, colour returning to his cheeks as the realisation began to dawn. 'Wait. Did *Deniz* hire him to beat me up? Why on earth...? What have I ever done to Deniz Pegasus?' He turned to Elizabeth, his expression a mix of outrage and wounded pride. She thought of the Bentley idling outside her flat, the Bruch playing inside, the flowers and the 'just checking you're okay'. She shuddered.

DI Watson poured the remains of her tea into the cactus plant pot. 'Yes. Deniz Pegasus hired him to do the job. Along with two other labourers on his site – all Turkish, by the way. Zoltan has given us their names and we're out looking for them now. But actually, it wasn't Deniz's idea. He wasn't the mastermind either. He was doing it on behalf of someone else. Someone who wanted you roughed up, as a warning. Someone who wanted you punished.'

Matthew's shoulders sagged. Elizabeth felt a new dawning horror. She was on the verge of being sick; she couldn't swallow.

DI Watson put a gentle hand on Matthew's shoulder. 'We have Deniz Pegasus here. We brought him in this morning. He was initially very resistant. He accused us of taking our eye off the ball with this mugging inquiry, instead of finding out who or what killed his best friend, Ricky Clough. But once he knew we had Zoltan in custody – we caught him last night trying to get on a flight to Turkey – his blustering all fell apart. He was in fact quite quick, then, to point the finger of blame elsewhere.'

'At Ricky?' Elizabeth whispered. Matthew turned to her in astonishment and then slowly back to the detective, his own mouth dropping open.

'Yes, that's right. I'm afraid Ricky Clough ordered your mugging, Matthew. He got Deniz Pegasus – his best mate, his enforcer – to sort it out for him. He wanted you punished for cancelling his show. And for hiring Hutch to make a new show. He couldn't bear to hear there was a new kid on the block. He told Deniz it was a total betrayal. He'd worked for your network all his life. In his book, he'd been loyal. But he didn't think you'd been loyal to him.'

Elizabeth turned that word 'betrayal' over and over in her head. The word Lorna had used. The word she'd used when confronting Hutch this morning in his flat. The word Lola had used to accuse her in the café.

'That's why Ricky came to see you in hospital the day after the mugging.' DI Watson went on. 'He'd heard from your wife that you could remember quite a lot of detail about your attackers. He wanted to check out whether or not you'd remembered Zoltan from his party.'

'But I didn't,' Matthew said bitterly. 'Or at least, not until Ricky brought it up again over lunch last Tuesday.' He looked up at DI Watson. 'God! Was Ricky trying to make me remember him? Zoltan? At lunch? Did he *want* me to work it out?'

'I'm not sure. I don't think we'll ever know.' DI Watson stood up. 'Ricky was a complicated guy – you two know that better than anyone else. He'd got away with the mugging. No one suspected him. Or Pegasus. But in a way, that sort of defeated the point. I think it's possible he did want you to work it out. He did want you to know.'

Elizabeth's head, now in her hands, was reeling with images: of a laughing, bicycling Ricky eating an ice cream; Ricky struggling down the street with an enormous white cock; Ricky winking saucily at the camera, holding up a satin make-up bag; Ricky in his yellow underpants, standing on a table;

Ricky doing up his flies in his dressing room; Ricky dancing with her on a moonlit lawn. Ricky! Crazy, complicated Ricky. Crazier than she'd ever realised. What was it Lola had said? Unhinged. Definitely unhinged.

DI Watson opened the door. 'I'm sorry, but I have some other urgent things to deal with. Matthew, we can organise a car to take you home now if you'd like?' Matthew shook his head. He had plans far more comforting than being taken home to his disapproving wife in the back of a police Ford Fiesta.

'Well, we'll be in touch. Elizabeth – you should go home too.'

'I was going to wait for Hutch. Can I wait? I mean, until there's news?'

'Go home.' DI Watson was firm. She more or less pushed Elizabeth out the door and down the corridor. Matthew took her arm and they trailed together back to the main front door.

'I'm so sorry, Matthew,' Elizabeth said. 'I just can't believe it.'

'I can. It didn't occur to me at the time, of course. But now? Well, actually, it doesn't feel that strange. Ricky had gone off the rails, Lizzie, we all knew it. We kept excusing him. But his behaviour wasn't normal. I should've clamped down on him sooner.'

'We all should. We're all to blame. I don't know why we let him get away with it. It was coercive behaviour. It was harassment. Everything about it was wrong. We thought he was a genius, but he was just a bully.'

Matthew kissed her affectionately on the cheek. He opened the main door to the street and the bright May sun blinded them momentarily. 'Let's talk about Hutch on Monday, yes? I mean, about what we should do.'

Matthew stood propping the door open with one foot and Elizabeth wondered if it was the sudden burst of light that was making her dizzy. 'I mean, we have to be fair here. Almost everyone else is doing it. Look at what we let Ricky get away with! It's just the difference between getting caught and not. Obviously it'll be hard to keep out of the press, if there are charges against Hutch. The family show we want him to make may have to be shelved for a bit. But I see no reason why we can't start talking again, once it's all died down, if he does the right sort of confessional interview. Kev can sort him out.'

Elizabeth leaned weakly against the door. When it's all died down? DIED down? What on earth was her boss thinking? How on earth would Hutch survive a murder charge? Perhaps the madness was catching. Perhaps they were all off their rockers – she knew that was what DI Watson thought. But Matthew was still talking. As if the worst thing in the world hadn't actually happened.

'Thanks for being there today for me.' (He seemed to have failed to remember she was actually there for someone else – that it was entirely an accident of fate that she was there for him – but she said nothing, since nothing was making any sense.) 'I really appreciate it. God knows what my wife will say when I tell her. It will confirm all her worst suspicions about television. See you on Monday.' And with that, Elizabeth's boss swept down the steps and off to the soothing embrace of his undemanding mistress.

It was as Elizabeth turned to go back inside, in defiance of

DI Watson, that she noticed her. She was standing across the street, outside the tube station. Her hair was blowing softly in the wind and slightly obscured her face, but Elizabeth recognised the dancer's poise, the slim legs encased in long suede boots, the cream belted mac. She seemed to be waiting for someone; she paced about a bit, and then stopped.

Elizabeth froze. What on earth was Lorna doing here?

Chapter Sixteen

Elizabeth ran towards her, just as she had started walking back into the deep shadows of the tube entrance.

'Lorna! Wait!' Elizabeth arrived panting at her side. Lorna was caught off balance. She frowned and her blue eyes moved from Elizabeth's face, red from running, to the police station framed behind her, and then back again.

'It's me! Elizabeth.'

'Yes, I know.' Lorna regained her composure. 'I'm just surprised to see you here. At the police station. Is that where you've been?'

Elizabeth nodded. 'They've got Hutch.'

'They've got...? Oh God, no.' Lorna closed her eyes and seemed to sway.

'Listen, Lorna, you don't fancy a drink, do you? I mean, a proper drink? I don't know what to do with myself. I don't know where to go...' Elizabeth had given up caring how desperate she sounded. She really, really, wanted a drink.

'But where...?' Lorna looked around dubiously.

'Anywhere that sells alcohol. Look – there's one over there. The Green Man. It'll be grotty, but it's bound to sell vodka.'

Lorna looked momentarily horrified but Elizabeth took her firmly by the arm and led her across the street. The saloon bar smelt of stale beer and sweat. Three or four men were standing nursing pints, fat forearms resting on the bar, engrossed in a football game up on a screen. A young couple with backpacks were sitting at a corner table, bent over a map. A woman of about fifty was sitting on her own with a glass of wine, confidently meeting the gaze of anyone who looked at her as if to challenge the notion that she ought not to be sitting there alone. Every so often, she muttered to herself and at one point, without asking, the barman refilled her glass. Two other men, both in leather, sat apart, at different tables, avoiding each other's eyes. Elizabeth planted Lorna on a stool in the furthest corner, and then ordered two double vodka and tonics. She carried the glasses to the table and made Lorna take a long gulp of neat vodka after a count of three. They both swallowed and shook their heads in distaste as the spirit burned its way down their throats. 'Okay, now we can have it with tonic.' Elizabeth topped up their glasses. Lorna sighed and leaned back in her seat.

'So. I'm here because of Hutch. But why are you here?'

Lorna took another gulp of vodka and then pulled an envelope out of her bag. She put it in front of her on the table. It was the same envelope that Elizabeth had seen on the table two days before in Surrey. On the front, in Ricky's distinctive black sloping handwriting: '*MRS Lorna Clough, Tetherdown, Maple Lane, Surrey*'. She looked up at Lorna quickly but she was staring straight ahead with a strange unblinking expression.

Eventually, Lorna said slowly, 'The police think Hutch killed my husband? Is that why he's in there?'

'Yes.'

'Strychnine.' Lorna's voice was oddly flat. She took another swig of vodka. 'That's what killed Ricky. They came to see me yesterday – DI Watson and Sergeant Rafik. They'd got the toxicology report. They had to tell me, I'm next of kin. The poison, the strychnine, was in his bloodstream.'

Elizabeth reached for Lorna's hand. 'I'm so, so sorry.'

'I googled it, you know, after they'd left. Strychnine. A lethal dose first of all gives you head and neck spasms, then you get convulsions as the poison begins to work on the nervous system so that you can't breathe or swallow. Then your heart collapses, exhausted from the spasms.' Lorna sounded as if she was reading from a chemical textbook. She'd learned it off by heart. Elizabeth remembered Ricky shuddering on the studio floor beside her, violently gripping her hand. It had seemed so much like a heart attack. But then she'd had no previous experience. She hadn't been there when her dad's heart attacked him.

Lorna nodded at the letter. 'Ricky posted it the day he died. Look at the postmark: 4.25 p.m. Wednesday.' Lorna's eyes had regained some of their animation and two spots of vivid colour appeared on her cheeks, but her lips were bloodless and her voice was a whisper. 'A letter! Not an email. An old-fashioned letter. Like a love letter. Like the ones he used to send me...' Lorna rubbed her forehead. 'I feel so tired, Elizabeth. I've barely slept since Tuesday night. I drove myself to the hospital that night. I know you told me to get someone to drive me, but I couldn't bear to call anyone. I couldn't face it. He was in a private room, on the bed. They left me alone with him and I held his hand. But it was so cold, like steel. His face was already gone. So waxy and yellow. And his mouth was shut – you know how his mouth was always moving? Chewing, talking, smoking. But it was all gone, long gone. It just wasn't my Rick lying there. I left after only a few minutes. I could see how surprised the nurses were. They wanted to hear me weep and wail. Everyone's wanted me to do that. But I can't, Elizabeth. I can't.'

Lorna took up the letter and sat gently tapping it against the table. 'I drove straight back home at dawn to be with the boys. To be there when they woke up. They were so sleepy when they came down. Their hair was all tousled – Rick liked them to keep their hair long, he thought it made them different. More creative, he said. And I realised Josh had grown out of his pyjamas. His limbs seemed so long – he's so tall. Just like Rick.' She faltered. 'Telling them was the hardest bit. They looked so confused, so bewildered. We just sat there, hugging.'

Elizabeth thought of herself, her mum and Vic, curled up on her childhood single bed, sick with shock and grief, each of them wearing one of her dad's old shirts, watching the evening light creep across her bedroom floor, the shadows lengthening and spreading before fading to black.

'I kept wandering round the house, looking at all our stuff. All the junk from our twenty-year marriage. Photos, LPs, Rick's awards. Things the kids were forced to make in pottery classes. I cried, then. I cried for what we once had. As well as for what might've been.' Lorna hung her head. 'I know you were in some ways his professional wife, Elizabeth. I could tell from the way he talked about you that he adored you. I never once suspected he was sleeping with you. But I think he was very hurt that you betrayed him. And that you betrayed him with Hutch. And that Matthew knew all along. Our friend Matthew! Who came to our wedding!'

There it was again. Betrayal. Elizabeth said nothing. What could she say? She was guilty. Guilty as charged. Elizabeth, irreligious as she was, felt a sudden longing for a priest to confess to – someone to offer her three Hail Marys and an absolution. Vodka seemed a poor substitute, but at least it was available. She got another round.

Lorna downed the second glass without being urged. She ran her tongue over her lips. 'Deniz has been around a lot, you know, at home, since Rick died.' Elizabeth nodded, not daring to speak, knowing what she did. 'He's the boys' godfather, of course. And they adore him. I mean, he's always so free with cash and Xbox games, and always turns up in fast cars to take them out. But... there's more to it. He's always wanted me, too. For years, now. He's always made these lewd suggestions, caught me off balance, tried to kiss me. He told me if I ever breathed a word, he'd tell Ricky about the stable boys. Well, I mean there was nothing much to it really – just silly larking around. But Deniz witnessed me kissing one of them once and that was enough. So I never did tell Ricky. And now he's gone... and Deniz is all over me. I don't agree with him on anything: his ideas for the funeral, how we should be dealing with the press, the boys even. He'd become Rick's manager, so he seems to assume he has a right to tell me what to do, to manage me as well.' Lorna swallowed hard. 'You know, I think he reckons he'll have me, too, in the end.'

'Have you – how?' Elizabeth put down her glass, horrified.

'To live with him. Be his wife. Have sex with him. He told me I'd need his "protection". His breath was on my neck, I could smell how sour it was. He put his hand on my waist, he moved it down…' Unconsciously, Lorna rubbed the white skin on her neck as if to remove a stain. Elizabeth thought how revolting it would be to have Deniz Pegasus leering in at you, using grief as a weapon to seduce you.

'You see, Deniz wanted everything Rick had. He had the money, sure, but he wanted the fame, the attention, the celebrity status. He had no idea. He didn't realise how it poisons everything. But Rick knew. In the end, he got it. He knew it was meaningless, it just distorts everything. But fame was like another addiction for Rick. He still couldn't give it up. Even though he knew it didn't make him happy, he couldn't let it go.'

Elizabeth looked again at the envelope, at the thick black ink, the bold handwriting. 'What does it say? The letter from Ricky? Can you tell me?'

Lorna lifted one page of creamy notepaper from the envelope with its blood crimson flap. Ricky's writing covered both sides of the paper, sloping down the page, filling more space than was strictly necessary.

'I brought it here to show DI Watson. But I lost courage. I was about to go back home when you found me. I just don't know what Ricky meant me to do with it. But actually, I'd like you to read it. I want to hear what you think. Of course, it's a private letter. I think it's meant only for me. But I just wonder…'

Elizabeth gently took the sheet of paper from her.

My darling Lorna,

I miss you and the boys. More than you will ever know.

My show has been cancelled. That ignorant bastard Matthew finally had the courage to tell me, today, at lunch. But I've known for weeks. The morons, thinking they could keep it secret. I know they've all been plotting against me.

No one knows how to run things properly any more. No one understands television like I do. No one trusts their instincts any more. It's all about fucking focus groups and audience numbers. Although God help them if they ever had to spend any real time with the people they're making the bloody programmes for.

But I know my fans. I know how to speak to them, what they're thinking. The top brass just didn't like how powerful I'd got. They'd rather have me off the air than deal with my power.

And now, even you have lost faith in me, Lorna. My own sweet child bride.

But you know me, babe, I've always done things on my own terms. And that's how I'm going to go. Not on their terms. On my terms.

I've talked to Barty – you can call him.

Don't tell the boys. I don't want them to think their dad did this.

I want them to remember me as a hero. Think of me as your hero, too, babe.

Know that I've never stopped loving you.

Yours always, Rick

Elizabeth read it once, quickly, then again more slowly, her eyes widening, biting her lip. It was so plaintive, so accusatory, so self-deceiving. So Ricky.

'What do you think?' Lorna took the letter from her and folded it up.

'Does he mean... Is he saying...? Lorna! Is it what I think it is?'

'Yes.' Lorna's eyes filled with tears. 'I think he intended to kill himself. Rick couldn't live with failure. You know that, Elizabeth. He couldn't live with not being a big star. It meant everything to him. He told me he was suicidal a few weeks ago – before the party – but I just assumed he was being dramatic, as usual. His moods were so awful, it was hard to tell what was real with Rick. And then of course he was the life and soul at the party, so I thought he was better. I thought the black dog had moved on. I should've got him help – I know I should – but I was so angry with him most of the time.'

'We should all have got him help,' Elizabeth said firmly. 'None of us realised how bad he was. Honestly, Lorna, we just thought it was part and parcel of being Ricky. You know, crazy, complicated Ricky.'

'Yes. I fell in love with a crazy guy. A crazy, funny guy. But I didn't fall in love with a bully. And that's what he'd become, Elizabeth. I'd become scared of him. The boys were scared of him. His mood swings were so violent. I never knew where I was with him.'

Elizabeth nodded. None of them had known where they were with Ricky. He'd put himself beyond the pale and had assumed his power would protect him. Instead of calling him out, they'd all just gone along with it. Matthew had confronted him only after it was clear the audience themselves were getting tired of him. Elizabeth was very struck by how far they'd all gone along with Ricky's own narrative of the way things were.

But the letter! Surely this was now the thing that could save Hutch? 'Lorna, don't you think you should show the letter to the police?'

Lorna sighed but she said nothing. Elizabeth felt a sudden rush of impatience at her hesitation. She imagined Hutch, head bowed, sitting in one of those police interview rooms she'd seen on television, where the iron tables are bolted to the floor.

She stood up. 'I'll come with you, Lorna. Let's go together.'

She held out her hand and Lorna slowly gathered her things. It was more than Elizabeth could do to stop herself grabbing her and running out the door and down the street. She couldn't help wondering how Ricky, impatient at the best of times, had dealt with this slow grace of Lorna's, this cool calmness, this total lack of animation. It was so opposite to everything he was. How odd that they had ever found solace in one another... Elizabeth felt that she still had much to learn about the business of being a couple.

PC Ginger gave Elizabeth a cheery wave as she steered Lorna to the blue plastic chairs. She was beginning to feel very much at home in the waiting area of Paddington Police Station. It was time for the second half of the show. The climax.

'Could you please let DI Watson know that Lorna Clough and Elizabeth Place are here to see her?'

PC Ginger immediately picked up the phone. They didn't

have to wait long. DI Watson came half running through the barrier. She ignored Elizabeth.

'Lorna!' She gently lifted her by her elbow. 'What are you doing here? Are you alright?'

Lorna did seem to stagger slightly. Elizabeth jumped up to offer more support.

'Thank you. I feel a bit light-headed.'

'Come.' DI Watson steered Lorna skilfully through the barrier, down the corridor and back into her office. Elizabeth tripped along behind them, carrying Lorna's bag and coat.

'Well, here you are again, Elizabeth,' DI Watson said drily. 'Tea?'

This time Elizabeth said, 'Oh, yes, please.'

'Can I get you something else, Lorna? I think we could probably rustle up some toast?' Lorna shook her head but Elizabeth said, 'That would be lovely.' DI Watson raised her eyebrows but picked up the phone and ordered some toast.

'We met outside,' Elizabeth explained. 'It's funny, if you loiter for long enough around a police station on a Saturday afternoon, you seem to bump into quite a few people you know really well.'

DI Watson ignored this. She sloshed some water and milk into two cups. She added a paper finger of sugar to one and handed it to Lorna. 'Drink!' she said imperiously. Lorna drank obediently. A policewoman in uniform came in with a paper plate of warm white buttered toast. Elizabeth ate. After a few moments' silence, Lorna reached slowly into her bag and pulled out the letter. She lay it on the desk in front of DI Watson: *MRS Lorna Clough*… DI Watson glanced at it and then sat on the edge of the desk, lightly swinging one leg. Waiting.

Lorna took a deep breath. 'You know, Deniz Pegasus came round after Rick died. Round to our house. He kept saying it wasn't right, Rick dying like that, it didn't make sense. Well, of course, it didn't. But then he kept going on and on about Rick having enemies. People who wanted to bring him down, as Deniz put it. People who wanted to take everything away from him.' A delicate blush spread over Lorna's very pale face. 'I wondered if he meant me... I'd asked Rick for a divorce. A week ago.' She looked up quickly at DI Watson, whose face registered nothing. 'I'd assumed Rick had told Deniz. He was very upset, at the time.'

'Upset how?'

'Well, wild really. Furious. He lay on the kitchen floor and ranted at me. He accused me of all sorts of things: affairs with God knows who, moving in my parents to block him out, turning the boys against him.' Lorna's eyes filled with tears again. 'But he just hadn't been there. For years, really. The boys saw him less and less. I'd just had enough. I wanted a clean break. There were so many stories about his affairs. All the other women. I just wasn't going to be a doormat any more.' She wiped her eyes. 'But then I realised Deniz wasn't talking about the divorce. He was talking about Rick losing his shows, about him not being able to get work. He said something about Matthew not returning Rick's calls. And then he said something about me being too close to Matthew. It was so ridiculous! I mean, Matthew's been a good friend to me, for sure. I've asked for his advice a lot during the bad times but that's all he is, a good friend. But Deniz seemed to be jealous of him. I think maybe he wound up Ricky with talk of me and Matthew being close.' She looked up at DI Watson earnestly, whose eyes were fixed on her with an X-ray intensity. Elizabeth dropped her toast on to her plate, no longer able to swallow.

'And then Deniz went on and on about Hutch. Said he and Rick were "on to him". That he was behind it all. It didn't really make any sense to me. I mean, we knew Hutch and his wife, Sue. We've had dinner together several times. Sue's helped out with my horse shows and they both came to the party. Rick told me their marriage was in trouble, but Sue had never said anything and to be honest, they seemed happy enough to me.'

Elizabeth didn't dare look up for fear of catching DI Watson's eye.

'I said to Deniz, "but Hutch is a friend of ours!" And he said, "No, Rick just keeps his enemies close."' Lorna shrugged. 'And then I asked Elizabeth to come and see me in Surrey. And well, she confirmed it, didn't you, Elizabeth? She confirmed they were making a new show with Hutch. And then I realised that Rick must've known all along! I knew how much he would've hated it. I mean, we've been out with Hutch and his wife in the last few weeks and all the time he was working on this rival show! And he never said anything. And Matthew... He never said anything either – and he came to our party, too!'

Elizabeth very much wished someone would just put her in the spotlight, announce that she was Guilty, Guilty, and that the final curtain would come down. DI Watson, on the other hand, didn't take her eyes off Lorna.

'I mean, Matthew must've commissioned this new show

with Hutch! I'm not surprised Rick thought it all a betrayal. I thought it was a betrayal.' Lorna's voice was very quiet. 'I'm sorry. I should've said all this yesterday, when you came to see me. But I… I suppose I still feel loyal somehow to Rick. To my husband.'

'You know,' DI Watson was surprisingly gentle, 'the one thing I've learned about Ricky Clough since Wednesday night is that somehow he drew the most extraordinary loyalty from people.'

Elizabeth thought both that this was true and also no excuse. They'd covered for Ricky and liked to call it loyalty, but in the end, she felt, they'd covered for him mainly because they were scared of him.

But Lorna looked up gratefully, as if to say, you see! You see why I married him! 'Rick wrote me this letter. He posted it the day he died and I received it the day after. Funnily enough, I'd tried to call him on the day of the recording, the day he died. But he didn't pick up. We didn't usually speak when he was recording the show and I knew he never had his mobile on the set. But, well… I wish I'd made more effort, that day.' Lorna bent her head, and her shoulders shook.

DI Watson laid a hand on her shoulder and said gently, 'What's in the letter?'

Lorna looked up, her face tear-stained. 'I wondered perhaps if you'd found a copy? If he'd left it for anyone else to find? But it's so personal, sending a letter, isn't it? It's not like an email, with all its traces… I know, really, he intended it just for me. He used to write me letters in the beginning. And now, he's done so again. At the end.'

'No, we haven't found a letter. We do have his laptop. But someone deleted everything at 6.30 p.m. the evening he died. His inbox and all his sent items. His history, all his desktop apps. Our IT department has been working to restore it all.' DI Watson frowned momentarily at the apparent slowness of the police technology department.

Lorna sighed. 'I wish in a way you'd found it. Then I wouldn't have to be the one to break his confidence in me. I think he wanted me to know – and he didn't want me to tell anyone else. But well, Elizabeth's read it now. And I think you should read it.' She pushed the letter towards DI Watson, who quickly picked it up, looked closely at the postmark and then pulled out the sheet of paper. Elizabeth watched her face carefully but it was a complete blank. She read it once, turned it over, read it again. Then she folded it and put it back in the envelope.

'I take it you know for certain that this is your husband's handwriting?'

Lorna nodded.

'I recognise it too! I have several notes from Ricky you can compare it with,' Elizabeth added eagerly, but DI Watson didn't even glance at her.

'Who's Barty?'

'He's our lawyer. I did call him yesterday. Rick apparently went to see him last week to make sure his will was in order. Barty said everything's been left to me and the boys. Once he heard about his death, he assumed Rick had received some kind of health warning or been to see a doctor and that was why he'd gone to see him. That he'd wanted to make sure everything was in order. It seems Rick had never told him about me asking for a divorce. Barty had no idea.'

DI Watson sat still, watching Lorna, who let out a sob. 'Can we keep the letter, please? Of course, you'll have it back – I realise it's precious. But for the time being, we need to keep it.'

Lorna pushed the envelope towards DI Watson. 'I don't really want it. I don't want to put it with all the other letters he sent me. Those were love letters. I've got them tied up with a ribbon in my bedside drawer. But this? This feels like another bit of poison. It's another bit of madness. How could he do it? Abandon our boys rather than face his demons?' Lorna looked wretched. 'He says don't tell them… but how can I stop them finding out? Of course they'll know! I'll have to try to help them forgive him. To help them understand him, although God knows, I hardly understand him myself!'

'What are your plans, now? Can we help you in any way?'

Lorna picked up her bag. 'I want to go home. I've got to be with the boys. They want to make a playlist of all Rick's favourite music. We're going to do it together – this evening. A soundtrack for all our photos. The good times.' She stood up and looked at Elizabeth and then she turned to face DI Watson. 'I saw Hutch, here. When I was hesitating outside – I saw him coming in here, with you.'

DI Watson's expression was opaque. Lorna bit her lip. 'I just couldn't have lived with myself. I had to say something. Rick almost certainly didn't want me to, but I can't go along with it. I realise now that Rick hated Hutch. For what he thought Hutch had taken away from him.' She looked at DI Watson very directly, her eyes brimming with tears. Then she turned back to Elizabeth and said softly. 'But I don't think Hutch took away his life. He didn't do that.'

It was Elizabeth's turn to dissolve into tears. She flung her arms around Lorna and DI Watson was left standing between two apparently strong women, both of whom appeared to be crying helplessly for men who, Karen Watson felt, were entirely unworthy of anyone's tears. It was more than she could do to control her impatience. But professional as ever, she produced tissues and soothing words and even managed at one point to rub Lorna's back. After what she regarded as a decent interval, she said she would organise a car to take Lorna back to Surrey and offered to walk her to the door.

To Elizabeth she said, tersely, 'Wait here for my return. I'm not done with you yet.'

Chapter Seventeen

When DI Watson stalked back into her office a few minutes later, she caught Elizabeth prowling furtively around the room.

'Oh, come on! I'm a detective! You think I'd leave evidence lying around?' Her expression was stern but her eyes were bright and Elizabeth felt she detected in them a hint of amusement.

She shrugged apologetically. 'Well, before I was made ringmaster of the circus, I made proper documentaries. And no journalist worth their salt would sit in a detective's office and not have a bit of a snoop.'

'And what have you learned?' DI Watson sat back in her chair and stretched out her legs.

'You have some really revolting juices in your fridge. Broccoli and kale? Seriously?'

DI Watson laughed, a genuinely uncomplicated laugh that rumbled up from deep inside her. Elizabeth was beginning to like DI Karen Watson very much indeed. If only she would now release her lover and apologise and say it was all a terrible mistake, she thought there was a chance they might even be able to go and have a drink together. She even thought in the circumstances she might be willing to tackle a spinach and ginger smoothie. Maybe even agree to go and watch some netball. But DI Watson turned to look at her appraisingly and she wilted slightly under the new scrutiny.

'Is Hutch okay?' she asked pathetically.

'Tell me, Elizabeth, just how well do you know Harry Hutchinson?'

'Well, I've been sleeping with him, on and off, for nine months. But I've begun to realise there are probably an awful lot of things I don't know about him.'

'He and Ricky Clough shared a coke dealer. Did you know that?'

Elizabeth looked at her flabbergasted. 'Hutch? And Ricky? Shared a coke dealer? Are you sure?'

'You didn't know?'

Elizabeth shook her head numbly.

'So the reason you went to Hutch's flat this morning was not so that you could take cocaine together?'

Elizabeth shook her head again. But thoughts of the wine glass, the smeared coffee-table top, the rolled-up note, made her head swim. How stupidly blind she'd been these last few months! 'He shared a dealer with Ricky? I mean, I know you're a detective – but really?'

'Yes. That's why Hutch went to the pub on Tuesday night. He went to get cocaine from his dealer – and Ricky was in there.'

Elizabeth wondered about this. Hutch had taken cocaine before he came to see her? She remembered him striding into her sitting room, taking off her T-shirt, pulling down her jeans, urgent, breathless, the spaghetti uneaten in the pan. How they'd fucked, once, twice, three times – Elizabeth feeling entirely flattered by his desire. She gave herself a small shake and tried to concentrate on what DI Watson was telling her. 'So Hutch didn't plan to meet Ricky that night?'

'No. I believe in fact he was on his way to supper with you?' DI Watson raised a questioning eyebrow and Elizabeth nodded. 'It would seem that Ricky, on the other hand, *did* plan to meet Hutch in the pub that night. He knew Hutch was going to be in there. Their dealer had told him so.'

'Okay,' Elizabeth said, comprehending nothing.

'He needed Hutch's fingerprints, you see. On one particular plate of food from Culone's restaurant – the food that was going to be laced with strychnine. That Ricky himself would eat. The dish that would kill him.'

Elizabeth began to shiver. She gripped the sides of her chair.

'Ricky was blackmailing Hutch. Had been for a while. We have the texts. Ricky wiped everything on his computers, but not his mobile phone – because he wanted us to see the texts, I presume. And those texts suggest that Hutch had a motive for killing him. Ricky was threatening to reveal Hutch's coke habit, to Matthew and to the press. Once that came out, as you know, it would stop Hutch from working on the sort of big family shows you were planning with him. The sorts of shows that Ricky himself had made a career and a fortune from.' DI Watson stared at her. 'And Ricky was also threatening to tell Hutch's wife about the affair with you, Elizabeth.'

Elizabeth hung her head. Oh, Hutch! Why hadn't he told her? Why hadn't he lain down with his head on her shoulder and told her everything, in that lovely low mellow tone his voice always had after sex? Why hadn't he trusted her? Elizabeth bit her lip. She'd wondered over the last few days how well she really knew Hutch and now she had her answer. He had a cocaine habit, and she hadn't noticed. Despite telling her over and over that his marriage was a sham, he was so worried about his wife finding out about his affair he'd allowed himself to be blackmailed.

'One thing about this case always bothered me,' DI Watson mused. 'The thing that several of your cameramen mentioned in their interviews, the thing they all heard Ricky say on talkback when his microphone was on before the start of the show: "Let's make this a show to remember." It seemed so odd; so, well, *knowing*… How could he possibly have known that this would be a show to remember?'

'Yes, but you can't read too much into that. It's just a TV thing!' Elizabeth blinked her tears away. 'It's just a saying; people say it just before they do a show. It's like "break a leg".'

DI Watson looked at her pensively. 'I don't claim to know Ricky Clough better than you, but I think over the last few months he'd become very paranoid. And none of you really noticed. I don't know much about television, your world, but I think that sort of mania can be overlooked by people in your industry, regarded as just a symptom of a kind of comic genius. And you're all so frenetic, so excitable – I guess that sort of extreme behaviour doesn't look that unusual.'

Elizabeth looked at her wordless, ashamed.

'It's not an accusation, Elizabeth. It's an observation. But Ricky Clough was also spiteful and a bully. He was capable of violence. Did you know he was expelled from school for beating up another kid?'

Elizabeth didn't.

'Yes, he and Pegasus. Both expelled. The kid had his kneecaps smashed. Nasty. The school report said Ricky had a terrible temper – he'd been warned several times about bullying – and I don't think as a grown-up he'd ever learned to control it. God knows how his wife put up with it for so long! God knows why any of you put up with it…'

DI Watson went on, her voice steady and low. 'Matthew told Ricky at lunch the day before he died that he was cancelling his shows. Ricky admits that in his letter. Matthew also confirmed that Hutch's new show, the one you were producing, was destined to replace it. It was devastating news for Ricky.'

Elizabeth's hand covered her mouth.

'I don't think Ricky Clough could face a life not being in the spotlight. But he decided if he was going to go down, then he was also going to bring down the man he thought was stealing the limelight from him. The man who, to compound it all, was also sleeping with you, his long-term producer.'

'What do you mean?' Elizabeth whispered. God, was Hutch still not off the hook?

'I believe Ricky Clough intended to kill himself. I think he'd been planning it for weeks; he was just waiting for his moment. And Matthew unwittingly gave him the moment when he delivered the final piece of bad news, the day before the studio recording. And being an egotist and an exhibitionist, Ricky decided to make his suicide as public as he could, in his own studio, recording one last show.'

DI Watson stood up, as if addressing a jury. 'And because he was also a bully and a brute, Ricky decided to implicate someone else in his death. He would point a finger of blame beyond the grave. He wanted someone else to suffer, to be accused of his death, even if only for the short term – but, he reckoned, long enough for the stain to linger. Long enough to ruin a career. He decided he would make sure that it looked like Hutch was responsible. He found out from his dealer that Hutch was going to their pub rendezvous. He invited the production team to meet him there. He persuaded Zander to bring the food from the restaurant to the pub. He made sure Hutch fingered the dish he'd selected. He made Zander cover them with clingfilm and then in the studio the next day, at some point, Ricky himself put the strychnine in the dish Hutch had handled.'

Elizabeth stared at DI Watson. She was desperately trying to process her words, but her head was spinning.

'Our lab tests were able to pinpoint the poisoned dish. It was only half eaten. Ricky made sure the dose was heavy so that it would definitely kill him, but he also needed to leave some of it behind as evidence. And he did well. The evidence against Hutch all stacked up. His fingerprints were on the poisoned plate. He hated Ricky, who was blackmailing him. They'd also been embroiled in this row over the footballer Marcus McManus and his wife. And a few people, including Lola, had told me that they didn't think Hutch had ever recovered from his humiliation at the hands of Ricky on *Bonkers*.'

Hutch! Ricky! Elizabeth held on to the arms of her chair.

'So by this morning the evidence all pointed very clearly

to Hutch and we decided to arrest him. But we also had the Pegasus line of inquiry to pursue – we wanted to get to the bottom of Matthew's assault. It always felt too coincidental to me – Ricky's boss beaten up, apparently with no motive, just a week or so ago.' DI Watson looked pensively at Elizabeth. 'And I mentioned to you and Lola on Thursday that we knew someone had been on Ricky's laptop on the night he died, and deleted a lot of recent stuff. So we've been wanting to get into his computer, have a look at his internet history. And we were waiting to get to some CCTV camera footage, because yesterday we managed to pinpoint where the poison had been purchased and when.' DI Watson allowed herself a small smile of triumph.

Elizabeth's untouched tea sat cooling, a film of sour milk yellowing on its surface.

'Sure enough, the CCTV cameras caught Ricky's car, the afternoon of his lunch with your boss.'

'The afternoon he missed our production meeting.'

'That's right. We got footage of him outside a hardware store in Acton. He was wearing a baseball cap. No one in the store recognised him. And he used cash. He did what he could to cover his traces.' DI Watson smiled to herself. 'But once we finally got into his computers, we discovered that over the course of the last few weeks he'd spent quite some time on websites researching poisons and their effects. He wanted something that would be visual and dramatic. It was going to be on camera, people would be watching. He needed it to be deadly. And he needed the timing to be precise.'

Precise. On camera. Dramatic. Visual. Of course, Elizabeth

thought, he wanted it to be public. He wanted his final moment to be in the spotlight, the place he was happiest.

'Ricky intended to implicate Hutch in his death all along, but I'm not sure Pegasus was in the loop. Ricky just got him to believe that there was enough bad blood between them so that once the forensic evidence turned up, Pegasus would add his voice to the fact that Hutch had enough reason to kill him. He would be entirely convinced. Ricky was spinning a web and he made sure everyone close to him gradually got entangled. And Deniz Pegasus, now very ready to tell all, has said that he and Ricky intended to finish off Hutch's TV career, whatever it took.'

A silence fell between them, DI Watson rolling her neck, loosening her shoulders. They sat for a while, the detective watching Elizabeth closely as she struggled to make sense of it.

'I realise this is all quite hard to take in.'

'I don't know what to think. I don't know what to do.' Elizabeth's voice was unnaturally high. She felt like screaming.

'Why do anything? Why not just go home? Rest. Eat. Do you have someone you can call?'

Elizabeth thought for a moment about her empty flat and shuddered. She didn't want to leave. She wanted to curl up under DI Watson's desk and stay there forever. But the detective was standing up.

'Look, can I still wait for Hutch? I really want to see him. I want to hear it from him. I can't leave without speaking to him!' Her voice faltered. She desperately wanted to see that lopsided smile, those amused eyes, those lips telling her that it was all a terrible mistake, his arms spread wide, his chest broad and welcoming.

'You can't wait here. Go home and let him call you.'

Elizabeth registered the slightly scolding tone. But you don't understand, she wanted to say to that straight back, as it strode ahead of her to the dismal reception, things are not always so black and white, right and wrong. Sometimes, it's messy, muddled, mixed-up; the pieces don't always neatly fit together, two halves don't always match perfectly to make one whole. Quite often there are torn threads floating free, waiting to snag you.

At the front desk, she said goodbye to Karen Watson, a woman who dealt only with certain truths and incontrovertible evidence. She found herself saying in a shy way, 'Perhaps we could meet up – um, for a drink or something – a Diet Coke? I mean, when this is all over?'

She was rewarded with a big, unambiguous smile. 'Yes, I'd like that. I'll get in touch.'

Karen Watson pumped her hand firmly. 'Don't worry, Elizabeth – I know where to find you.'

Chapter Eighteen

For the third time that afternoon, Elizabeth found herself walking reluctantly out of Paddington Green Police Station. Who'd have thought she'd find a police station the most comforting place to hang about on an otherwise bright May Saturday afternoon? She took once last glance at the unwelcoming reception area with its yellowing walls, plastic seats and civic notices. It wasn't really that different from the civic register office where she almost got married a year ago. Another May day.

Just as she opened the door to face the sunshine, she heard a familiar voice saying 'Where do I sign?' She turned quickly and there was Hutch, at the desk, with DS Rafik beside him. He signed something and then turned around to face her. He stopped in his tracks. He looked shrunken and crumpled, his face was pale and a shadow already forming on his jawline and his lips. Elizabeth smiled at him. She wanted to hold him, she even held out her hands. But his face was frozen, there was no returning smile, he didn't move. Elizabeth moved impulsively towards him, as if flying, her arms outstretched, her face full of smiles and tears. Her foot caught the plastic chairs as she blindly ran and she stumbled slightly, reaching for his strong grip, as she had so often in the past. But there was no strength or steadiness there; this time, his hand was limp and helpless in hers. They both breathed deeply, heads bowed, almost touching.

'Hutch! Hutch!' she whispered, her voice full of urgency, forcing him to look at her. 'Why didn't you tell me? Why? Why so many secrets?'

His eyes were weary and half closed. 'Have they told you everything?'

Elizabeth nodded. His voice was slow and hopeless. 'I thought you wouldn't want to work with me, Elizabeth. I thought we'd lose the show. All you ever did was talk about how worried you were every time you saw Ricky, about whether he'd be drunk or high – what mood he'd be in. I thought you'd feel the same about me, if I told you. You wouldn't trust me to do the job properly.'

Elizabeth's gaze was unforgiving. There was no more looking away. 'What happened last night? In the flat?'

He shrugged. 'She was a PR girl for one of the guests on the show. I don't know why I brought her back to the flat. She came on to me really strong. She had some coke… I don't know, Elizabeth, I guess I'm just weak.'

She understood that in confessing to weakness, Hutch was hoping to be excused. She realised that he hoped he might deflect any more confrontation by admitting to be what she least wanted him to be. She was infuriated by him.

'What, and you thought you'd have a bit of that? Another

sweet from the sweet shop? You thought you could have it all?' She flushed red with the force of her feelings. 'It's greed, Hutch. That's all it is. That's what a little bit of fame does. Of course, you get it all offered on a platter. It's too easy! But the clever thing is to say no. You have to resist all that shit. And if you don't care enough about what I think, let me point out that's what your fans want from you as well. They want you to be a hero. They don't want their heroes to be the sort of people who don't pay their taxes or who fuck anything that moves, or do drugs… That stuff's all too easy. They want you to be better than that.'

Hutch winced. His whole body seemed to sag, his chest caved, his shoulders hunched.

'I thought we had a future, Hutch…' Her eyes spilled with tears. 'You made me feel like we had a future. You told me your marriage was over. I believed you. But you were just taking what you could get, weren't you? From me, as well? For God's sake, Hutch! You were just like Ricky!'

She turned away from him, tears running freely down her cheeks. Hutch reached out for her, but she shrugged him off. 'What's going to happen?' she asked in a small voice.

Hutch misunderstood her. 'They're charging me with possession. They searched the flat and found a stash. But it's a first offence. I think it'll be just be a caution and a fine. But I'll have a criminal record.' His voice was full of self-pity and Elizabeth cringed. But she suddenly realised what Matthew had been talking about. He'd known about the coke dealer, of course! He'd known that Hutch was using the same dealer as Ricky, and that the police would have to do something about it. Matthew hadn't known that Hutch was facing a murder charge. He couldn't have known. When he left her at the station door, he was simply talking about how they would deal with Hutch once it was known he had a rap for cocaine.

'I know the future's ruined. I know I can't do the show, now. With you,' he said.

The show! Again! As if she cared about the show! But that was the ruined future he was thinking about. His professional future. Not their future as a couple, maybe as future parents. Not that ruined future.

'So Ricky was blackmailing you – about me?' She was going to force him to address her, them, their relationship.

His eyes suddenly blazed. 'Christ, Elizabeth! You have no idea how fucking awful it was. Threatening to tell Sue.' Bang. Crash. There was her name again. 'I just tried to keep ignoring it. Ricky and I kept on meeting in public as if nothing was going on, pretending like we're mates. Even that night in the pub! But the thought of Sue finding out…' Elizabeth flinched and Hutch went on quickly. 'I mean, finding out like that through Ricky Clough! It was unthinkable.'

Unthinkable. She registered the word. He couldn't bear the thought of his wife finding out like that. Nor could he tell her himself. It was all unthinkable.

'None of this needs to be your mess, Elizabeth. You don't owe me anything. We're not married. You can distance yourself from it all. You don't have to be hurt by any of this.'

'I don't have to be HURT?' She was shouting now. 'You

think I'm not going to be hurt by this? Really? Hutch, we've been sleeping together for months! I thought we'd be together. How can you *possibly* say I won't be hurt by it?'

PC Ginger was looking over at them, excited and curious. And Hutch looked at her, as if groping his way towards a previously unseen light. But then, behind her, Elizabeth heard the front door bang open and running steps. Someone dashed past her, not registering her, almost knocking her aside, crying Hutch's name. Elizabeth unconsciously stepped aside and couldn't help but watch. Later, much later, during endless, sleepless nights, the scene played over and over in her mind in slow motion. The shape materialised into a woman with blonde hair wearing a long red raincoat that fanned out around her like a cape. She threw herself at Hutch. Over her shoulder, as she rushed to embrace him, Elizabeth saw his face lighten with relief as he murmured 'Sue! Sue! Thank God!' They stood hugging, connected; their tears and sighs merging, their bodies locking into old familiar positions: her arm around his neck, his hand gripping her coat as if hanging on for dear life, their heads close together. They were utterly united, sharing each other's heartbeats. Hutch had eyes only for his wife and Elizabeth stood a fraction longer, willing him to look once more at her. But he didn't. He wouldn't.

Backing away, still barely able to tear her gaze from the embracing couple, Elizabeth clenched her fists in her pockets. She felt a sensation rise from the soles of her feet and gurgle its way up through her stomach. She didn't always know herself well, but she recognised this feeling. It was relief. She was free. She was under no obligation. She could take matters into her own hands, she could make her own decisions. She owed him nothing.

She turned on her heel and ran out into the bright May afternoon, alone.

Chapter Nineteen

Four weeks later

Elizabeth was due to meet Matthew at 10 a.m. She'd woken late, feeling exhausted. Her limbs felt like lead; simply lifting one leg felt like a supremely challenging exercise. Her head was swimming uncomfortably and her gut heaved at the prospect of movement. She couldn't drag herself out of bed. She had to have two stale dry biscuits with her cup of tea, which she drank without sugar or milk. It was 9.30 by the time she left, which left her little time for crossing town, north to west, at the tail-end of the rush hour. She drove fast down the Euston Road, weaving in and out of traffic, flashing the Uber drivers crawling along looking at their sat navs, glaring back at the black cab drivers who resented her lane hopping. She crept past Marylebone Town Hall, silent and shrouded in scaffolding, its stone face obscured, but then the jam miraculously cleared and she felt a sense of freedom as she accelerated into the open space and sailed up and over the Westway. She screeched to a halt outside the network's offices at 10.15 and left her car parked jauntily half in and half out of Matthew's private parking space.

Elizabeth had called her boss to ask for this meeting as

soon as she'd heard he'd returned from his three-week break in Italy. They hadn't been in the same room since that day in the police station four weeks ago. As she stumbled through the door, bumping into the table, and dropping the contents of her bag on the floor, she realised how pleased she was to see him again. She ran to give him a hug, crushing lipsticks and pens in her wake.

'Oh my GOD!' she cried. 'How are you? How was your break?'

Matthew shrugged. 'We went to Santa Maria di Castellabate, a village on the Naples coast – a drive away from Pompeii and Paestum. My wife suggested it. She thought some Roman ruins would restore me. I needed to get away, you know, after all the revelations. And the shock of finding out that one of my closest friends had wanted my skull bashed in.' He sat heavily on the leather sofa.

'I'd thought we'd maybe go to St Lucia, or Necker – you know, one of those places where they have guards with guns at the gates of your hotel, to keep out the savages. But my wife said I was being paranoid. The cultural hotspots of Europe would do me fine, she said. I got a bit bored, to be honest. I suppose that's good for me.' Matthew pulled a face and Elizabeth laughed, despite herself. He looked at her gratefully and then said nervously, 'You seem pale, Lizzie. Are you okay? I mean, after everything?' In that moment, Elizabeth understood, finally and certainly, that he knew. She nodded, but she couldn't speak.

'My wife thought I should try mindfulness. Have you ever tried it? God, it's horrible! But I sat in the village square café every morning practising this deep breathing, feeling like shit. Then one day this old Italian, who was drinking grenadine and smoking a gauloise, came running over to my table, shouting at me, '*Signore! Signore! E il tou coure?*' and before I could stop him, bent over me and started giving me mouth-to-mouth! Christ, his breath stank!'

Elizabeth laughed again, a spontaneous snort of derision, which restored colour to her cheeks and a brightness to her eyes. Matthew smiled back at her.

'Other than that, Italy was uneventful. The heavy breathing made me dizzy and anyway, I didn't like emptying my mind since it just meant that there was more room for the monsters to roam. Turkish-looking monsters with wooden clubs, and a manic, laughing clown. I can't stop thinking about him.' Matthew bit his lip.

'Has DI Watson told you when the trial will be? For Pegasus and the muggers?'

'Not for six months or so, I don't think. I've been able to identify the other two, though. They were also employed on the Pegasus building sites. The police have found some transfers into a bank in Turkey, issued from an account they traced back to him – to Ricky. Apparently, mugging me commanded quite high fees.'

'Well, that's comforting,' said Elizabeth. Then after a pause she asked curiously, 'Like, how much?'

'Five grand apiece.'

'Not bad for one hour's work! Turns out mugging you pays better than producing your television programmes. That might be worth thinking about.' She smiled at him but it faded very quickly. She took a deep breath. 'Matthew, I don't know what you've decided to do about the show with Hutch, but I don't want anything to do with it. I've no intention of ever working with him again.'

He looked at her carefully. She was once again very, very pale. 'No, of course not. I think we're going to put that one on ice, Lizzie. Don't worry about it. You're my first concern. I want you bouncing back. We've missed you spilling your coffee and tripping over the chair legs. When will you feel ready to come back to work?'

Elizabeth couldn't look at him. She stood up abruptly, and started walking around the room. He watched her warily.

'The thing is, Matthew, I've been talking to DI Watson. Trying, you know, to make sense of it all. And...' Elizabeth paused. 'She's been giving me some advice.'

'Oh?'

'Yes. I'm thinking of doing something a bit different.'

'Bloody hell, Elizabeth! Tell me you're not joining the police force. I don't think my heart could take it.'

Elizabeth allowed herself a small smile. 'Don't like the idea of me banging you to rights? Fair enough. No, not the police. But I do need to do something a bit more useful. Well, more useful than tipping green sludge on people's heads and avoiding close-up shots of sex toys.'

'Careful, Lizzie. Don't underestimate how much people want some lightness in their lives. I don't like the idea of you po-faced. I know it's been traumatic – for all of us. Especially for you.' He looked at her kindly. 'But your career's just taking off, Elizabeth. Don't let this thing spoil that for you. You deserve the big time – and that's where you're heading.'

Despite herself, despite all her promises, Elizabeth felt her chest swell with pride and temptation threatened to upend her again. But there was no going back. 'You know, Matthew,' she said slowly, 'I think I need to pay more attention to my personal life. It's been a bit of a car crash. And I don't seem to be able to do that and work at this job. It seems to be all or nothing for me. And Karen Watson's right – we're always so frantic, so hooked on the idea of adrenaline, it blocks out everything else. It's not normal, we just think it is.'

Matthew sat with his head bowed.

'I don't want you to take this the wrong way – I've loved working with you all these years. But I don't want to work for someone else, any more. I want to try and do things on my own terms.' Elizabeth took a deep breath. 'I'm going to set up my own thing – my own production company. I've got the offer of some backing from someone, an American woman that my brother-in-law Mark put me in touch with. She needs someone to make some campaigning films for a children's charity she's involved with. And she wants to turn it into a big television fund-raiser – I think I can help her do that. I'm going to ask Lola to come in on it with me. And well … I think I'm going to try and set it up as an all-female thing. A co-operative, where we all share equally in any upside, any profit. Without breaking any laws on sex discrimination, obviously.'

Despite the quip, Elizabeth could hardly bear to look at Matthew.

'Funnily enough, it's what Jamie – my ex boyfriend – always

thought I should do. I think I can bring something a bit different to campaigning – you know, make it funnier, maybe, more impactful. And you know, the television light entertainment department has yet to find any use for my thesis on Jane Austen's women!' Now she smiled as merrily as she could at Matthew, who was not smiling at all. She could hear her own earnestness and thought how many times in the past she too would have shot down in flames an idea so worthy it must automatically be dull. She sat dreading what he was going to say. But after a long moment he stood and took her hand.

'You know what, Lizzie? I think it's a terrific idea. Seriously. You'll be brilliant at that. You're good, because you care. Now you can direct all that energy at something really worthwhile. I admire you for it.'

'Really?' Elizabeth flushed with pleasure. She really, really wanted his approval.

'Yes. Truly. And if it doesn't work out, you can always come back here!' His eyes twinkled.

'Actually, probably not, Matthew. I'm moving out of London.' She looked away, pulled her hand from his. 'I've sold my flat. Sold it in a day, actually. I realised for what that Islington cupboard's worth I can buy myself a small house up north. I'm going to move closer to Vic – my sister.'

She had a sudden vision of Vic, still in her severe court clothes, sitting in Elizabeth's galley kitchen with a glass of wine that was making Elizabeth feel sick, listing with a fountain pen (only Vic would still use a fountain pen) all the reasons why moving to Manchester was the best thing she could possibly do. 'Family,' Vic said firmly. 'That's what you need now. Family.'

They were trying to persuade their mum to come too, although she was reluctant so far to substitute the long sandy beaches of Frinton for the narrow paths of the Manchester ship canal. But she didn't know the whole story, yet.

'Up north? Really?' Matthew couldn't keep the disappointment out of his voice. 'I'm sorry to hear that, Elizabeth. I hoped we'd deal with this thing – this terrible thing – together. I assume Hutch is to blame? That you don't want to bump into him? With his wife?'

Elizabeth visibly winced. She understood that Matthew felt abandoned, but even so the mention of Hutch's wife seared her like a flame across skin. She leaned against the wall, shaking her head and closing her eyes. The Hutchinsons had done a spread in one of the glossy weeklies a fortnight ago. An exercise in damage limitation, once the drug charge had been slyly leaked to the tabloid press. They'd been photographed at home, in their kitchen, by the Aga. Sue Hutchinson, who said she'd known nothing of her husband's drug use at the time, said she'd forgiven him for 'everything'. They were 'stronger as a couple' for dealing with it, she said.

In a weak moment (Elizabeth had endured more than a few of those), she'd googled Hutch and had seen the piece. She'd sat for a long time and stared at that photo on her computer screen, the two of them arm in arm, beside the Aga. Mr and Mrs Hutchinson. She'd read the words 'we're stronger as a couple now' over and over. And she knew that whatever the outcome, whatever the result, she wouldn't splice in half something that now seemed whole. She wouldn't say the thing that would shatter for ever that mirror of perfect domestic happiness.

'Do you know, Lizzie,' said Matthew warmly, regretting his outburst a little too late. 'I'm a bit jealous! A whole new world. A different kind of challenge. It sounds great. I'd quite like some moral one-upmanship of my own – if only to shut up my wife.'

Elizabeth realised this was probably the best she would get from Matthew. He stood up. 'Have you seen Lola? How is she?'

'Yes, I saw her yesterday.' Elizabeth smiled at the thought of Lola's mouth dropping open, her eyes wide and unbelieving, the burst of happy tears. She was going to run the new company from London, while Elizabeth based herself in Manchester. 'She's channelling Monroe at the moment. She feels they have a lot in common.'

Lola had still not published her kiss and tell, and Elizabeth was hoping to persuade her not to. Elizabeth had gone for supper in Surrey a week ago with Lorna – the first time she'd met her since the events in the police station. It had been a slightly awkward evening in truth – Lorna was again distant and hesitant – but Elizabeth had brought a showreel she'd made of Ricky's best moments, as well as some of his scripts and doodles from the office walls. His sons had pored over them, searching for the funny, impulsive, affectionate dad they remembered from their childhoods. Lorna had finally thanked her with tears in her eyes and Elizabeth had hugged her tight.

She glanced at Matthew. He was fiddling with his mobile, struggling with his next question. 'Elizabeth, are you going to the funeral? To Ricky's funeral?'

'Yes, I think I will.' Elizabeth sighed. She'd been wrestling with this, ever since the coroner had finally released Ricky's body and Lorna had decided on a burial at her local country church. 'For Lorna. For his boys. To help Lola. Because Ricky taught me a lot about television, because he was once funny, and generous, and because I once loved working with him. And because I didn't spot his neediness. The fact he'd sunk so low. I don't know if I can shed any more tears for him, but I will go and pay my respects.'

Matthew nodded. 'You can represent the network, then. That's good.' He straightened up. Elizabeth moved heavily towards the door and he noticed again how tired she seemed.

'Elizabeth?' She turned back, her hand on the door handle. 'Stay in touch, won't you?'

'You bet! I'm going to be sending you notes on all your programmes, whether you want them or not! Try and stop me!' She smiled at him and her eyes were neither mocking nor teasing.

She was halfway out the door when Matthew stopped her with a smile.

'Oh, and Elizabeth? If you are going to the funeral, I suggest you remember to put on some knickers.'

Epilogue

The last of the boxes have disappeared with the van ('*We'll Make The Earth Move For You*') and Elizabeth thinks of it trundling up the North Circular towards the M1. She tucks the Yeats collection back into the box and closes the flaps. The doorbell rings. It'll be Vic, come to drive her home. Elizabeth checks the flat one final time: the dents in the carpet where Jamie's chair had once sat; the vacant cupboards in the brothel-painted bedroom, their doors gaping open; the empty shelf above the mantlepiece. The flat is now a blank canvas, waiting to tell someone else's story.

She walks into the bathroom, flooded with summer evening light. She leans once more against the window, resting her cheek on the cool, fragrant-smelling glass. Everything is scrubbed and polished, the whisper of stains removed, all hints of another life expunged. She turns and opens the mirrored cabinet door for the message that's waiting there for her. She knows what it'll say. She's not running away from it any more. She's going to embrace it. Her new life.

When Elizabeth first told Vic of her suspicions, she simply asked, 'Will you tell him?'

'Yes. I suppose so. Eventually. But I'm not asking anything from him. It's up to him what he does about it. I suspect he'll never tell. You know him, he likes to have a secret – or two.'

Now she pulls the packet from the cupboard shelf and glances inside.

Clear blue. Ten weeks.

She's found a little house, two up, two down, close to Vic in Manchester. It's got a small neat kitchen, with a run of Formica-clad cupboards, looking on to a cobbled backyard. There's no room for an Aga, but soon it'll be filled with brightly coloured plastic, two-handled cups, teething rings, milk bottles, a highchair. *All that domestic stuff.* If things go smoothly, a few months after the baby's born, she's going to share Vic's au pair and she'll go back to doing what she loves. The thing she's good at. There won't be anyone to take out the rubbish, fix the lightbulbs, or share the night-time feeds. She knows that independence comes at a price. It's not the life she thought she'd have, it's not the life she planned. It's messy, it's complicated. The cracks could become fissures down the years, she understands that. But it is a new life. There's already a small beating heart. And from this day on, Elizabeth understands, that little heartbeat will govern her every move and inform her every decision. Her life will dance only to its demanding pulse.

The bell rings again, more insistently, and Elizabeth remembers another bell, in another flat, at another time. A lifetime ago. May, she thinks. Of course. It would've happened in May. Another Mayday. Elizabeth smiles to herself.

Perhaps if it's a girl, she'll call her May.

Acknowledgements

I started writing this book in the summer after leaving ITV and in many ways it's turned out to be my love letter to Television. I worked very happily for many years as a TV producer and then a commissioner – and yes, it was mostly bonkers, but I loved every minute.

So firstly, I should say thank you to anyone I ever worked with: thank you for some of the best times of my life – as well as some of the worst.

And NO, you're definitely not in this book. No character in this book is based on you. Doh! It's *fiction*.

I'd also like to thank anyone who's managed to get through this book but has never worked in Television. Thank you for indulging me. And by the way – it's ALL TRUE. Honestly – that's what it's really like!

There are many people I need to thank for getting me here: my mum, Iris, who taught me to read and took me to the library every Friday evening so that I could borrow another three books; Clive James, who taught me how to craft a sentence (and no one could do it better than him); Lynda

Edwardes-Evans and Gordon Wise, who generously gave me early clear notes and a good steer.

I want to thank the gorgeously stylish Caroline Michel – the only woman I know other than the Queen who can carry off a brooch – whom I've known since my twenties and I'm very glad to say is now my friend *and* my agent. She has been a steady provider of wisdom and calm.

I'd like to thank everyone at HQ for being so enthusiastic from the start about the book, especially Lisa Milton and my editor Charlotte Mursell – who gave me very firm notes and when I protested, didn't give an inch. As a result, she has made the book a better read and I'm very grateful.

There were three important women who kept me going while I wrote this book: Amanda Bruckshaw, BBC news editor extraordinaire, who read drafts of this book and quietly corrected some of the live gallery sequences; my sister Geraldine (thank God for sisters), who is herself a brilliant writer and is wiser, wittier, and better than me at almost every single thing, but who constantly supports and encourages me nonetheless; and Polly Coles – also a wonderful writer – who has been a tireless reader of various versions of this book and has saved me from my worst excesses (mostly by writing things in the margin like *'Now, Elaine! Come on! Really?'*). She's been metaphorically by my side, holding me up and keeping me going in ways I can't even begin to describe. Girls, I couldn't have done it without you.

Finally Clive, the best script editor – and after all these

years still the funniest man I know – thank you, thank you for being my biggest supporter.

And Joe and Flo, thank you for letting me be a TV producer as well as a mum. None of it would have been worth it without you. You are my proudest achievement.

ONE PLACE. MANY STORIES

Bold, innovative and
empowering publishing.

FOLLOW US ON:

@HQStories